Y0-ABT-225

THE LIONS

THE LIONS

PAUL S. SUNGA

Orca Book Publishers

First Edition

Canadian Cataloguing in Publication Data
Sunga, Paul S., 1956–
The lions

ISBN 0-920501-70-2

I. Title.
PS8587.U53L5 1992 C813'.54 C92-091209-5
PR9199.3.S96L5 1992

Publication assistance provided by the Canada Council.
Cover design and artwork by Nyla Sunga

Orca Book Publishers Ltd.
P.O. Box 5626, Station B
Victoria, BC Canada V8R 6S4

Proudly Printed and Bound in Canada
by
Best Gagne Book Manufacturers Inc.

For their gifts of belief and trust,
I am indebted always.

Nyla Sunga
and
Sharon Mylod

PART ONE

ONE

I

When Conrad Grey was a boy he saw his mother awaken from death.

It happened late one night when he was four years old, more alert than he wished to be, and spooked by shadows. In a corner of the kitchen, beneath a metal-legged table, he crouched. Here he was concealed at least, although the thick, toilety smell ruined the flavour of the thing he ate. It was stolen, the thing, cakey and iced, discovered by accident in a canvas bag in the hallway. Like a wolf, he had withdrawn to the safety of his den to devour it. So he chewed fearfully, part of him awaiting discovery, another attuned to the mysterious stirrings of the alleyway. A creature howled while another laughed. A bottle shattered.

Then he felt, rather than heard, a sound which made him drop his loot. It was not the boom of a big freighter, nor the foghorn across the bay, although it was that loud. It was lower and closer, and raised the hairs on his neck. Grey stood, bumped his head beneath the table and sprawled to his knees.

Four-legged, he crept from his cave, moved out into the dark until he came to his mother's closed door. He bumped the door ajar and the vibration ceased.

Mary Grey lay upon the bed, naked and still. A stranger hovered over her, surveying the body with eyes as remote as those of a dockyard rat. It was from the stranger that a wordless boulder of a sound rolled forth, breathless and immense, then suddenly dropped off into silence. Then the stranger moved so quickly that the boy saw only a peculiar dance, not sensible actions. He saw his mother tumble through the air and slam to the floor on her back. She moaned, breathed and her eyes fluttered.

Mary Grey called her son to her and spoke to him, thinking she was finished. She whispered words to him that he had heard before, once when she had fallen in the street and could not rise, and once when she had lain in a hospital bed. She reminded him that he was destined to be hunter. In the days of his grandfather they had hunted whales, lions, moose and bear, she said. They had known the animals, as well as a boy knows his mother. They had known the spoor and the magic of their prey. And they had learned from the animals, too, as a student learns from a wise teacher. Yet the animals would be gone by the time he was grown, she told him. Only men would remain.

What would he hunt then? he whispered.

Death lifted from her at that moment; he saw it, watery drops flickering into the light, and he told himself that this was a thing which he must never forget.

II

During the days, men appear, smelly, large and loud. A woodsman with one leg who brings a kitten that runs away. Another man who pulls down his fly and caws like a crow.

The hunter waits, learning the spoor and the magic.

At night the air is hot and alive. A river of sounds flows through the broken door, down the hall, through the kitchen. Nearby night-creatures play, cursing the moon. The cracked voice of radio erupts from a score of windows, and down the alley the old fireman sings his Jeez songs. Used to be a fireman.

"Jeez is king, yes he is. Jeez, Jeez, he's the lord . . . " Dead-string guitar chugging in the dark.

Closer still, within the confines of the house, is the wild rustling of prey. Now the cry of hawk, now the bark of seal and the purr of lion. Below, beyond, in the darkness, wheels sing in the railyard and below that, the frightened contortions of his lungs and heart.

I am a bird, thinks he, but my wings are inside.

"God help me, I know men," says Mary Grey. "Long as it's in a skirt you follow it. Never good enough, never enough. I know you. I know men. Never satisfied with nothing . . . "

The grunt of bear, the splintering of wood. The huge claws tear at the door and walls of his room. He runs from his bed and seeks his place in the kitchen.

Then the back door bangs open and Darlene comes in, face shiny with the night.

He waits, hugs himself laughing, then rolls out of his place. He loves Darlene more than Mom, or Jeanine or Cookie-dog.

"Hush, how come you're up?"

"Voices," says he, the hunter.

The door to the bedroom opens and light pours out.

"Who's in there?"

"Bears . . . " he whispers, eyes wide.

Darlene picks him up. He wraps himself around her, for she is not twice his size. She carries him to her bed, shutting out the sounds for him, lulling him into his dreams.

They first come with pens and papers and a perfume as sweet and sickening as rotten fruit and church pews. They swoop through the house, writing, and they leave. But after they leave the hunter cannot sleep, smelling this new spoor. Darlene explains that this is the way of witches. They bring bad smells, make sleep impossible.

More than ever the sounds of the forest fill the house, then Mary Grey goes away. Darlene must be mother, burning things on the stove, experimenting with pilfered make-up. Aunt Jeanine arrives from the North Shore, blasting through the house like a storm, leaving food and a clean kitchen. . . .

The second time they come, Mary Grey is home again, ready to fight, and the witches say nothing as she fends them off, screaming.

The hunter watches. He knows the witches by now, but does nothing. He is not surprised that they sneak back when his mother has not been there in days. He is not surprised to be taken to the witches' lair. Darlene is taken somewhere out of reach. He knows but does not understand that they will keep him from seeing Darlene. That is the way of the witches.

III

One morning he awakens in a room of pink. It overlooks a garden, trees and other houses. Light floods in through the windows; it is green light, from the trees.

He tells himself that the toilet-smelling hiding place was a dream. But the smell sticks like dirt to his memory and he longs for that safety.

Darlene is a dream. Mother is a dream. Jeanine and Cookie-dog. . . .

His heart pops unsteadily in his chest. He is the prey. He will die. He lies in a bed pink and immense around him, mountains of pinkness stretching away on all sides, and he sees Darlene, sitting cross-legged beside him, telling a story. He will die here. His heart will pop open and he will be dead.

A man, a woman and a boy own the house. A family. The man is tall and square-shouldered like a downtown building. That is where he works so that is how he looks. The woman piles her hair up on her head and smells like Aunt Jeanine's medicine roots. And the boy is older than he. They are kind to him and watch everything he does. They sit together and look at a television, drive in a car, ride on a ferry-boat. The hunter watches the family, learning their spoor, and they watch him.

The boy comes into the pink bedroom and sits near the dream of Darlene. He, the hunter, watches the dust dance in the stream of sunlight at the window.

"You're my brother now," says the boy. "Daddy wanted a girl but we got you instead. Now you can call him Daddy too."

"Daddy," says Grey.

He wonders how the tall man will take this news. He tries to imagine the man and woman fighting like animals, snarling and biting and laughing at the same time behind the bedroom door. They seem calm enough.

The boy calls him Conrad-Grey, as if it is one name.

"Conrad-Grey, you spilled your milk."

He is always spilling. After a time he stops eating, the better to watch the others.

A rosebush grows beneath the window of the pink bedroom, tended by the woman. She wears leather gloves and a scarf over her pile of hair.

"Come down and play, dear. Why don't you come and play?" she calls. "Connie dear."

The hunter hears but does not answer. He watches the air from the garden pour through the window like water. It's ghostly and molecular, cleansed by the greenery, oozing like syrup from the leaves and blades of grass. He tells himself that this is mere air that he sees, but he knows better. He knows that he has seen this upon his mother. It is death, watery droplets that flash in the sun, coming to wash him. He will never forget what it looks like. His legs are numb and his throat parched and bitter. Beside him lies the empty bottle from which he has eaten the perfect white buttons which taste like dirt.

Darlene is a dream. Mother, Jeanine and Cookie the dog.

IV

It was twenty-four years later that Grey met Jaswant Sijjer.

It was the beginning of a Pacific winter, the rains not yet begun. The sky was low during the day but reflected mauve as night approached. In the middle of the roadway, in a trench, Grey and the other men shifted lengths of pipes, chaining them to the arm of a backhoe.

The men took note of Sijjer on his first day with the crew. They silently observed the thin limbs, red-rimmed eyes and the untried skin on his hands. To the crew Sijjer was distant, and to the foreman he paid as much attention as he would a street sign, obeying without acknowledgement. He made the other men nervous.

One day the sides of the pit, shells and fossils and the wet stone of an old sea bottom, slid in on a section of the trench. Three men leapt to safety, as startled as hares. But Sijjer let the ground come until it stopped at his knees. He wore an expression of forbearance, his instincts gone. It was then that Grey saw the familiar droplets that had settled upon Sijjer's shoulders and head. Death rode him like a tick sapping his strength.

The crew but for Grey stayed well clear of Sijjer from that day on. Grey, who had worked for fourteen years with men like the men on this crew, who had been ridden by that same tick and who had made it his slave, did not stay clear. He watched Sijjer quietly, sometimes curious, quite indifferent. He spoke to him one day, then helped him when he needed help. Grey did not fear death's glitter. His strength was a storm that had driven him to extremes in his life, but he did not regret that. It had made him, like his mother, an oilskin to death's watery approach. That which Sijjer absorbed, he repelled. But he had a knowledge of death. He believed in his knowledge of it, believed he knew where it came from and where it hid.

So Grey believed, from the beginning, that he would see Jaswant Sijjer die.

TWO

Jaswant Singh Sijjer

I

November 1983
In the eyes of lions

Dear Mother,

I am in a state of decline. I look in the mirror and I see the signs. Thin as water, you once said of me. I can no longer eat food. Eating is a task I would gladly be free of. Talking is a chore that exhausts me. Yes, I've always been thin as water, always weak in comparison to Gurjit. But now it is different. Some dim, inexplicable force drains my substance away. In my blood I am cold, and of this I am afraid. Coldness is the essence of Mohan, is it not? With this coldness I see similarities, the way he was after you left us, the way he froze from the inside. What had been cold became burning dry ice. Ice that turned to smoke and vanished. First his eyes faded, then his hair and his skin. His cheeks were sucked into his mouth by the things he couldn't say. His body dissolved where he sat behind his newspaper. Yet even after all that Mohan somehow recovered and remarried.

Now Mohan's race is almost run. This is the real reason I am writing you. To tell you that the man who destroyed you is finished. Gurjit sent a telegram – he must have given up phoning (I won't pick up the phone). He says it's my last chance. He says Mohan doesn't have much life left in him. I laughed. How much life does anyone have in them anyway?

I've been wondering if people change when the end is nigh. Do they see their mistakes suddenly and take on a new, final perspective? Does impending death endow us with a generosity that their worldly concerns wouldn't permit them? Do they abondon pride and vengefulness? I don't know. I do know Mohan though, even if I don't understand him. I know there's no generosity or warmth in him. He is cold. He is hard as stone right through to his soul. I care less for him than I would a complete stranger on this earth.

your son, Jaswant.

II

At the bottom there is an arm of the sea they call Burrard Inlet. On the north side of it the land rises up sharply so that the human settlements seem to cling there precariously, ready at any moment to slide into the water. This is how Piara's store is: perched, ready to slip. But the store resists gravity and has remained through the years, neither failing nor flourishing. It's immutability is one of those things that Jassy Singh Sijjer has always taken for granted. There is a Pepsi sign that says Perry instead of Piara, the faded Marlboro cigarette ad in the window, the pungent aroma of *masala* wafting from the kitchen into the two short aisles. And above all there is a quiet contentment which emanates from this Punjabi couple who grow so gradually old that no one can see the mark of time upon them. All of this is a good and decent mystery which has never interested Sijjer in the least, even if the couple are his kin.

From his uncle, Piara, he accepted a brimming tumbler of rye and drank off the top inch. From his jacket pocket he retrieved the telegram, offering it crumpled and in disdain. Piara waved it aside with a closing of his eyes.

"I know all about it, Jassy. Don't you think I would know? I know your Dad better than anyone in this world knows him. When he feels pain, I feel it, just like always. He's sick as an old snake now — cancer, they say."

It was late. Naseeb had served their *alu pranta* and *lassi* on a tray before tottering up to bed. Now the rain came, hissing in the trees. Sijjer rested his gaze on the portrait of Guru Nanak that hung in the parlour. The colours of the print were bright to the point of luminousity; Nanak's cheeks were like red lightbulbs, his eyes like candles.

'Saintliness', thought Sijjer. But he said, "The last message I received from my father contained six words. You want to know what they were. YOU ARE NO MORE MY SON; that was all."

"I know that, Jassy. Gurjit told us the whole story. Your brother has always included us." This said with a pointed glance. "Anyway, you are here, you came to us and that is the important thing. Now is my chance to explain everything finally. There is always an explanation, right? It is a tragedy when a father and son don't speak. It is painful and sad for everyone. People die off, you know, and then they are gone like . . . like rockets in the bottom of the sea. Gone!"

"Rockets?"

"You know. Cape Kennedy . . . "

"My father disowned me, Uncle. He has disliked me from the beginning. He made it formal when I married . . . "

"He's your father, Jassy. Which is why you're here. Why you care. He will die off soon so now is the time to end this painful thing between you. Now is the time to go and make peace. Forgiveness! That is the difference between a man's love and child's love. Look at you. Big university scientist, a real *sahib*. You make everybody proud with your doctor degree, Jassy."

"Don't patronize me, Piara. I know what I am."

"Please Jassy. I am a simple man. But I'm trying to help. I loved your Papa like a brother. I still love him. We're brothers, sure! As close as brothers! And some brothers love each other so much they can't stand to be together. That's me and Mohan.

We're like this." Piara clasped his hands together. "Like the right and left hand. Same but different, part of the same machine. See, that's why I care about you and Gurjit – you're like the sons of the other hand!"

"You're not in the least like my father and of that you may be proud. To his own flesh and blood Mohan is gangrene."

"That's what I want to explain to you, Jassy. See, it isn't his fault he got like that. He's that way because they made him that way."

"Who?"

"His own family, that's who. His father and brothers. Don't forget he's someone's son too. See, what he did to you wasn't near as bad as what he got. He couldn't help but be mean. It's funny the way things in a family get passed on down like that. Seen it lots of times. You get my age and you start thinking all life is just a bunch of dizzy circles. History, history . . . all circles. You don't know. Sure you feel bad. But your dad never meant to be mean to you. He couldn't help it. He got to be so tough he couldn't let his real feelings get past the toughness, see. He loves you really, but he just can't show it. That's what you got to realize before he dies. You got to realize he can't control how he feels and then you got to go and try to make peace with him before he dies."

'You are no more my son', Sijjer remembered. It was as though he had held that letter in his hand all these years and could not put it down. It pierced him as much as the day he first read it.

"Me and Mohan grew up together," Piara was saying. He paused to fill the tumblers once more, then sank into his chair, eyes glistening with nostalgia. "Yep. Same village, same schools we went to. Same fields we worked and played in. Not brothers. Cousin-brothers. But just like two hands anyway, always together experiencing the life. You can't imagine what Punjab is like where we grew up. It's beautiful like nowhere else. All flat and green and golden with a big sky above, and in the north those icy mountains standing straight up just like a great wall of a house that a giant started to build but never finished. Yep, one big dark wall in the north with Punjab as the floor. And such a fertile floor of earth you never saw. Crops growing all year round, winter and summer, just like a sea of growing stuff that won't stop. Four harvests a year we used to get. Wheat, corn, sugar cane, mustard, vegetables all purple and red and all kinds of colours you never see here. Lemons and oranges. Sun pouring down all year round, except the monsoon, of course. Then it would flood up like someone up there had busted the dam open. Rivers would form where yesterday was a cow trail. The snakes would come out then. We had to call the snake charmer once and he came with his flute and brought two giant cobras out of our place. Male and female. Husband and wife. Out they came behind him, as proud and brave as you please. We saw it was the old couple who founded our village, come back as regal cobras. People greeted them. *Satsriakalji*, everyone said, and we followed the snakes to a field and left them buffalo milk in bowl. No one here would believe the things we saw. Nobody could imagine it.

"Me and Mohan saw all kinds of strange sights. We watched a lady catch fire once in a field. No reason. Just stood there and burned. We tried to put her out but she just burned down to ash and bone before our eyes and never made a peep either. Kind of thing you never in your life forget. Big, strong lady she was too. Tough as steel, whoever she was. Another time we watched some young men tear apart an Englishman's house because he lashed a Sikh boy with a horsewhip. I heard they faced a troop of soldiers for doing that. They didn't care. See, our people, the Punjabis are like that, Jassy. Rough and rowdy. Farming folks. Jats is what we call ourselves. Farmers. Salt of the earth. You, me, Mohan: we're all the same stuff. Jats. Back home we work our land and see that green stuff coming up over and over again. Sometimes go to war. A lot of Jats travelled off to other countries just for the hell of it. Ah, but most of them stay and farm the land in Punjab.

"That's what Mohan and me did when we were kids. We used to reap the harvest with long scythes, then bundle up the wheat. Or sometimes we worked at the water hole where a bullock pushed this wooden spoke round and round to draw the water. We went to school sometimes. Other times we wandered the countryside fields like two ghosts, watching, getting in fights. When Mohan fought, I was there with him, just like we were two hands."

"I don't understand what was so difficult for Mohan," Sijjer interjected.

"I'm coming to that. I wanted you to know what it was we came from. The tough part was in Mohan's home. Outside he was fine but his home was hell. See, Mohan's dad, your Baba, Jasbir Sigh Sijjer, hated Mohan because he didn't think Mohan was his own son. Said as much to Mohan's face. Said he was a bastard dog and nobody cared if he lived or died. And it was almost true, too, at least as far as the old man was concerned. If anything happened to Mohan, the old man didn't want to know. Now Mohan had three older brothers and they all listened to their father. They hated Mohan so much they wouldn't let him sleep in the house with them. They made him sleep with the old man who swept out the stable. They made Mohan eat in a corner of the courtyard away from the kitchen, even when he was small. Mohan had to learn to live with this pain every day, every hour. He never would talk about it to no one, even me, but we knew, we saw how hurt he was. My papa was Jasbir Singh's brother, see, and we lived right across the lane. We knew everything that went on in that house. Papa felt sorry for young Mohan — used to tell me to stick with him and watch out for him, and that was no easy task sometimes.

"They played tricks on Mohan — that's the kind of men they were. They got this wild bull one time, this big mean devil of a thing with two spears for horns and red eyes that looked like they were bleeding. Brought Mohan over — he was just four or five then — and they gave him the lead of the bull to hold onto. Told him he wouldn't get no supper if he let go the bull. I still remember the way that bull started to swing his head back and forth and stamp his feet, Mohan holding on for dear life to this short lead until his feet came right off the ground and he still wouldn't let go. I called for my papa then and he came running. Got Mohan out of there. Papa was always coming and rescuing poor Mohan, never saying a word to Mohan's dad or brothers. They never passed a word between them in all the years I was there. My papa told me to watch Mohan all the time because they might really try to kill him some day. And he said if they were going to kill him, they better do it right away because some day Mohan was going to be a grown man and would turn around and kill them instead."

"He must have done something. He probably deserved what he got."

"In our village we had a *panchayat*, a council of five, but they were weak men. They were afraid of Jasbir Singh. But no, he never deserved what he got. I was told a story, once, about a caravan that came down from the mountains. They would come sometimes, traders, from China or Afghanistan. This one had a lunatic chained like an animal in a big box without food or water. Mohan's mom, that's your Dhadhi, Parmjit, she was a kind-hearted woman who hated to see suffering things. She always gave to beggars and helped old folks and even tended to dogs and goats if they were sick. The way the story goes, she took pity on the poor animal-crazy, chained-up man and somehow let him off his chains. And as soon as he was free he leapt on her and raped her — and that was the start of Mohan. Well, it's a story anyway. Who knows how true it might be? I only know that that poor Parmjit-Auntie suffered more than she ever deserved. She gave up trying to stick up for her son because she would get beaten so bad by her husband. He used to beat her almost every day and we would hear her cry like a child at night.

"Papa used to say sometimes that it would have been better if Mohan wasn't born at all, he had it so rough. There was this other time he did something to this school pal of his brother and the guy brought out an ax and said he would chop off Mohan's hand. He held Mohan down and would have done it too because the brothers just stood by and encouraged him. I had to get my papa that time, too.

"Your dad survived it all. He grew up tough and mean. We became young men. I think everyone just hoped he would get out when he grew up, just pack up and leave without a fuss. But Mohan claimed a part of the land which was his right. It caused a big fight. It went to the district court and before that ended there was big knife fight and he almost killed his own dad. Stuck a knife in his side. They tried to kill me, too, that time because I was right there with Mohan. I ran away. I was a good runner in those days. Anyway, your dad decided to leave Punjab. Didn't have any idea where he could go. People came back from the wars and someone mentioned this place called Canada, saying the land was fertile and cheap and there were huge empty places where no man had ever walked. The name sounded strange to us back then. I tried to find out what I could but he kept saying the name Canada over to himself. He finally decided one day that Canada was where he was headed. I didn't have to think twice. Mohan was like my other hand and you never heard of one hand going off by itself did you? Even my father told me with tears in his eyes that I had to go. That was my *kharm* he said — my destiny. Don't get me wrong. We loved Punjab. We knew there was nowhere more beautiful. But we knew we needed a new start somewhere and, well, we were young and full of spunk . . .

"Imagine it. Two village boys with no idea of the world. Hardly any English. There we were on a Japanese boat, steaming in from Hawaii. I will always remember how the peaks popped out of the water. Hell, I was scared. Not your dad, though. Tough as a bobcat he was. I don't think I ever saw him really scared in all the time we were together."

"We knew nothing. We stared at the people and they stared back. We stayed in the Gurdwara at first, in Vancouver, then we got jobs in the mills and camps. Mohan saved money from day one so he could go to university. Me, I used to buy whisky and stuff. Then one day he went off on his own. He changed in those years and he didn't have much patience with me, I don't know why. Seems like he grew smarter than me somewhere along the line. He went off to school while I stayed behind in the lumber camp. We were never together after that. It was never the same . . . "

Piara's voice trailed off. He stared at the blackness beyond the window. Then he came to life and hopped to his feet. "Boy, I got something you will love." From the shelf he pulled down a worn photo album, opened it and dumped it into Sijjer's lap.

The photos were the yellow of another era. Villagers were poised ceremoniously before a flash, eyes unnaturally wide. In one corner was a picture of two small boys in turbans, arms on each other's shoulders.

"That's us," said Piara. "Two hands, left and right. We were in school then. It was Urdu in our school. Sort of like Persian . . . I forgot it all now. And this young woman is Mohan's mama. She looks sad, see? Parmitjit-Auntie always looked just like that, pretty and sad. I used to think she was the prettiest woman in the world. She never deserved to get what she got in life. Last time I saw her was the day we left the village. She came running after us when we were miles from home, crying her pretty eyes out. We looked back and there she came, running in the dusty road, bawling like a child, just so she could give Mohan and me a little bunch of rotis and some chicken she made. She'd dropped the stuff in the dust somewhere and it was all dirty and wrapped up in newspaper. I thought her heart would bust when she gave that dirty little packet to Mohan. Then she just watched us go. Ladies always get the worst of these things . . . but I guess you know that."

"Yeah, I know."

"A person must be forgiving, Jassy. A grown man must learn that his strength is the root of kindness and he has to give that kindness to stubborn and foolish and proud old folks. Especially with the old folks. It's up to men like you to make peace, Jassy."

"And what about Mohan," Sijjer countered, "He never forgave his father. Why does he wriggle out of his responsibility to everyone. He's never made an effort to heal things between us."

Piara nodded and sank lower in his chair. He seemed to cock his head and listen for a moment to the hiss of the rain on the roof. "Pride," he said, "is a terrible weapon to wield."

III

When he left Piara's it was dawn.

Sijjer drove over the Narrows which open onto the Strait, and up through the deserted streets towards his home. As he rolled down the block, he glimpsed a bounding flash of gold in the overgrown brush of his yard, but, when he came closer, he saw that it was nothing. The apparition was both there and not there like the clicking of claws on the kitchen floor and the light sigh of a sleeping child in the night. He endured these presences as painfully as a smothering man dreams of air.

He turned on the lights of the house and lay in bed listening to the rain. Through his mind walked a teenage girl, Piara's daughter, clad in a swimsuit. He had been in love with her as an adolescent boy one summer, long ago. Up the beach he followed her one day, following the flash of her smooth legs into the woods behind the dunes until he lost sight of her. Then he had wandered in the woods like a lost puppy, finally coming to a clearing where a small patch of sunlight fell through the canopy. He saw his cousin lying next to his older brother, Gurjit's hand tucked into the crotch of her swimsuit.

No one had seen this but he, and the incident was never mentioned. It was strange how distant those sensations were, yet familiar. It was the sensation of a stranger in a land where the rules are not apparent. Was that what Mohan and Piara had endured in Punjab, the powerful wills of adults storming around them, threatening and incomprehensible?

Sijjer envisioned his father. He saw a tough and sinewy street urchin with hard and watchful eyes. His mean streak was there, taught him along with sharps wits and reflexes in his struggle to survive.

As the light of morning filled the room, Sijjer fell asleep and dreamed of Punjab. He dreamed of a bearded man with an raised ax who waited for him to reveal his hands. In this dream it was a great effort to keep his hands behind his back; they kept straying out to meet the axman.

THREE

I

There had always been trouble with Mohan. When he reflected on his childhood, Jaswant Sijjer reflected on war. The high points were skirmishes over pride; the defeats, humiliation and ignomy. Above it all towered the indelible, harsh face with winged eyebrows that flew outraged over marble eyes. This was his adversary: clipped voice, steel hair and the temper of a blizzard. This was his shadow and his judge. This was his father.

"Ditch-digger." Mohan hissed this word with such relish that the muscles in his jaw quivered and the spit dried on his tongue. "You are not a doctor or a lawyer or even a dog-headed clerk. Ditch-digger is what you are. You will wear boots full of cold mud and a rag for a shirt. You will smell like rotten meat, have a sore back and you will hate, I say HATE, your life."

There was a tuft of hair growing from his father's nostril. It was gray, that tuft, and inexplicable like so many things about adults. More than this, it was obscene. The more he examined this wiry hair, the less Jassy listened. Who cared what one was when one grew up? Adults were nostril hairs and misery and . . .

" . . . poor habits, slouch around like a *bandar.* Even your teacher says you slouch. Ditch-digger! You will end up a wretched . . . " Mohan swallowed and evidently could not go on. Fast-blinking, mad, he slapped the report card into Jassy's hand and returned to the *Globe and Mail.* Small wrinkles around his eyes and nose formed and vanished as he read, and the tuft of hair in his nostril twitched. From his body came the bitter scent of burning spice.

He had heard this many times. Jassy's dreams had become a ditch. Muddy water seeped and stagnated. In his sleep he walked black pits, slime sucking at his boots. In this vision there was no sky above his head, only endless walls. He understood well enough the destiny of ditch-diggers. With Gurjit he passed through the low rent project below the hill. This was where it led. This hovel. This humiliation. Ditch-diggers, garbage men, dog-headed clerks . . . "They're all here," Gurjit whispered, and Jassy felt himself drawn to it like a bug to a drain. When he brought home his report card, the muck dragged at his legs. When he was caught sampling a cigarette, his back ached. "Even your hands are those of a labourer," Mohan pointed out.

Behind the house, behind the yard and garden and behind the wooden garage, was a small patch of concrete with the date 1951 imprinted in it. Beside the date was a crack. Sijjer owned three stones, one glacial white, another pink, the third a deep, liquid blue. These he tossed against the garage time after time. When they crossed the crack, there was hope. When they failed, there was no escape: a ditch-digger he was.

II

Children. They screech from the trees like monkeys, rattle bicycles over the sidewalks, raid gardens, spit, fight, poke things in each other's eyes. They form packs to rove the summertime streets in search of trouble.

"Dog-children," Mohan says of the children. "They look and act no better than pie-dogs."

Jassy imagines the pie-dogs eating pie. Free, joyous, roving pie-dogs. He stares at the yellow stains in the armpits of his father's shirt. The summer heat smothers him, yet Mohan wears the heavy black pants and stiff white shirt that he wears year round. And his sons must dress exactly the same.

Oh, to wear a raggedy tee-shirt. Oh, to be a roving pie-dog.

III

Jassy sings a song. The song spins around, a tiny loop of a song in which he searches for big brother, perpetually lost. Miles from home down a country lane, Mohan finds him sitting in the middle of stream stranded on a rock, Donald Duck lunch pail suitcase containing his three stones. Mohan asks his son what in hell he is doing here, and the song plays: hasn't Gurjit come this way? He never, ever finds Gurjit, for it is only a song. . . .

And so the song hums and he is captured one sun-yellow afternoon by the spoked glitter of the bicycles in the playground bicycle rack. Bicycle wheels have a power over his hands. His hands turn to creatures, walking the rubber ridges, sliding the perfect rims. His own bicycle he never rides because the tires are flat. Gurjit has pumped them but they are flat.

A pie-dog-children gang, a gang known to all as the Ander-can gang (there were also the Kleins and Beavers) appear in the flash of the afternoon sun. They surround the rack where he squats in his hot black pants.

"Chocolate-face," says the pie-dog leader. "Whyn't you go back to Chocolate-land." Sijjer stands but someone pushes and someone crouches behind him and he finds himself sitting hard.

"He did it to my bike before. I seen him doing it," says a pie-dog. Someone is slowly shoveling sand with his foot into his lap.

"He's queer," says the shoveler. "What we gonna do to him?"

The sun blazes. The squeal of children on swing sets and slides bounces from walls of family dwellings that surround the park. The Childs, the Berries, the Goodsons and the Pattersons. Each house has its own maple sapling, planted in the front yard by the city. Everywhere is child-happiness. Everywhere, love. Only the midst is spoiled by this odd vortex: a small exploring creature which hides in the sand. . . .

"Let's wash his face," suggests a pie-dog.

Gurjit pushes his way into the circle of boys and hauls his little brother to his feet. "Go home," Gurjit hisses.

At dinner Jassy sits across from Mohan in silence. Father studies son with a frown of curiousity, as though watching the behavior of a captured pest. He observes the small brown hands, one clenching a spoon, the other inching along the edge of the table. The boy does not eat, but watches the finger-legs of the exploring creature.

Gurjit is in the bathroom with Prito. Hushed voices, water running, then they emerge. Gurjit's lip is fat, his forehead scraped.

"They tore his clothes, Mohan," says Prito quietly. "What is wrong with them? Are they animals? Why, why have they done this?"

Gurjit shakes his head and looks away.

Jassy mechanically brings his spoon to his mouth with one hand while the other, his creature hand, labours along the table. It is this same creature that seeks the tiny buttons on the rims of bicycle wheels, pressed them in to feel the cool, watery rush of air. Why does it do that? Neither insect nor spider nor worm, it creeps into Jassy's lap to hide.

"You," says Mohan. "What do you have to say about this?"

IV

White women were immoral. "They'll trick you," Mohan said. Strange women were not permitted into the house. He became infuriated when the boys gaze fastened on a pair of legs scissoring up the street.

Gurjit batted his brother's ear if he saw him sniffing perfume or peering at the curve of a woman's breast. But then one day Jassy discovered Gurjit in the cellar with a mouldy Playboy magazine and a flashlight. The two stood in the dark poring over the shiny pages.

"Mr. Klein says anyone who hates women as much as our Dad is a fag. I heard him."

"When?"

"He said it."

"Do you think he is?" asked Jassy.

Gurjit shrugged his shoulders and flipped the pages up to

the centrefold. "They never show anything really good," he murmured. "They cover up the important part."

"I saw him looking down a lady's dress once. At the store. He was looking at her boobs."

Gurjit slammed shut the magazine punched his brother's arm. "Don't lie, Jassy! If you tell lies, I'll tell him what you said."

"Tell who? Tell who? How do you know who I was talking about?" sniffed Jassy. It was hard to know how far to take it with Gurjit. Jassy wanted to tell Gurjit about Marilyn but it was too risky. He wanted to tell his brother about cello class but he was never sure.

Cello classes were the result of his father's nightmare. In the nightmare a colleague discovered that Mohan's son was a recipient of welfare, an alcoholic, a parasite on society. Mohan burned with a humiliation that lasted for a short period after the dream ended. He embarked on a search for an honourable vocation for Jassy. Some newspaper article or theory planted the idea of music lessons in his head and the next day he returned home with a cello. Jassy was to learn the instrument and make it his life. "It is time you learned at least one skill."

But from the beginning Jassy hated the boat-like instrument and would not practise unless threatened. After a few weeks even Mohan was reluctant to endure the yawing scrape of hair on string. Evenings, the cherished peace of his newspaper perusal, were shattered.

Jassy faithfully attended the classes. There was a freckled-faced girl named Marilyn who often sent a sweet, inviting smile his way. Jassy could do nothing but smile back, conscious that he was living dangerously. He could not summon the nerve to talk to this Marilyn, but went to each class in a turmoil of fear and joy.

V

When the cello lesson is finished, he drags the encased cello over a field of snow. The air is so cold that it aches to breath it. The trees are made of glass: they crackle in an Arctic wind. Snow crunches like sand under foot and the cello voices hollow, toneless concerns as it bounces behind. Too cold even for hockey; the rink is abandoned, the ice heaved like seismic rock at the centre line. The fields are empty and dark.

When toes and fingers are numb and sore, warm them by muttering a child's oath, something about "old bum-breath," against Mohan, then stop and look about to make absolutely sure.

He climbs a mountainous snow-bank created by a plough and, straddling the cello case, sleds down the other side into the dark pit of a street.

"If Mrs. Ryerson saw you, she'd scream," says a voice. Girl's voice. Jassy dismounts and sees it is her, Marilyn, against the bank of snow on the other side of the street. She holds her own instrument proudly by the handle, as though it is as light and delicate as an icicle.

"Hi," says Jassy. "Cold, huh."

It is perfectly still and empty in the street, everyone around warm stoves, eating warm supper in the warm light. It is one of those evenings when the cold deepens with each passing minute, as though the earth were being laid bare to the cosmos. Air is brittle, sounds are perfectly clean and loud over miles. As they crunch up the street, unblinking stars appear, frozen in space.

When they come to Marilyn's house, Sijjer is not halfway home and, like the stars, he is frozen stiff. He goes in to get warm, cauldron of fear and joy.

The house smells of bacon fat and cigarettes and coffee. Marilyn's mother says, "You're not going to play those here, are you?" and holds her cigarette away from her to squint at the cellos bumping through the door. She has freckles like her daughter.

"My mother hates the cello. Hates it!" says Marilyn in a voice that her mother can hear perfectly well. "She says it's sucky."

Marilyn's mother blows smoke and turns back to her T.V. "Take your friend downstairs, Honey. I'm expecting company."

"Ray? Are you having Ray? Oh Christ, Mommy, he's so creepy . . . "

"Go on, Honey. Don't talk like that. Go on."

"It's freezing downstairs."

"Take the electric heater then."

Jassy bangs the cello downstairs and sits beside Marilyn with his toes on the heater. For the first minute it is like boiling water being poured on his feet, then the blood warms and the toes are sore.

"They do it right in the living room," she says glumly.

"What?"

"You know. I've seen them a few times. Ray's her boyfriend. I hate him."

"How come you go to cello class if your Mom hates it?"

"My Dad pays for it. He's a jazz drummer. My Mom and Dad are legally separated. Do you ever listen to jazz?"

"There's a guy called Bird. His real name's Charlie Parker, but everyone calls him Bird." Marilyn puts a record on and when she sits again, she squeezes Jassy's hand and gives him the smile. "You sure are shy."

The sounds from the record are stranger than Jassy's cello music. Above, the frozen house creaks, mingled with this is the faint sound of voices and laughter.

Marilyn listens with her whole being to the sounds, then turns up her record and cocks her head. She is a real musician, even Jassy knows this. As the music plays, she stands and gives herself to the strains, dipping and swaying around the basement, eyes closed, long red hair swinging around her. She hums high accompaniment and her face is tranquil and pretty.

The lights are out upstairs but for the television set. It is already too late when he sees them. A light comes on. Cauldron of fear. Marilyn's mother is on the couch but her clothes are on the floor. She is a few stretches of bare naked flesh and on top of her is a man. He is poised with one arm, pure muscle, outstretched, his hand on the lamp switch. His pants are at his ankles which rest on the end table. Jassy stares at the man's white, sinewy, naked bum.

"Well, I'll be," says the man. "I thought I heard something."

Please turn off the light.

"Oh, it's just one of Marilyn's little friends, Ray."

"If it ain't a Hindoostani kid with a bull fiddle."

"Cello," Jassy croaks in a small, cauldron-of-fear voice.

"Oho," says Ray. He rolls off of Marilyn's mother and Jassy looks away. "Oho. How about playin' a tune for us, little fella. I don't think I've ever heard a . . . "

"Oh Ray, for God's sake. Go on, dear. You go ahead."

"Now wait a sec. I wanta hear this. I like music." Ray has his pants on. He grabs the cello by the neck and unsnaps the case. Ray is huge and heavy and smells sour-sweetly of beer and meat. His hair sweeps into a messy pompadour which hangs in his eyes. Now he takes up the bow and the cello and scrapes away for a minute, gives up.

"Come on, little Hindoo. Let's see you play."

"Leave him be, Ray."

"He's gotta pay for busting in on us. Play it, kid."

"I can't," says the cauldron of fear voice.

"What?"

"I can't. I don't practise."

"Play it, ya little gook, before I get mad."

He pushes the cello into Jassy's arms roughly.

"Play it now, kid. Let's hear."

Jassy plays so badly Marilyn's mother begins to laugh. She tries not to at first but after a few minutes she holds herself and bubbles where she lies in the shadows.

"I like this," laughs Ray.

No one is sure whether Mohan knocked at the door. Jassy feels the cold, still air at his back and sees Ray and Marilyn's mother looking past him, mouths agape. He knows who it is. Even in the cold puddle of air that flows in, he smells Mohan's bitter *masala*. Stronger than bacon fat or beer or cigarettes. Without looking back Jassy packs his cello and follows Mohan into the night.

He never asked Mohan how he came to Marilyn's house that evening.

Mohan cancelled cello classes, though, and sold the cello. "Ditch-diggers are rarely musicians," he told Jassy. "I should have known."

FOUR

Prito

I

Her full name was Pritam Inder Kaur Johal Sijjer. At her home, those who cherished her referred to her as Prito (and they spoke of her often even though she had not been seen in over ten years). Home was the Punjabi district of Patiala which was once a powerful Sikh kingdom. There was a history of political intrigue in her family, but Prito cared little about that man's world of betrayal and violence. For she had been raised in the warm and protective nest of the village, nurtured by parents and kin. She had not known anything but love and kindness until the day she was betrothed to Mohan and sent away for what horrible crime she could not imagine. It was part of the man's world, the world of betrayal and lust and violence that had decided her fate; that was what she understood of it.

She avoided the intrusive gaze of strangers. She wore a clean *chuni* and *silwar-kemiz* the way she had been taught, and wore her flat-heeled, pointed shoes which tapped neatly the concrete sidewalks as she pulled her wire grocery cart. And wondered what in the world her crime had been that she had been exiled to this place of Toronto. Nothing had prepared her for this barren suburban landscape.

Nothing could have prepared her for the harsh temperment of Mohan. He became enraged when she was mistaken for his daughter, or eyed by some stranger. This or any other slight would spark his smouldering fury against her so that she existed for days in isolation, neither spoken to nor even looked upon by her husband. So she survived with a spirit flagged until her sons were born. Then she lived for her Gurjit and her Jassy.

She knew that her boys were all she had. She could not lay claim to anything else in Mohan's domain. Her energy was concentrated on the love of the two things that were undeniably hers.

Her boys.

They are obsessed with war. They open their mouths and follow the white tracks of jet fighters in the winter sky, lust and man-violence stopping their breath.

"Don't be a fighting boy. Don't be rough," she implores in her quiet voice.

But they are preoccupied with the hydrogen bomb and machine guns and sit transfixed by the American police shows on television. They love hockey, and learn to master the ice themselves. She watches them one evening, charging up and down the rink, unleashed from gravity and friction.

It must be stopped, this man-lust, this hunting. She strokes their brushes of black-blue hair and knows they do not hear her. In the evenings, in Mohans' presence, they are quiet, but she sees the pulsating energy in their tired limbs. Their eyes brim with light.

They only listen to her when Mohan is not there. Then she tells them the stories of the Sikhs. Like two furry animals they curl before the fire, their hunting and lusting done for the day. The snowy winds howl in the eaves.

"There were no Gurus but the ten and the tenth was Gobind. He himself decided that ten was enough and decreed that he be the last. Gobind was a fierce fighter and was extremely strong . . . "

"Stronger than Rocket Richard?"

"Much stronger. But strong as he was, he was also a gentle kind man who loved small and meek things and loved his family more than anything. His strength was the best of strengths: it was deep and could not be sapped. His kind of strength was like love because it came from the heart and when a person's strength comes from the heart the strength is not harmful and is never angry."

"You mean there's angry strength and calm strength?"

"Of course. Now the Moghuls were in Punjab in those days and they wanted to be rid of Gobind and his Sikhs. The Moghul leaders thought that anyone who was not a Moslem must be converted or killed. Gobind, as leader of the Sikhs, was forced into a fight. Like any strong, loving person, he did not want to fight unless he absolutely must."

They are two creatures of the forest at her feet. Gurjit: long-muscled and tall, and strong. And Jaswant. Jaswant like a goggle-eyed otter caught in a snare. Jaswant: fearful, watchful and uncertain. In their minds they fight, track and hunt. They swell in man-glory and violence. She has seen this thing tamed in the village. But she does not know how to stop it and is afraid. She is afraid that boys who start out as innocent as forest creatures end as cold, wrathful men. Like Mohan.

II

"In this story I want you to see that you can have great courage and your courage will spread to those you love.

"Guru Gobindji knew that his Sikhs were afraid of the Moghul chiefs who threatened to attack at that time. So he called a big meeting under the open sky on Baisakhi day. All the Sikhs were there and they all looked nervous and worried. Gobind had set up a tent on a little knoll and now he came out and drew his sword and said, 'Let there come forward a true Sikh who is willing to die for our cause.' No one stirred. People looked at one another not knowing what to think. Gobind asked a second time. 'Is there a true Sikh of mine who will give me his head as an offering of his faith?' Everyone looked away from each other in real fear. Then Daya Ram stood up. He was tall and beautiful, with flowing, uncut hair and a beard. He said, 'O my king, my head is at your service.' Gobind took Daya Ram into the tent and a mighty blow of the sword was heard. A stream of blood flowed from the tent and Gobind came out with his sword dripping. A hush fell over the Sikhs. Women wept and old people were moved and said silent prayers. Gobind called again and a man named Dharm Das stepped up. He too was taken into the tent whereupon another great blow of a sword was heard.

"Gobind requested three more Sikhs, and at the end of it the crowd was in awe of the courage and faith they had witnessed. Gobind told them, 'This is the courage of the pure, and the pure can never be beaten because God is in their hearts.' Then he opened the tent to reveal five dead goats and the five Sikhs with not a scratch upon them. He then baptized the five and gave them all the name Singh, which means lion-spirited.

"The other Sikhs took inspiration from this and went on to fight well and with great courage."

"Did they always win?" asked Gurjit.

"It is important that they fought with faith and courage."

"They would have won if they had the H-bomb," remarked Jassy.

"Don't be stupid, Stupid. They didn't have bombs in those days," scoffed Gurjit.

"I said if, Stupid."

"The story is about courage, not weaponry, not who won. The Sikhs got courage because they saw that faith could give them strength . . . "

Prito was tired. Deep inside her she detected a weakness concentrated in one place and of this she was afraid. Faith in God could not correct this flaw. She beheld her sons, full of wonderment and fear. The pages of a letter floated on her thoughts like dead leaves on the surface of a pond.

She spoke to her sons of the courtyard where, as a child, she played under the loving eye of her *Massi*. She told of her handsome brothers, of the sweet buffalo milk and the syrup of mangoes, of the fields burgeoning with sugar cane and how a cobra came to her bed one night and swayed over her without striking. When her stories were finished, she laid her hands on her son's heads and gazed out the window.

Under her hands their young hearts thumped.

"I'm going to Punjab, boys. My furry boys."

"For good?" asked Jassy in alarm.

"I must go and see to some things."

She pulled the boys up to her and pressed them close.

"Do you have to go, Ma? Are you sure you should go alone?"

"There are times when everyone must go alone," she said softly. She pulled them to her and felt the weakness tugging from inside.

It was coming spring; the snow falls were wet and heavy. Warm blasts of April wind portented summer and growth.

Then, before anyone quite realized it, she was gone.

III

Mohan explained nothing about Prito's departure during the following weeks. He was stony faced and surly, but that was usual. He made the announcement that there would be a vacation during the first week of summer. But Mohan didn't believe in vacations and everyone knew it. "Time, money and energy down the drain, that is vacation." The boys were skeptical when they were told to prepare for a week at a rented lakeside cottage, and distrustful as they piled into the aging Vanguard.

They drove up a long dirt road from the highway, the old car chugging in the dust, through birch forests, past shimmering rivers and dark ponds. Even this was not enough to fill the void where Prito had been. Not for a momentary scene of bull moose in a swamp. Not for the sight of the cabin on the lake where they were to vacation. Mohan cooked something with meat and masala. Only he could eat it. The boys went to bed hungry. When Mohan had turned in, they sat on the beach under a star-painted sky and listened to the sounds of the forest and gentle waves of the lake.

In the morning, the vacation dream began to unravel as tranquility gave way to a peculiar madness consisting of speedboats, water skiers, and rock music. Gurjit and Jassy sat on the dock watching Mohan. Then Gurjit winked at his brother and plunged into the busy lake and swam boldly out.

Mohan stalked along the beach near the dock, pretending to examine the lake bottom. He muttered to himself, his face twisted into a sneer of contempt.

"What is he doing out there? Did I say he could do that?" Sickness, this place. Foul, disgusting, play like children . . . " He fumed and snorted, uncaring of Jassy. "They're all the same. *Kotu.* Unreliable shits. See what I care. Hey you," Mohan suddenly turned to Jassy. "Get your brother out of this cesspool. We're going home."

"He just got bored because he finished his newspapers," Gurjit whispered to Jassy as they got into the car, and Jassy sighed and said, "Our kind of people don't know how to have fun."

Mohan took a swipe at Jassy, but Jassy ducked behind the seat and stayed there the rest of the drive home. . . .

A long time passed and they filled in the space where Prito had been. Jassy wore a suit his first day at high school, knowing that no one wore suits to school, but knowing, imagining, what she would have him do. The suit came to him in a dream. He'd thrown his stones against the back of the garage and borne out the wish of Prito and the wish of the stones.

The stones, one blood-red, one white as ice and the other a blue of the centre of sky, he tossed each day. It was part of life without Prito. Like Gurjit's long hair and moustache and his late hours, and Mohan's growing seclusion behind his wall of newspapers.

"We'll survive," Gurjit assured Jassy. But Mohan was changing. He seemed to forget, after a time, his sons. Each evening he returned from work and sought refuge in his papers, slumping behind a barricade that read SOVIETS INVADE PRAGUE. The barricade arose for increasing periods, rising higher each day until Mohan resembled a park bench bum shielding himself from the storm.

Gurjit claimed that Mohan was dying.

"I have to shake him awake in the morning," he said. "He wouldn't make it in to work if it wasn't for me. We would starve. Mohan would rot in bed. And he forgets things. He forgets to wear his tie some days. And I saw him drive right through a red light. He's dying. When your mind goes, you die."

Jassy watched his father die. He saw Mohan's hair grow out and stand in an unruly silver wave on his head. He saw the thin face become drawn and sunken as though the flesh were being absorbed into the mass of hair. Mohan did not eat. One day the newspaper pages didn't turn and Jassy knew the end was nigh.

"He's finished," confirmed Gurjit sagely. "His mind is blown . . . "

He did not see how it was that Mohan began his affair with the bottle. It was sudden and was marked by the newspapers lying unread one evening, the chair empty. Then Mohan came home and took a tumbler to his room — a bottle was never seen by the boys — and some time later his voice droned out in Punjabi as he paced behind the closed door.

On Christmas Eve Jassy heard a crash from Mohan's room and he buried his head under his blankets and awaited his brother's return. In the morning he and Gurjit cautiously opened Mohan's door. The air was thick and harsh inside. A table and a chair were in pieces. Mohan lay on one side of the wide bed, staring at the ceiling. Strangely, Prito's side of the bed was immaculate, the covers unwrinkled as though Mohan had managed to avoid touching them all the months of his wife's absence.

"Is he . . . ?"

"No, Stupid. His chest moved. There, he blinked." Gurjit stepped ahead into the room, crunching pieces of wood beneath his feet, Jassy on his heels. They stood breathlessly over their father.

"She's not coming back, is she, Papa?" said Gurjit.

Mohan shook his head slowly, and Jassy felt tears welling up.

"Why?" Jassy sobbed, "Why?"

"It is not a matter for . . . " Mohan began but Jassy, overcome, sat on his father's feet at that moment. "Ow, hai! For the sake of God, are you a baby? You sniveling girl. Stop that weeping before I go crazy! Ditch-digger! Stupid digger of dung!"

Jassy and Gurjit skipped from the room as Mohan, awakened into his old blazing anger, threw off his covers and stomped after them. The door slammed.

Mohan did not speak to them for a long period after this.

The door to his room remained closed and locked more than ever and when he appeared his body was noticeably diminished. His skin took on a yellowy-green pallor and was rough. His silver wave of hair reached upward like the upturned blade of a snow shovel.

"He's on his last legs." observed Gurjit.

But another spring came and then at the beginning of summer Mohan emerged. He came out, not to die, not to wreck the house or beat his sons, but to pack them up and send them away to the West Coast to stay with Piara.

That was the summer that Jassy saw his brother's hand tucked into the swimsuit of their cousin. It was then that he suspected that Prito, Mohan and even Gurjit were not really his family after all. It was then that he first suspected that Jassy Singh Sijjer was alone in the world.

FIVE

Mohan's Bride

I

At the end of the summer Jassy and Gurjit returned to find their father and their home transformed. Gone were Mohan's deathly pallour and his blade of hair. The furniture had been changed, the house repainted. Even the locks were new. In the midst of it sat a strange woman in a pink, silver-sequined sari. Introductions were not offered.

Gurjit dropped his suitcase, the blood draining from his face.

"Where's my mother, Mohan? Tell us. " He said this quietly, but Jassy saw his hand tremble as he took down an ornate musical instrument that hung from the wall. It was a sitar. "You went to India, didn't you? Did you see her? Why didn't she come back?"

Mohan smiled a slippery, cold smile. Jassy saw the meanness in that smile, but Gurjit was looking at the sitar. "You have a new mother now." Mohan said.

The sitar dropped, the gourd cracking like a huge egg. Gurjit roared, then the roar became a string of obscenities, erupting from somewhere in his chest. But Mohan was ready for this. From behind his back he brought forth a short leather whip of the kind used by mahouts. He brought it down with one abrupt motion on the crown of Gurjit's head, the blow stunning everyone into silence. A drop of blood fell from Gurjit's hairline, then Gurjit crouched and his fist shot into Mohan's stomach. But Mohan barely recoiled from this. He seized Gurjit by the hair and pants, marched him out of the house and deposited him in the street. Jassy heard Gurjit roar again, even after Mohan had come back and shut and locked the door. A window broke upstairs and then Gurjit was gone. Left to fend for himself, Jassy elected to stay quiet rather than suffer the whip. When Mohan glared at him in challenge, he looked down at his shoes, then retreated to the back of the garage.

For the first few days Jassy watched and waited until the facts of the situation became clear.

Late one night he wrote a letter to his mother.

October 2, 1969
Under Mohan's guard

Dear Mother,

It is hard to know where to start because so much has happened here. I still can't believe it but Mohan has gone crazy and kidnapped this lady and brought her home to be his new bride. I will try to begin at the beginning.

To begin with there is the size of new bride. She looks sort of like the Michelin man with arms the size of Mohan's legs and, no kidding, thighs the size of Mohan's chest. Her chest looks like two Rocky mountains and, when she moves around, it rustles as if she's got two rabbits and some dry grass in there. You should see her bum. It is so wide it takes up half the sofa and it sags down like the bum of an elephant. She's got this voice that kind of shrieks and makes you want to hide in the closet. I swear one of the China plates broke one day when she was shrieking at Mohan about something. I never know what she is talking about because she does not speak English and never speaks to me anyway. She will not even look at me in fact.

So far I have only seen the new bride do four things. Eat, cook, sleep and watch television. And sometimes talk to Mohan. I think if she keeps eating and watching television the amount she does she will soon grow too fat for this house. We are all skinny people here, as you know, and the house probably is not used to the strain.

Gurjit left home and has not come back. I would have left with him, but I saw that there was a lot of weird things going on in our house and someone has to keep a look out. I thought it over and decided the best thing to do is call the police, but I am going to wait until I hear what Gurjit thinks about it.

In the meantime I am laying low and writing everything down for the police file they will need on Mohan. I haven't decided how to handle going to school yet. A thing like this is pretty hard to hide. You end up thinking that everybody knows and then you spill the beans by mistake. What would the kids at school say? What will they think of me? There is something wrong with all this, even a fourteen-year-old knows that. I sure don't know how Mohan can go around with that funny smile on his face. He has really gone crazy this time.

your loving son, Jaswant

Weeks later Gurjit returned under the cool gaze of his father. He told no one where he had been. He took Jassy aside and advised him not to speak to Mohan's bride. "We'll make her leave," Gurjit said confidently. . . .

That evening he took Jassy by the arm and led him out of the house. They rode a street car to Yonge Street. The streets were like a carnival. Stores were open late spilling light onto the passing throngs. Prostitutes leaned into car windows and teenagers gathered on the corners to smoke and share rotgut wine. Orange robed Hare Krishnas danced and chanted in the midst of ringing chimes. Gurjit led the way at a leisurely pace as if guiding Jassy through a museum. Someone greeted Gurjit and offered him a bottle and someone else approached with a hand-rolled cigarette. They went on and a woman in red skin-tight shorts came to Gurjit and kissed his mouth. Jassy stared.

Gurjit finally went into a pizzeria where he sat his younger brother down and dove into the back room to return with two cold bottles of beer.

"Initiation, Jassy. Your first beer. If you turn it down, then you're a pious man, but if you love it, you're a real Sikh."

Gurjit was seventeen. His hair flowed in a black mane and he wore a bright Navajo headband and complicated sandals of leather. "I think Mama went crazy," he said.

"How do you know?"

"You believe everything I say, don't you, little brother?"

"Of course not," retorted Jassy but this was a lie.

"I know you do. I'm glad you do," Gurjit said seriously. "I think Mohan drove our mother crazy so he could get a new wife. I'm going to bring her back, you know . . . "

"Come on."

"I am. I got a job. It's simple. I'll save my money and go. I calculate it'll take me until next year."

"Come on. What about your scholarship?"

"I don't want it. There are more important things than university. Even more important than philosophy."

Jassy laughed nervously. He believed Gurjit and was afraid. It meant being left alone with Mohan and his fat bride. He watched Gurjit gulp his beer, his throat working. It was hard to point to any one thing that Prito had done that was a sign of madness. All memory of her was clouded at that moment. But she was beaten down by Mohan, just as he and Gurjit were.

"How could we let it happen?" he whispered.

"It's Papa. He drove her away. The bastard."

They drank another beer and Jassy felt at once conspiratorial and queasy. From without came the sounds of the busy street, merged together to sound like crashing waves. It was a complex, dangerous sea, surging at the door, and Gurjit forged ahead into it, swimming boldly away from him like that day at the lake.

Gurjit brought still more beer.

"I guess they know you here," Jassy said.

"Hell, I practically own the place," Gurjit grinned.

II

Jan. 2, 1970
In Mohan's Prison

Dear Mother,

Gurjit has become a fencepost hole digger instead of a philosophy student. Each night he tramps in sweaty and muddy, wearing a secret grin which means, you watch and you will see me swim.

Mohan does not not seem to care. He is only interested in his new bride and seems to have lots of money all of a sudden. He buys her all kinds of clothes that look like they are made for elephants and enough candy and chocolate to feed my whole school.

The new bride is growing fatter every second, and her voice is going through a change. Now it is deeper than it was before and does not warble so much. Gurjit says she's either having late puberty or she's going through a sex change. Whatever it is, her voice still makes me want to put a pillow over my ears. Even though I do not understand what she says to Mohan, it sounds like she is asking to buy her more stuff. Her throat is as thick as a telephone pole and she is so wide she has to squeeze to get through the kitchen doorway. When she rides with Mohan in our poor old Vanguard, it leans to one side and the springs and stuff scrape the road. The only place they ever go is not too far, lucky for our car. They go every second Sunday to Montgomery School where all the Sikh have begun having Gurdwara.

So now Mohan's new bride has five things that she does. Cooks, eats, sleeps, watches T.V. and goes to Gurdwara. She forces Mohan to do what she wants by crashing around in the kitchen and bellowing like a bull elephant in her new deep voice. One day he was forced to pull out his mahout whip and threaten her, and we thought that was the end, but we were wrong. Another time she shook the house so bad we thought the whole place would fall down. That was the only time Mohan ever refused to go to Gurdwara with her. Now he just shuts up and goes. Then he got this idea to make me go too (they wouldn't dare tell Gurjit what to do). I only put up with it so I can keep an eye on them. I'm biding my time before I make my report to the police.

Gurdwara is nothing like you described in India. Instead of smelling like incense, it smells like gym class since it's in the gym of the school. So they read from the Granth Sahib and we look at the basketball hoops and the ropes for climbing and sit on the wood floor. There are only a few people who come, so we are always lost in the middle of this giant room, the Shabads echoing with a kind of lost, lonely sound, and on cold days the wind whistling outside. It makes me sad really. It's like the end of Gurdwaras everywhere. I always think of you as I sit and listen to the singing and the wind. I wonder what kind of Gurdwara you're sitting in and I get this peaceful feeling, because I know it's better than here. . . .

Believe it or not the Gurdwara people actually seem to like Mohan's bride. I wonder if they know she was kidnapped. I wonder why she never tells them or why she has never tried to escape. Gurjit just laughs when I ask him. He thinks she came of her own free will, but that would be the day. Who would go off and marry someone when he was already married? You would have to be nuts!

Anyway she loves the Gurdwara and is often asked to go up and sing in front of everybody. My skin crawls when I hear her sing. I cannot understand what they see in her.

So I watch them and wait. Every fourth Sunday I take my shoes off and cover my head, bow down before the Granth Sahib, and I pray and dream and listen to the words. Then there is buttery Karah Prasad, which has a taste which, despite everything, gives me hope.

Best of all, the thing I like is the way Mohan hates Gurudwara. You can just see him squirming all the time he is there. He sits as stiff as iron and with that bird-like expression on his face, as if he is just about to pounce on something. You see all the other men in the place have beards and turbans. Except for the kids, Mohan is the only one with cut hair. So he ties an old napkin around his head and looks really ridiculous, like a scrawny chicken right out of the freezer. I think he must know how he looks. Even at the Langar, when everyone greets Mohan's wife, no one there really has much to do with Mohan. I can see that this bugs him like crazy. Gurjit says that, if his new bride can make Mohan suffer every second Sunday like that, then she must have something on him. I cannot see what that is. She still never talks to me and Gurjit, but Gurjit says she is just biding her time.

love, Jassy

My sixteenth birthday
Trapped

Dear Mother,

For my birthday Gurjit gave me an old book which has changed my life. It is called The Art of Questioning *written by an obscure and ancient writer named Pia. It is the kind of book that contains the really important things to know about life. It makes the stuff we learn in school seem silly. I always have about a million questions in my head, but none of them much to do with school. Pia teaches that asking questions is the most important part of learning. Most of his book is questions. But he also wrote these things called aphorisms in which he says things like that the amount of knowledge in the world depends on how many people have died. And he says there are two kinds of questions. Questions that you ask out of knowledge and those you ask out of ignorance (the knowledge kind are 'questions of discovery' while the other kind are 'questions for the dead'). I could read Pia all day long.*

Mohan's bride finally decided to make her move on us. One morning she told Gurjit, IN ENGLISH, that he should start wearing a turban like a grown man. She said he couldn't go around looking like a 'shippie' and we all looked at her until we saw that she meant 'hippie'. This made Gurjit laugh, so she ran away to her room which made the whole house shake like there was an earthquake on. Then she came back and started ordering me and Gurjit around, telling us all these jobs we had to do, and, when we ignored her, she started to shriek. She said she was the mother of the house and not just a 'crackplate' which sent

Gurjit running out of the house laughing. She finally went to her room and turned on the television.

Mohan will drive his bride nuts sooner or later anyway, without any help from us. She's all alone here with him, and me and Gurjit are against her, so what can she do? She'll go crazy. They'll have to send a special huge white truck to take her away in, and a specially made straight jacket to wrap her in. She'll be babbling about shippies and crackplates and no one will know what she is talking about.

I have also been reading about evolution. The universe, the earth, and all biological life evolves continually. That means that we must evolve too, in our lives. What comes later depends on what went before. I fear what I will become, to tell you the truth. I fear that I will become a ditch-digger, of course, like Mohan has always told me. But more than that I fear that I will end up like Mohan, trapped in a tough shell, and driving everyone crazy with my misery.

So my question is this: does evolution ever take a break?

your loving son

Jassy picked through the laundry looking for his socks. He found a strange silken garment with three great holes of equal size in it. It was Mohan's bride's underpants, big enough to be a vest for Gurjit. He held up the thing and imagined her huge, shaking flanks as she pulled the ridiculous garment on. And, for some reason, he felt sorry.

III

Nov, 1971
Abandoned

Dear Mother,

Gurjit is gone. One night a short time ago he hoisted his rucksack on his shoulder and said good-bye. He said if he got lost in India I was supposed to come and get him. I'm not sure if this was a joke or not. He was all laughing and smiles, but I couldn't look him in the eye. I know how mad he would get if I cried.

Mohan was in his chair behind his newspapers when we came downstairs. He knew something was up. He put down the newspapers and looked Gurjit over like he hadn't seen him before. I knew how Mohan was thinking. He was thinking that Gurjit was full grown and he wouldn't be able to thrash him again. You see, Gurjit is way bigger than Mohan now. He looks as wild as a pie-dog in his jeans, boots and rucksack. Mohan asked Gurjit why he was dressed like he was, even though Gurjit has looked like that for years. Gurjit just looked at me and laughed, then he said to Mohan "I'm going away, Old Man. What do you have to say about it?" But Mohan wouldn't say anything. He just put up his paper again.

So now I'm alone with my questions and my book by Pia which I read every day. 'Many false questions,' Pia wrote, 'are about balance. For balance refers to the simple comparison of value and the human mind is such that it prefers simplicity. In fact, there is no such thing as balance in the real world, because no one thing is similar to another.'

love, Jassy

March 1972
Toronto

Dear Mother,

Gurjit has not written. It has been four months now and I am worried about you both. I am also worried about myself, I must admit. I let my hair grow these days but it has not gotten long and impressive like Gurjit's. Instead it has formed this set of weird-shaped earmuffs that just grow straight out sideways. It looks stupid but I can't do anything to make it different. I hold my hands to the sides of my head a lot when there is nothing else to do, to press the earmuffs down, and this caused Mr. Ross, the chemistry teacher, to think I had a migraine. He sent me to the nurse. So I am sort of disappointed in how I look. I always thought I would look more like Gurjit by now but something has gone wrong. Not only is my hair different but my whole body is not what it really should be. I am just a stick, Marilyn says, meaning skinny. Not to mention not nearly as big as Gurjit. I figure that my hair and my skinny body are the reasons I have never gotten the same attention Gurjit always got. I always hoped to be sort of rollicking and streetwise like him and have some older women who liked me or something. I always hoped to plunge into the water and swim away the way he did.

To be really honest, I am worried about my virginity most of all. I have this friend Marilyn who is my age but she is miles ahead. She has fallen in love numerous times and already had an abortion once. She goes out on dates with men who are a lot older and is able to drink and so forth with no problem. She even looks older. Her life is full of passion and love. Beside her I feel like a plain brown pebble next to a diamond. I expect any time to be kicked along down the hill into the ditch. No one is interested in plain skinny little stones, are they? I fear that I am destined to endure my life without ever being moved

your son, Jaswant

Alone in the house one day Jassy resolved to find the letters Mohan claimed Prito had sent. He rifled his father's desk and found Mohan's bride's passport. She was twenty-nine years old and in the photograph was thinner than he'd seen her. He found a Playboy magazine which he studied in detail, and he found his own birth certificate. Lodged in the slit between the back of the drawer and the side he found a single small photograph of Prito. She was not much older than Jassy in the photo. Her eyes were moist, her expression one of betrayal and mourning. There were no letters and nothing else of Prito's. The drawer was like Mohan's heart: unsentimental and austere. Except for this one small photo. Did the photo belie a secret niche where Mohan perhaps laid his hand now and again to remember Prito? Or had it fallen from somewhere to lodge there forgotten?

He stole Prito's photo and in the safety of his own room considered it further. Who did she mourn at that time? She was full of secret, silent mournings her whole life it seemed. And who would not grieve. He recalled how Mohan's voice lashed Prito as viciously as he had lashed Gurjit with the whip. He thought of how Mohan made her suffer by ignoring her for weeks on end. It sickened him to draw on these thoughts. It seemed Mohan could get away with anything and no one, not even Gurjit could stand up to him. Grieve then, she did. There had been no escape for years. Jassy stared at Prito's tender face and anger boiled up in him. There was no fairness in any of this. He saw her warm eyes and imagined the pain she'd endured because of Mohan. His limbs trembled with a sudden violent rage. . . .

He stormed back into Mohan's room and looked about with the bloody eye of destruction. He seized an old vase that had been in the house for years and hurled it against a mirror. The crash of breaking glass echoed on in his mind for some minutes. Jassy was transfixed by what he had done. He wished he were far away where Mohan would never find him.

Locked in his room he fell asleep and dreamed of a cache of gold which became smaller as he guarded over it. In the middle of the night he awoke to the shouts and concussions of Mohan beating his bride. She wailed and sobbed and the door slammed but his father's voice could not be heard.

It was days before the swelling of her face went down, and before she could rustle through the house without a groan of pain.

June, 1972

Dear Mother,

You will be proud to know that I matriculated and won a scholarship to U. of T.

Since the night that Mohan beat his bride I have been awakened every night to the sound of her warbling out a Hindi love song to the rhythm of lovemaking. The house bounces along with a shudder and slap that sets the plates jingling and furniture bouncing. I can't help but imagine the unclothed expanse of Mohan's bride with skinny Mohan riding atop her with his mahout whip, whipping, and riding and hanging on.

Last night in the midst of this spectacle I realized I can't stay in the house. I've become an intruder here and Mohan's bride is here to stay. My family doesn't exist here any longer. I am on my own. You and Gurjit are so far away I can't even picture your faces anymore. So I am leaving. When I finish this letter I will pack up my things and move into town.

your son

Jassy cried when he finished the letter. Then he cleaned himself up and packed his things. It did not take long. A few books, his clothes, along with some stolen utensils. Lastly there was his old wooden box of most prized objects. These were his baby teeth, some special marbles called crystals, a recent letter from Marilyn, a broken toy gyroscope, the photo of Prito, a *kirpan* Prito had given him, and in a matchbox his three stones: one iron red, one the white of alpine ice, and one the blue of the deep sea.

SIX

Questions

I

The room is a scuzzy hole which is worse than any slum dwelling he has ever imagined. The backdrop consists of rats, roaches, hallway racists and drunks, all of it pervaded by a urine-decayed wood smell, the odour of failure and neglect.

And there is not one person who knows about it.

Can one convey to a school mate, an acquaintance, a stranger that there is a grease-stain on the wall of the kitchen which takes the form of a leering face, which will not be rubbed away? Can one describe a concoction of masala, beans and bread which make a good appetite wither? Are there words for the way the heart sinks on winter nights in the face of darkness? Or the way one must soothe oneself day and night by pulling on the sex until calm. Would even a mother understand this? Would anyone care?

He switches off the light and tries to sleep. A draught whistles in under the door and across his bed. It is stale air, laden with the ripe stench of garbage. He buries his head under the covers and shuts his eyes tightly. His mind fills with half-learned chemical formulae, Schrodinger's Wave Equation and the name *Serratia marcescens*; the voices of professors mingle with the laughter of a woman and some red, floating spots appear. Now comes an upwelling of anxiety about an upcoming test in the craft of calculus, and this combines, strangely, with a stubborn sexual yearning.

One plods and plods with eyes to the mud, hoping for a glimpse of sky. One is stone.

February 1973
Free in T.O.

Dear Mother,

I know that you must worry about me. I live in a clean place, eat well and I have many reliable friends. I think of you often and still hope for the day when you and Gurjit return home.

I've been wondering how well you ever know someone. Do lovers ever know each other? Do mothers understand sons? I am beset by questions and dreams.

You probably wouldn't recognize me if you saw me now. I must wear these quite thick glasses and I have a moustache which is not quite satisfactory. I'm not especially tall or short, which is not quite satisfactory either, but my face and physique are, I like to think, dependable.

your loving son, Jaswant

II

July 1974
Lahore, Toronto

Dear Mother,

It is now summer here and in the neighbourhood where I live it is hot. Tar in the street is running in streams. The lake is a bath. I was lucky enough to secure a summer research assistantship. Each day I go to work at the university. I go through a city grey with smog. The city people have fled the heat like a pack of scared lemmings, heading for the cool lakes, I suppose.

This weather brings to mind the old walled city of Lahore which you described in detail: the seething crowds of the bazaar, the noise and dust and confinement of it. It was there, you told us, that Guru Arjan was tortured for not giving his son in marriage to the daughter of Chandu, the Emperor's minister. Arjan, you said, was asked to give up his beliefs but I always thought he was kind of too proud. After all, they tortured him to death. It was like here, at the height of the hot season, with a blazing sun, and dust all around. You told us they put Arjan into a cauldron of boiling water, then made him sit on a gigantic skillet over a fire. I wonder if it's really true that he suffered in silence, received his torture and when he was released, walked on blistered feet to the cold river. What kind of vision possessed him, to make him die over a principle? Are people like this human? Are we really all made of the same stuff after all?

Other questions have grown in magnitude. I now wonder how it is that ordinary things like dirt and air and water can possibly come together to form living, thriving cells. I remember you saying once that living things are really one and that the thing that makes everything run, living or not, is God. I find this unsatisfactory, to be frank, even if it is an interesting idea.

I've also been wondering what makes people dependent on the attentions of others. Why aren't people content to be alone? There would be more time, I feel, for important matters such as science, if people didn't have this need to socialize.

your son, Jaswant

When the sun was low, he sauntered down University and along Queen. Heat lightning flashed on the small horizon between the buildings. The air was thick and still.

In his apartment fires had broken out six nights in a row. A fire engine waited on the corner, the firemen looking pessimistic and sweaty in their gear. The fire escape of the ancient building groaned under the weight of tenants who had moved outside, refusing to risk the possibility of an inferno. They had moved mattresses, sofas and colour televisions, onto the iron structure. Beer spilled down through the gridded floors onto the heads of those below and there were fights. The police had come when the fifth floor tenants formed a defence brigade to battle the Sixth Floor Vigilance Committee. A riot had threatened to erupt.

Jassy pushed through the grillwork door and was descended upon by a marauding band of dogs and naked children who had taken control of the hallways since the fire crisis had begun. They begged a can of Coke from his bag of groceries, then stampeded away.

His room was a blast furnace. He popped open a Coke and stepped through his window onto the fire escape. It creaked unsteadily. "Easy. Walk soft or you'll bring us all down," a voice above intoned.

"Don't tell him what to do," said someone else. This he recognized as Sally, the woman next door.

"You people on the third are a bunch of shitty wimps," said the voice above.

"Don't answer," said Sally, "we don't have to answer that kind of crap!" she yelled.

She moved into the glare from the window and Sijjer stared at her. She was clad in a skimpy bikini and held a beer in her hand. "They've been doin' this all day. They want another rumble."

Something dripped down through the grating and someone said, "Assholes . . . "

"Don't stare so much. You give a girl the goosebumps."

"Sorry."

"I'm just tryin' to keep cool same as everyone else. Look at those jerks. They wear anything they want and get away with it clean."

Jassy peered across the alley into the dark.

"When you're a fee-male, you gotta dress up for forty below all the time."

She sat beside Sijjer and offered him her beer. The fire escape shook as someone walked along it.

"I thought maybe Bud threw you out without your clothes again."

"Oh Bud. He's ancient history, man. Gone-o. I told him to piss off, frappez la rue, vamoose."

The alarm sounded then and the tenants leapt to the rail to see the fire. The building shuddered. Pieces of concrete broke away from the mountings of the fire escape and someone gave a yelp. Jassy and Sally dove through the open window, but the commotion eased and the fire escape remained.

"You're starin' again," said Sally. Then she winked, moved sveltely to the door and returned to her own flat.

Jassy sat down on his bed. He was trapped. He saw Sally's long legs and the shape of her nipples through her bikini. He sat still and tried to control his agitation. Questions budded in his head. What was her skin like in the heat? How smooth were the insides of her thighs? Why had he never made love? Why?

The streets erupted again as a fire engine clanged, red lights flickering over the faces of the haunted tenants of the fire escape. In the corridor the band of children and dogs stormed by and through the wall Sally could be heard telephoning, begging someone to please come and get her, she is about to roast or fry, and please, please give her a break.

At the end of that week Jassy returned to Mohan's house. He had vowed not to capitulate. But it had now been more two years and, like Sally, he needed a break. He could not think of anywhere to go but back.

In the suburbs, under the trees, it was cool. He used his key and entered Mohan's house through the kitchen. Mohan's bride stood by the stove frying samosai. She had prepared a cold pitcher of lassi to go with it. "Oh, my dear boy. My son," she cried when she saw him. She wrapped her tire-like arms around him. She smelled sweet, like spiced candy. "Mohan, oh Mohan, look who has come. Like a lost bottle he has come. Just like that!" Jassy allowed himself to be stroked and pinched for a moment before he took a large glass of lassi.

Mohan stuck his head around the door. "Well," he said shortly.

Jassy accepted a plate stacked up with samosai and sat beside his father who was in the depths of the *New York Times*. The two sat in silence for some time.

"This Trudeau should resign," Mohan said with great effort.

"Uh-huh."

Mohan's bride came and sat next to Jassy. "Eat. You are thin as glass," she said. "Is university fine?"

Now she turned and spoke in Punjabi to Mohan. Mohan glanced over his paper.

"Soon you must think of marriage," she ventured.

Jassy laughed.

"Not to worry about it. Only think about it," she said with a plump smile.

She stuffed him full of *roti, dal* and *achar* until his belly ached and his mouth burned. She was fatter than ever. Jassy imagined Mohan riding her with his whip, no longer a mahout, it seemed, but a mere flea upon her back.

Mohan sat with Jassy and watched the evening newscast. He paid his son no more or less mind than he ever had.

III

Oct. 1975
Toronto

Dear Mother,

I am finding these studies of the grand questions of life alternately intense and dry. I get the distinct impression sometimes, of being on the wrong road, that I am somehow missing the point. I know that you would make me keep on with my studies though. "Learning is changing," wrote Pia. "Change reminds one of growth and so gives the illusion of perpetual growth."

"Learning is for those conceited enough to believe they are improvable," says a rather cynical professor of physical chemistry who builds bomb shelters as a hobby.

Most times this learning, this indoctrination in the scientific method, is a soothing habit at least. Some students never want it to end. Change! Growth! Perpertual youth! For a quavering temperment, there is safety in the temple of learning. I have my doubts.

You taught us to study all we could. "Be like Nanak," you told us, "and search the edges of the world in search of the truth." I wonder what Guru Nanak would have thought of Pia? Maybe they knew each other.

I go back to Mohan's these days and who knows why? They've developed — I should say she has developed — this routine of introducing me to a lot of young women. I can't quite decide how far to go along with this, since I know what is going on in Mohan's bride's fat head. She's got me pegged for an arranged marriage, I am sure. She keeps dropping hints about how old I'm getting and how lonely I look. I've never even considered an arranged marriage. I'm independent after all. I don't need anything arranged for me.

But when I return to my flat downtown, I am indeed lonely and strange. I have not known women. This scares me. I am as virginal and unmoved as ever. I peer down the road into the upcoming years and I realize how possible it is that I will endure solitude. I see myself as a nattily dressed, middle-aged bachelor, and still later as an old bachelor, pathetic by then, without people around me, nattily dressed still and hoping. I will be a lonely stone of a thing, gray and spavined. Without highs or lows. No children to fret after. A withdrawn and cold stone of a thing. I have never found the secret of taking hold of real life and making it my own. I'm sure if I did I would find a girl. It works on the mind. I see the aging process already beginning. My hands are growing scrawny, like Mohan's. My life has only begun, yet already it has begun to end. Perhaps the purpose of surrounding ourselves with people is so we don't see time fly by. The touch of others, the chatter and confusion, distracts us from time. I too wish to be distracted.

So I keep going back to Mohan's like a gambler going back to the races. Maybe if my life isn't arranged for me, nothing will happen. That is a horrible thought.

J.

P.S. By the way, all that past stuff between me and Mohan seems forgotten now. One must have a family after all. It is tough to get by without one.

"Someone is here who you will like, Jassy. You will see what a gentle, soft mind she has." Mohan's bride was cooking in the kitchen and as she shuffled about the floor the pots and plates jingled in their places.

"You mean, 'soft heart'."

"Yes, that too. All of her is soft and nice."

The young woman who sat in the living room with Mohan wore a traditional silwar kimiz and wore her waist-long hair in a single thick braid. Her name was Manjit. She had large, slanting eyes that shifted downwards when Jassy looked at her. Her shyness she wore like a veil: her smile was cautious and her voice so soft and small it could not be heard above the jingle of Mohan's bride moving around the kitchen.

Without a word, Mohan suddenly left the room. The two sat through an awkward silence. The girl was panic-stricken, he tongue-tied. After no more than five minutes Mohan's bride came and took Manjit to the kitchen. The two women remained there, conferring quietly in Punjabi.

After Manjit had left, Jassy sat next to his father watching the evening news. Mohan's bride entered, causing the men to bounce in their chairs and the television to flicker. She let herself down close to Jassy and gazed intently into his face.

"You like her Jassy?" she whispered.

"She's very beautiful."

"There's a time when a man must become serious, Jassy. It's no good on your own, you know. Not for you. You cannot be a lone wool."

"Lone wolf," Mohan corrected.

"You can't, Jassy. A man without a family is just part a man. Not a complete, finished man. A man needs a wife to finish him."

Mohan glanced sidelong at his bride.

"Well, I can hardly be serious about someone I've never had a conversation with," Jassy pointed out.

"Think about it. That is all we ask. Oh, she is a shy girl. Just a soft donut of a girl, really."

"You just consider what's right," Mohan threw in.

As Jassy made his way to the bus stop later, he looked upon the streets where he had grown up and saw that changes had occurred. Houses were shrunken, and trees which he remembered as saplings had trunks like pillars. And he had changed too. The nerve and muscle in his leg tingled as he walked, and he imagined the cells of his body going through the strains of senescence. He saw his reflection in the window of the bus: two enormous eyes set in a triangular, thin face. There was an air of solitude and hopelessness. 'Like one of those stones' he thought, 'that remain in one place through the millennia, gradually yielding to time, and crumbling away to nothing.'

He descended from the bus and moved through the streets. A sad-faced boy manned the counter in the grocery store. He had long, dark eyes that reminded him of Manjit. Both revealed the same destructible light. Sijjer paid for his groceries and left quickly.

In his apartment block a woman was bellowing heartily in French against a resounding singular voice of a hundred televisions. The gang of children and dogs swept by in the hall and yet another quarrel ran its course in Sally's room. A voice begged her to "Be rational" and Jassy could not help but laugh. Do lovers ever understand each other?

Jassy had become accustomed to the fights next door. He eavesdropped with interest, certain there was a pattern to be discerned in the line of argument used by Sally and against her. She had a new lover every two weeks. "I blow through men like they was Kleenex," she boasted.

Now her door slammed, someone shuffled off down the hall and there came a tapping on the wall. A moment later Sally was at his door, her face drawn. She smelled of beer. Her china doll eyes were smeary, her teeshirt rumpled.

"Everything alright, Sally?"

"Sure. Sure I am. He was just another psycho anyway. Another psycho bites the dust! Hah! This was one of those quiet ones, the kind who's nice and gentle, then you wake up one night and he's starin' at you like maybe he'd like to see you without no head or somethin'."

Jassy watched her curiously, held back, but smiling a little at her intensity. "How do you get mixed up with guys like that?"

"It's always the same. Don't you know? Don't you really know? Psychos go for me. Lunatics, madmen, they love me. Didn't you notice that? I go for them too, I guess. I enjoy it. I enjoy lunatics!"

She was like a bound wild animal. Jassy was never sure what she would do. He laughed nervously and put a pot of coffee on while she described in detail her latest suitor. As she talked, she slid around the floor doing a dance step and trailing cigarette smoke. She stopped in front of Jassy and laid her hand on his chest.

"Anyway, where's your little bit of something? How come you don't have a girl? You look like enough of a nut to have a girl hidden somewhere . . . "

"Yeah, I have a girl. Sort of."

"Sort of? What's that mean? Sort of a friend or sort of a girl? What is she? A sheep?"

"I'm just getting to know her. Sort of."

Sally blew a cloud of smoke into his face. "Probably one of those Miss Campus Chicks, huh. Sort of, he says. How come she don't come up? Place not exciting enough for her? She a good lay? Oop! Sal, you and your mouth. He don't know that. You better find out if she's a good lay, is my advice. You don't know that, you don't know diddly squat. She might be frigid, for all you know, or one of those ball-breaking hold-outs. Nothing worse than that. So I've heard anyway . . . " Sinuously she moved around the room to a tune in her head, smoking and blowing clouds at Jassy. She wore a skimpy pair of jean shorts that did little to cover her lean flanks.

"Know what my problem is? I can't resist lunatics. They're always turned on."

Sally took Jassy to bed. It happened in a way that reminded him of the way the air was released from bicycle tires. In one blurred and uncontrolled moment he was between her legs. The sensations of warmth were as pleasing as the rush of air on fingers. There was the warmth in his loins, then the wetter, hotter warmth of hers. A dry hairless warmth of her belly and breasts. Different warmths: the pulsating warmth inside her, and a cool, twitching warmth of her nipples as they stabbed up under his palms.

'This is what I've missed all this time,' he thought. 'I've missed out on warmth.'

Sally and he slept together for two weeks before she abruptly spurned him.

"You don't own me," she sneered one night, and Jassy knew from his long term of observation not to argue or throw her out into the hall. He retreated to the science library once more and concentrated on his studies.

SEVEN

I

June 1976

Dear Mother,

You would say, 'What good is all this science with the way it abuses faith.' But I remember how you were in awe of anyone with Doctor in front of his name. So I will keep studying. I can't think of anything else to keep me from being a ditch-digger besides. I graduated with honours and have accepted a studentship to continue in the doctoral program in biochemistry.

Dreams, Mother, and questions fill my mind.

I dreamed about the girl named Manjit. She's so beautiful she scares me. In the dream she is clothed in crimson and gold silk. Her gold jewelry looks as though it were poured on like syrup; it drips from the crown of her head and from all the folds of her sari. She sits cross-legged on the floor, looking down. I see her eyelids, not her eyes. After a time she stands and spreads crimson and gold wings, then she folds them and sits again without taking flight. The dream ends with a hand. In the hand is a lit candle. It ignites this woman and she flares, swallowed in golden-crimson flame. I never see whose hand it is.

Is there such a thing as common human experience? Is there language outside the realm of our minds? Do human bonds exist?

love, Jaswant

One morning at the end of the summer, sunlight streamed through the skylight onto his table, when his eye detected in the periphery a point as brilliant as polished gold. It came from the head of a young woman. She worked in the study cubicle opposite and sent this beacon of reflected sun. Her small shoulders were squared and she wrote with deft, soldierly movements. She finished her perusal and moved to the little glass door of the compartment. The door was jammed shut. She wrenched at it unsuccessfully, then calmly placed her chair on the table, scaled the high partition and let herself down via the bookcases on the other side.

Like an animal returning to her hunting ground, she returned to the same ground to study every day. Like Jassy, like all the students. What do they track in the hunting grounds of the library? His eye was pricked by the points of the shining gold head every day. Every day he studied the crisp, light movements She climbed the wall often, but seemed to enjoy this travail. From the beginning she reminded him of elves or the peculiar witch-ghosts Prito used to speak of.

"Do you read Sanskrit?" She places an open book of Sanskrit before him. She handles it delicately, as if it were an ancient and sacred book of scrolls. From this close it is clear that she is an elf. Her feet make no sound, her hair sparkles with elf dust.

He scans the pages, searching, hoping for an insight he knows will not arrive.

"Punjabi," he offers dumbly.

"Oh, you know Punjabi."

"Actually, no . . . you don't belong in this library, do you?". . . .

"I hate the anthropology library. It's full of anthropologists."

"Ah," he says and inhales pixie dust.

She calls herself Karla. She explains that the anthropologists are a stodgy group. The students are uniformly conservative in spirit, while their radical, shaggy-haired professors are obsessed with seduction.

She takes up one of Jassy's notes and wrinkles her nose at a biochemical scheme. "This means something to you, I suppose."

"It's the biosynthetic pathway of acetylcholine. It's a neurotransmitter important in, well . . . " he breaks off, embarrassed for the suddenly obscure discipline of biochemistry.

She leaves behind a potent, yet light scent and fine pinpoints of light that buzz in the air like sparks from a tinder fire.

Jassy cannot work. Her fairy perfume has adsorbed onto his concentration, and saturated it. He stares at Karla's desk. With her head bowed her hair hangs in a curtain of perfectly straight golden hair. Her tennis shirt reveals the torso, not of a young woman, but of a wiry ten-year old boy. Eventually she closes her books, packs her papers and makes to leave. The door is jammed. With her tote bag on one shoulder she scrambles with the agility of a cat onto the chair, onto a table and up the wall.

Jassy drops his pencil and goes after her. He follows her scent out into the cold autumn air, down the street past joggers who puff forth snowy clouds. Then he continues on for a half a block until the scent is lost amid the foul exhaust of traffic.

She hunted on her ground every day, her round head with its golden curtain bent over the Mudmen of New Guinea, the Brahmins, the Yanomami.

Jassy's hunt ground to a halt. He avoided his laboratory, his professor and his experiments, simply to see the fairy-witch at her desk and perhaps contrive to share a few moments with her. When he was near her, he was immersed in her dust and scent. He found he could conjure her scent at will. He analyzed it as having the pungency of the halogens but not as sour. It was the scent of the sea perhaps. He experienced vertigo and life changed. The days were too brief to expend fiddling at the bench or thinking about molecules. He fantasized that he was a sailor or a jet pilot and wondered if he were capable of adventure and physical hardship. When he saw Karla, he was lost in dreams.

II

January 1977

Dear Mother,

I heard last night the Arctic winds howling through the fire escape outside my window and the radiator moaning as if it were an animal dying, and I heard hundreds of televisions speaking in a unified voice. I felt as bereft of family as ever, but there was a funny tone that cut through it and comforted me. It came through the walls and through the ceiling and floor. I began to think perhaps there was really a God on my side after all and he was speaking to me in this small way. I felt happy and safe.

I went next door to Sally's place, and I pushed at the door for some reason, sensing it was not locked. It gave inward to the sharp smell of Sally's hot loins. I screamed. For there, locked in her thighs was Baba Deep Singh himself, his head on his shoulders, his turban on his head, his beard wild and thick. He stood up, unashamed and laughed.

'Surprise,' Sally said, and then I saw that Baba Deep Singh was actually Gurjit. 'You weren't home,' he said, 'so your neighbour took me in.' Then they both laughed.

Gurjit is finally back! He is tall as a tree, and as wild-bearded a Sikh as you will ever see. In his riding boots and bright linen clothing he seems from another era.

'Satsri akal, Jassy,' he said to me. Later I realized it was his voice I'd heard in the walls. Gurjit was my God, you see. He has spread a bright red dhuri *on the floor and arranged his few belongings around him as artfully as a wandering* sadhu. *Everything just so. Boots at one end. The khaki hiking bag he left here with is now a pair of capacious leather saddle bags which he carries slung over his shoulder atop the folded*

dhuri. *In one of the bags he carries five black-bound volumes which he has stacked on at the head of his* dhuri. *He reads and writes in them every morning.*

That first night Gurjit took three objects from his saddle bags: a large, uncut diamond, a broad-bladed hunting knife of excellent German steel, and a length of magenta silk. He offered me my choice but I couldn't decide. The diamond was obviously worth money. The knife was completely functional and had a quality of immutability, and the silk was a thing of such vivid colour, it filled the room. I told him I couldn't decide so I wouldn't take anything. 'Oho,' said Gurjit, 'you've become a wise sadhu *while I was away.' But it is he who has become a* sadhu *with his waking at five each morning and the way he sits cross-legged on his* dhuri *on the floor writing in his books.*

He's been telling me all the tales of his travels. Of a child's head that fell from the sky and bit and killed a dog, and how one night he fought for his life against a band of yellow-fanged rats in Calcutta.

Five years he's been gone, and not a word, not a letter. I think in my heart I had given him up for dead.

your son, Jassy

"So how come you never wrote? I thought something happened."

"You were supposed to come and get me if I got lost, dummy."

"Oh yeah, I forgot. Tell me all about her, Gurjit. How is she? Is she really . . . deranged like we thought?"

Gurjit looked out the window at the gray winter dawn. "I want you to read these, Jassy." He tapped the tops of the five black-bound volumes. "They can speak far better than I can about this."

"I write her, you know. I haven't forgotten about her. In fact, I think about her all the time."

"I know you do, Jassy. Hey! I'm beat! Let's get some sleep, huh?" Gurjit lay back on his *dhuri* with his arm across his eyes.

"I've been thinging of making that trip too, Gurjit. I don't want you to think that I've forgotten about her."

"That's fine, brother. Read my books, okay, pal? Promise?"

"Sure, I'll read them . . . " Jassy watched his brother's breathing as the grey dawn light seeped into the room.

But he found he could not read Gurjit's books. When Gurjit was out, he took one of them up and found it as heavy as iron. The black cloth covering was worn smooth and each volume contained hundreds of fine pages. The heaviness and the worn surfaces made them monolithic and intimidating. For only the briefest instant Jassy opened each volume, then he replaced them exactly as he had found them. Whatever Gurjit had written was not for his eyes, he decided. Some days later Gurjit asked him if he had read the books and Jassy said he had.

March 1977

Dear Mother,

For the first month Gurjit did not visit Mohan or call to tell him he was back. I told him he can't ignore them. But Gurjit said Mohan doesn't give a damn whether he's alive or not. I kept on this for some reason. Maybe because I feel I've made a peace with Mohan and his wife. Maybe because I feel obliged to them or maybe because I want to savour Gurjit's return to its fullest. Everything, from his thick black beard to his knotted muscles and strange clothing, is triumphant. His hearty laughter, his saddle bags and books. When we were on the bus one day a journalist photographed him for his records. He makes an impression with his turban and Naga shawl. I want Mohan to see this. Finally Gurjit has agreed. We go tomorrow.

love, J.

When they arrived, Mohan's bride went into a fit of warbling, shrieking, exclamations in Punjabi. Her bosom jostled crazily as she beheld Gurjit through wide eyes. She was delighted with his dismissive, one-word replies.

Mohan was hidden behind his Sunday papers. He lowered them to inspect Gurjit, then put them aside. "Come and sit by your father," he said and the three men sat together, Jassy smiling for some reason not even he understood. Mohan and Gurjit were silent.

Mohan's bride, who had been bustling about in the kitchen, came in after a time and whispered to Mohan. She went back to the kitchen and returned with two young women. One of them was the shy-eyed girl, Manjit.

Gurjit stared at the women for a moment, then said plainly, "Shit."

Jassy had forgotten about Manjit. Now she smiled shyly at him and he squirmed with embarassment.

With Mohan's bride there Mohan and Gurjit finally began talking. While this went on, Manjit slipped something into Jassy's hand. It was a golden bracelet, a *Kara*. He flushed, then discreetly slipped it back into her lap without a word.

"Look what a bright future you young people have," Mohan's bride was bubbling. "I am so happy for these youngsters. They hold the world between their teeth. Nothing is beyond them, is there, my husband? And now the big boy has finally come. Returned just like a yo-yo. It is so happy. So very happy. Did you make money on your trip, son? I know he did. He has a pocket for money." This with a wink at Manjit's companion. "Jassy is a man of learning, but this Gurjit, he can get money . . . "

Manjit bolted from the room. Her friend took up their coats and with a stammered apology, fled after her. Mohan's bride drifted towards the kitchen after a moment, her hand to her mouth.

"They didn't want dinner," she said softly. "Please Jassy, *ajao*. Come."

Jassy went to the kitchen.

"Why did she leave?" she asked him. "Did you say something?"

Jassy shrugged. "I didn't say a thing."

Mohan came in. "What happened? Why did the girls run like that?" he demanded.

Jassy shrugged. Gurjit came in.

"He made her leave," Mohan explained to Gurjit.

"So what?"

"We brought the girl here for him," Mohan's bride warbled, "from India. Nature was taking its course . . . oh, the poor child." She bit her knuckle and her eyes drooped.

"What was wrong?" Mohan demanded. "Nothing! I thought you had agreed to this Jaswant."

"To what?" asked Gurjit.

"I never said anything."

"You did not say no. You were as good as engaged!"

"Who said? No one ever told me . . . "

"Are you so dense?"

"I was only trying to do what your poor Mama would have done," sobbed Mohan's bride to Gurjit.

"Don't ever mention my mother," said Gurjit coolly. "You don't have that right." These were the first complete sentences Gurjit had said to her. She responded by pulling her *chuni* over her face and running bawling from the kitchen, the pans and dishes ringing in her wake.

"No one ever asked me about an engagement. I've got a girlfriend besides."

Mohan turned sharply on Jassy. His thin, hawk-like features were concentrated in a way that made Jassy step back. "You idiot," Mohan hissed. "Is it someone we know?"

Jassy took another step away and felt the wall against his back.

"You idiot. A complete stranger. A white woman, hm? How could you? How could you?" Mohan moved swiftly to the door, turned once to glare at Jassy, then vanished into the bedroom where his bride sobbed and heaved on the bed.

They returned home with empty bellies. Gurjit, his joviality gone, would not say a word. Once back at the apartment, Gurjit went directly to Sally's. Through the wall Jassy heard them talking quietly, then become silent.

Alone in his room Jassy realized he had neglected his

research for the mundane. He headed for the library, determined to stay until it closed. In the morning he would return to the lab and his experiments.

But by the time he arrived at the campus, he shook with cold and hunger. The elf place was deserted. The librarian's trolley creaked like the last oak of a ruined forest.

He set about to pick up where he had left off before he had become distracted. But he found he had brought neither pen nor pencil to make notes with. He decided to read instead, but concentration eluded him. He was dogged by hunger and fatigue. His thoughts romped off on a venture of their own, filled with images of Manjit. He saw her large, moist eyes, down-turned out of shyness. Perhaps she had come from Punjab on the promise of marriage. Who had made such a promise, he wondered. Had he? By his actions? Now her eyes filled with tears, her mouth trembled. He saw her running through snow-covered streets, bootless and gloveless and lost.

Jassy lay his head on the table. Lacking the energy and will to either search for a pencil or go home to his cold flat, he dozed.

When he awoke, it was dark and the place was silent. The doors had been locked. It was a windy December night and a sibilant whistle came from the windows. Jassy wandered through the dark aisles and stood gazing out at the unblinking winter stars. Behind him the books brooded in the dark. Each contained a particular life. He could feel them at his back, whispering their wisdom. He moved through them, running his hands over the bindings of hundreds of books. What was he but a worshipper of these lives? Could he ever achieve anything worthy? Would he contribute to the body of knowledge? . . .

He returned to the cubicle and curled up on the chair. Human relationships were confusing and banal. Not the sort of thing for him. He was the question-asker, the learner. He must put Manjit, Karla, Mohan and his bride out of his thoughts and concentrate on his work. He must fulfill his potential as a questioner. He would cut himself off, he decided, and live purely for the quest.

This time when he slept Prito came to him and told him a story. It was of the Sikh saint, Baba Deep Singh, who led a band of soldiers against the Moghul army. The Sikhs were outnumbered, but they fought tenaciously, for their lands were threatened. In the heat of the battle Baba Deep Singh was decapitated by a scimitar. But so determined was he, that he retrieved his fallen head and took it up under his arm. His mouth opened and rallied his men. Then he fought onwards until the end of the battle, guided by the watchful, shining eyes in his head.

In another part of the dream Baba Deep Singh reappears brandishing a sword. In the dream the face on the head is Gurjit's.

III

The image of Baba Deep Singh came into his mind often. He forged ahead with his research for several weeks, through Christmas, and on into January. He followed a line that went between the lab and his flat and avoided the compartments of the library.

But he stopped sometimes, in the midst of an experimental protocol, and, catching a whiff of a pungent fragrance, his chest would ache.

One afternoon he looked down from the lab window onto the campus. It was a sombre February day, the sky an even gray from horizon to horizon. He spotted, in the midst of this, the little fairy-witch Karla crossing the expanse. She wore a red jacket that stood out against the grey like a rose petal. Her shoulders were back, her spine straight. There was not a hint of a sway to her slender hips. She was marching, brave and defiant, but to where he knew not. And this piqued him. He was left out, he felt, of something significant. He could see only that her mind was set. And he could smell her scent, even from where he stood.

He remained at the window for a long time after she had passed from view. Then, that afternoon, he sought her out in the hunting grounds of the library, in the little room with the door that jammed.

EIGHT

I

July 1978

Dear Mother,

I remember a story you told me of a captured Sikh soldier who was allowed to wrestle the champion of the Moghuls in a bid for his freedom. The Sikh concealed a long copper pin in his hair and used it to kill his much bigger opponent by piercing through his eye during the fight. But you never told us what happened after that. What happened to this wily hero? Did he escape? Or did he escape defeat in the ring only to die at the hands of a torturous mob of his enemies? If so, I wonder if it was worth it.

These first days of marriage have not been without problems. In writing this I wondered what kind of marriage you had with Mohan at the beginning. I cannot imagine him as romantic or kind. Does this show a failing on my part?

My problem in this marriage is that I am your son. In my

brain I hold a reel of film from my childhood, a reel of film that stars Mohan and you and how you were married. You were nothing, of course. You were squashed. But even squashed, your love welled up and filled our home, quietly, patiently, timidly. And Mohan ruled, of course. Even knowing all of this, knowing that it is nothing but a reel of film from my past, I keep expecting to see you in Karla.

But Karla is not you, of course. She is nothing if not a vaporous elf-being, disdainful of the mundane. Which leads to a nasty knot of problems.

You see, Karla's main difficulty is that she is disappointed. Not with me, she says. My guess is that when we married which was immediately after she graduated, she expected her world to become delightful and extraordinary. Instead I fear I have hung her up on the ordinary problems of married life. She is very much like a fairy, entangled, if temporarily, in the dream of a sombre and lustreless child. I am that child. I know so little about the strange and delightful. I know so little about her! I have no sparkle in my hair, no spells to cast. Only my naive dreams. To a magical being like Karla, who knows she won't be held for long, it is but annoyance. She may not leave me right away, but she will someday. She has ambitions. They are stronger than mine, and she's frustrated if no progress is made. Progress to what, I'm not sure. I thought at first she was vexed because she wanted us to be richer than we are, but I now see that this is wrong. Even though she's accustomed to a big house and a car and a boat, she cares little for the material life. Elves, fairies, angels, whatever kind of creature she is, she is difficult to fathom.

But there are times when we are happy too. I have learned some of the things elves love. Small magic is better than no magic, as long as you don't give up. One day a flame-twisted piece of glass from the lab is good enough, and another day a midnight swim. Or I tell her one of our stories. Sometimes she comes to the lab and asks questions and we go for long, meandering walks to the lake front. Or she smokes her concoctions, which I have not yet been able to identify. She will asks hundreds of questions about Mohan, the Sikhs, Nanak, Gobind. She's a good question-asker, this Karla-elf.

Of questions: my doctoral research has become a confusing jungle of hypotheses which I can no longer organize. Pia would claim that this is the best question-asking environment, but I am simply lost. I keep on working ahead, remembering Baba Deep Singh.

There have been times of late when, standing at the waterfront, I have the feeling that a star is about to land at my feet. I look out at the rolling water and the sky full of birds and I think I am about to discover something big. Maybe I'm doing better in my experiments than I thought.

love, J.

II

Through the kitchen window he watched her as she ran home through a spring shower. Her bluejeans and running shoes were soaked and where her windshirt stuck to her, a patch of golden skin shone through. She skipped and sang a childhood song.

Pineapple Princess, I love you
you're the sweetest girl I know . . .

She pounded up stairs, burst through the door like a homecoming child. From her jacket she withdrew a bottle of wine and opened it and poured it into a pot which Sijjer was attentively stirring.

"You can't put wine in curry."

"How do you know? You probably never tried before. There are many things you haven't tried. You're a neophyte, a seed of the newest breed!"

"Seeds . . . you have smoked your stuff again."

Karla peeled off her wet clothes and dropped them in a sodden pile. She stood shivering, her skin flushed, her nipples the colour of his special red stone.

"Look at you."

"Yes, look. Can you see it?"

"I think so . . . "

"You're not looking deep. You have to look inside, Jassy. I'm pregnant."

Jassy's smile faded. He forced it back up again, mumbling, then he stepped onto the rainy balcony for a breath of air. He came back and kissed his elven wife, ran a hot bath for her and put her in it.

"We don't want you to catch cold."

Then he was alone and he took himself away from the apartment, walking through the downpour.

It was an unknowable, this thing that brought on the urge to cry. He was reminded of mortality. He was, by steps, being laid open to disaster and pain. And he knew he had no guts for it. His body organs were as fragile as dessicated leaves! And only he knew this.

In the rain his hands were wet and cold. The hairs on the knuckles were plastered down and he saw childhood scars as clearly as though through a lens. His hands had changed over the years. He recalled his hand as the mischievous creature which inched along the rims of bicycle wheels, searching for the nipple. He remembered how Mohan's claws had clutched his newspapers. His hands were becoming Mohan's claw-hands with time. Next, hairs would grow from his nostrils. That was the way of things. A miracle of the gene, or perhaps he was victim of an unconscious desire to assume an ancient pattern.

The rain came in a torrent but he walked swiftly and became warm. He came to an old section of the city. A man who had been walking ahead glanced nervously back.

It would be a son. This he knew with certitude. The pattern again? He looked around at the hulking, colourless buildings, at the factories and tenements, shapes blurred by the torrent. He had lived in Toronto too long, he realized. The city had become like his old apartment. He had grown out of it. It was colourless and shapeless, no place for an infant. Infants need colour, he thought.

Love and colour and warmth.

The young man ahead of him lingered in the rain. Now he turned towards Jassy and approached. His shoulders were hunched and he looked tired, as though he had searched for hours. He said not a word but placed his thumb in his mouth and began sucking on it suggestively. He stared at Jassy with eyes wide.

"Go home," Jassy said. "Please go home to your family."

Then he himself turned away and went home.

III

June 1979
Vancouver

Dear Mother,

Karla was inflicted with a degree of pain that no one warned me existed. She gave birth. All her potions and funny smoke did nothing to help her. In the final moment I thought I heard a clap of thunder, but it was indistinct, shut out of the hospital room. A signal of some sort, but futile in the city. Karla claims not to have heard the thunderclap. There was no storm that day, so I have come to doubt it myself.

I stood beside her and held her hand, coached her as she turned into a raging tiger. Through her narrow passage came a little thing covered everywhere with brown down, everywhere except for on its surprisingly large scrotum. I took him in my hands and he opened his eyes, slate gray, looked at me, closed his eyes again and began to moan. We have named this little fellow Joginder Kekule Singh Sijjer. 'Kekule' after the chemist who had a dream one evening of six snakes eating each other's tails, thus conceiving the molecular structure of benzene. We call him 'Bear' though, after his physical attributes.

It was hard to convince Karla that we should move. More of the mundane problems she would disdain. What was Vancouver, she said, what was the West Coast but a place full of reactionaries and rednecks where it rained all the time? It was the fringe, I told her. The centre of North America has become corrupt and has fouled itself so badly that it will begin to die from the centre out. I really believed it too. Toronto looked to me more polluted than ever after Bear was born. I imagined he began dying in it, even as he took his first breath.

I let the idea incubate with her for a few weeks. When we went on outings, I purposely led her through the grayest, most decayed sections of Toronto. But I said no more about it. I left articles on the inversion layer and the pollution of the Great Lakes around the apartment.

I don't think she took notice of any of this. Karla was concerned with other fathomless things. She made an ordinary claim, saying she needed to have a friend, a woman, whom she could "share the rapture and sorrow with", as she put it. But I know there were other reasons. She told me one morning, half in her sleep, that she feared the ocean.

Yet in the end she agreed. I accepted a post-doctoral fellowship in Vancouver and we moved into a three-bedroomed, sun-decked Point Grey bungalow. Karla insisted on the extra space so she could have a private study. She will lose herself in her papers, the way her professor father does.

your son, Jaswant

Aug. 1979

Dear Mother,

Let me tell you about my people.

Karla one day takes up a hammer and nails and builds bookshelves for her study. She says she wants to reconstruct the book-smelly ambience of her father's office. I express doubts. She wants to create academia and controversy, but all on her own. Determined, piqued, she forges ahead, makes huge mistakes and scraps half the wood, and when it is done, she has bookshelves which lean and which have odd bent nails protruding. Yet somehow it has an ancient, dependable look, like something made for a farm. She loads her precious books in, handling each as though it were made of glass. Sometimes she opens a favourite and reads a passage. Sometimes she simply holds the book closed and recites a passage from memory. Such unlikely volumes they are too. Fanon's The Wretched of the Earth, *Lee's methodical study of the !Kung*

San, Schopenauer's Essays. *Nietzsche. And some old things in an old forgotten script. This is the treasure of this Karla. Then she orients her desk so that it faces a blank wall.*

She sits at her desk, sharpens ten pencils and lines them up. You see, my Karla would be a writer of books. To her the urge to author is something like the urge to mother. She is perpetually pregnant, yet her embryo is a mystery to both me and her.

Which brings us around to the product of that other pregancy, our Bear. Bear! As Karla is about to discover the seed of her book, Bear squeals from his crib. He wants the breast now, and when that is done he wants changing, holding, warming up, cooling down . . . who can do anything but take care of little Bear? And all the while he assumes that we will surrender all to meet his every need. How does he know? Karla's ego is inside out with this Bear. For my part, I am filled with apprehension of this demand. I am afraid, even as I am drawn into the vortex of this tiny assuming creature, this sink for our love, this Bear.

My poor Karla. I feel her elven spirit already sagging. Her magic is fragile, it seems. She wants to follow in the footsteps of her father and conjure a world of abstractions and paper, but this motherhood draws the magic from her. Her pencil, she complains, smells of dirty diapers. She complains that her mind is devoid of thought. She misses the old rapport with her father, the endless threads of ideas they wove together into splendid tapestries. You see, when she tries her ideas on me, I have a way of nibbling everything to pieces with my questions instead of taking up threads and weaving.

Now the other difficulty in our life here is that we have no friends. And this problem is primarily Karla's of course; I am accustomed to solitude. To remedy this problem Karla introduced herself to the woman across the alley who bears a prominent smear of mascara over her upper face. We refer to her as Raccoon Face. Raccoon Face is friendly enough to Karla. But one dark night when Karla was out for a walk, she spotted Raccoon Face jogging along the street stark naked. Karla was intrigued. Her eyes lit and the elf dust sparkled in her hair. The next day Karla called on her and immediately asked about her night time run. Raccoon Face turned red and went stiff as a clam. This places Karla in a predicament. While she finds Raccoon Face compelling, she is not sure how to proceed. The mystery lies between them, untouched. Every night we see Raccoon Face jogging under the street lights, her plump breasts bobbing wildly. Karla picked up her pencil and wrote a few lines on nudity in post-industrial society, but it did not take her far. I do not know how well her friendship is progressing with Raccoon Face.

Then are some quiet people two houses down who sit perpetually on their sundeck for a portrait painter. These people are lost in deep contemplation whenever we see them. They exude a kind of perfection in their movements and expression but they dress unconventionally. Karla says she saw them clad only in underwear during the height of a rainstorm. I myself have seen them adorned in fluorescent feathers. Only the painter ever has the courtesy to wave at us as we pass by in the alley. I think this group depresses Karla. She says they seem moribund and give her bad dreams. We refer to them as the Stiffs.

July 1980

Dear Mother,

One day Karla was out for a walk with Bear, and it began to rain. She returned home, pushing the stroller, and discovered she had locked herself out. She ran across to the Raccoon Face's house and but there was no answer to her knock. They got wet and Bear began to cry. Karla says she had a realization in that moment of what it means to be friendless. She says it means you are a nothing.

So she pushed back her tears and marched the stroller back down the alley to the Stiffs' house. They sat out on their deck despite the rain.

"Hello," Karla hailed. She opened the back gate and crossed the lawn. "Hello?" She came under the sundeck. There was complete silence as though the people had decided to ignore her. But, with little Bear's cry in her ears, she climbed the

steps to confront these cold-hearted people. She found them sitting stock still, shining under a cloudy sky. For they were not people after all, but life-sized mannikins made of plastic. And their tea cups were full of rain water.

It turns out the painter of the mannikins was a woman named Sharon Sterns. She rescued Karla and Bear from the rain, dried their clothes by the fireplace, put them in a hot bath and made oatmeal cookies and cocoa to cheer them up.

Her house contains dozens of mannikins. They recline on the sofa, stretch out on beds, stare bleakly at a broken television. They attend to plates at the kitchen table and gaze out windows. In every room of this house there are canvases portraying mannikins.

Sharon Sterns wears ripped T-shirts and is rebellious, I think. She has a tattoo of a dragon across her belly and her black hair is streaked with orange. Karla says she is basically warm-hearted, but I have doubts. Today I saw Sterns shoplifting groceries at the supermarket. She saw me watching her and laughed that she did not believe in the cash economy. She has no money but inherited the house, the mannikins, and an old VW bus which she cannot afford to run. Everything else she steals. However Karla thinks highly of her. Finally she has a friend. Finally she has someone to weave her tapestries with.

My Karla began a chapter in her book on the artist in post-industrial society but the tip of her pencil has ground to a stop after one paragraph.

love J.

IV

October 1981

Dear Mother,

I remember we were in a field of long grass. It was so long that I could not see over it and I held Gurjit's hand for fear of getting lost. We rolled around until there was a little private place where all the grass was flat. We felt safe there, and I thought, no one will find us in this jungle.

You told us a story about a lioness and her two cubs. The lioness, you said, had no food and became very thin. The land was dry and the animals had migrated or died. But the lioness stayed because her cubs were too small to move. After a time the lioness's ribs showed through, then her teats dried up. Vultures with bald, pink heads circled overhead and the lioness was desperate, she spoke to her sons. "What must a lion do when confronted by vultures?" she asked them. "Not lose faith," they answered in unison, remembering their lessons. Mama lion then tearfully bit her cubs' necks and devoured them, thus saving them and her from the vultures. She survived and the next year had more cubs which she loved as much as she loved the first ones.

What a strange story it is. I cried for the cubs, and then you cried when you saw me cry. Only Gurjit didn't cry which, I suppose, makes him the only lion of the three of us.

It is a time of an abundance I never imagined. My work is a roller coaster ride of questions. My director, a mystery called Hotnik, has left me to my own devices here. I have the opportunity to explore and ask any question I want.

your son, Jaswant

September 1982

Dear Mother,

Our little Bear at two and a half: whereas yesterday he was a helpless bird, gurgling in his crib at some shiny pieces of paper Karla hung from a string, now he is a ball of spark. He has a robust yellow Labrador named Zephyr after the Greek god of the west wind, and he rides his dog like a horse. The two are inseparable.

It is autumn and the beauty of the land is mystical. The

mountains are blue and forests fires burn inland. Haze hangs over the dark waters of the inlets. A while back I bought the old red Volkswagen van from Sharon Sterns and I have fixed it up. What I love is the feel of the worn-out wheel under my palm, and the sound of Karla and Bear chattering over the sound of the motor. Who could ask for more than an elven bride with a hair of golden strands, and a bear cub of a son!

O, to see the power and beauty of the earth.

your son, Jaswant

They drove across the bridge into the mountains. It was a warm spring day and the peaks were laid bare under the vault of clear sky.

Bear clung to the collar of his bounding pup who dragged and carried the boy from the van across a swatch of grass to the edge of the ravine. Below, a narrow mountain river cut down to the sea. Sijjer ran to keep up as boy and dog squeezed under a fence, ran through the midst of a waddling flock of ducks and headed for the suspension bridge over the canyon. . . .

When he reached the bridge they were already half across it, the dog spraddled on its belly as the bridge swayed and Bear fearlessly peering through the slats in the wood at the raging torrent below.

They walked on, the three together now, through a cathedral of Douglas firs. Sijjer sat on a log overlooking the gorge and called his son to him. He put his hands around Bear's chest. His fingers touched Bear's spine, his thumbs were over his sternum.

"I scratched my knee, Dad. On the rock."

"You have to be careful, Bear. Do you listen to what Karla tells you?"

"I do listen. What's a lion say, Dad?"

"Roar. What does a whale say?"

"Eeeeeoooo."

Bear's heart ticked under Sijjer's thumbs. It was brave and steady, the ticking. It seemed to Sijjer it was a clock marking the passage of life. He tried to imagine his son as a man. He tried to picture Bear's face lean and angular with strength and purpose behind it. But the picture remained blank. All he could see was a small boy, his brown eyes trusting and serious, shining with vitality. And under his thumbs he felt the small heart ticking. . . .

NINE

Long Beach
Sept. 1982

Dear Mother,

In one day I have gone from life and warmth to stone.

Karla and I had problems. Nothing serious, I thought. Was I the problem for thinking that? I no longer grasp the laws of causality. I no longer understand temporal sequence. I no longer know the light of reason. I am kept alive by the idea that love exists. It was at Long Beach on the west side of the island. The end of summer in which we saw bald eagles soar from ancient trees. In the mornings the fog rolls so thick off the ocean you feel it like cool velvet on your skin. Then the fog burns off under the sun and the ocean appears as pure and wild as the first ocean on earth. One night I heard a cougar screaming in the hills. I sat up and listened, afflicted with primordial dread. Cause or effect, I can not tell. The hair on my back stood, my heart pounded. The unknown is always just beyond our vision, like a cougar stalking the edge of camp. So I did not sleep. So Karla and I fought. The spark was Karla's old dissatisfaction, which has always been there, suppressed. She wrestles with ghosts, burning up because she can't write. I could write if you would co-operate, she says. You don't want me to succeed, you want me to fail, she says. I'm not happy with this relationship, it's got to change. You're not a part of us, you never were. You come and go from work. When you're home, you're tired and where does it leave me? I'm nothing, she says. Effect or cause?

Bear was upset by this so I took him for a walk. The place was deserted except for the owners of our motel and they sat in a room behind a glass door and watched television day and night. Father and mother and kids. All of them with big circles around their eyes from watching constant television. The kids would not play with Bear — they had forgotten how, I think.

We went to the beach through the fog. We explored coves and the sandspit that runs out to a little island where there are tidal pools filled with starfish, crabs, sea cucumbers and octopi. I swam and Bear rubbed me with a towel saying, 'Goosebumps, goosebumps.' He looked out to sea. Serious, wonder-eyed, boy. 'What's out there,' he asked me and pointed out to sea. 'Just water. Japan and the Soviet Union past that.' 'Ship-pan?' He wrinkled up his nose and his mind went to work. 'I want to see a Ship-pan,' he said.

O, Bear. With eyes so big they swallow me whole and spit me out in pieces. He likes to sleep with Zeph when he can, the two of them curling up together in a brown and yellow ball. He must have imagined Ship-pan as a boat. He was always talking about tugboats, sailboats, power boats. He wondered why me and Karla fought. I cannot imagine what he thought about it. He had hardly ever seen us using hard words on each other.

We returned to our room and words began again. It came round to that mean talk about sex and power and how I didn't do this or that for her and how she was always on the bottom and subservient. On and on. We'd never done that in front of Bear. He must have wondered about it. He went off to play finally and Karla I kept at it for a while until I grew weary and walked out.

I walked down the beach, trying to cool down and looking for Bear. It was windy and the morning fog had blown off. The sea was mountainous. A fishing boat fought its way against the waves and current out of the bay. She rode up the huge waves, seeming to stand on end as she crawled up walls of water. Around my ankles a stinging sand storm blew. Huge surf breaking. I called out to Bear and Zeph, and they did not come. I was miserable from the fight. Along the beach I found two sets of tracks, boy track and dog track, and I followed them, became calm. Tiny boy footprints meandered back and forth on the beach. Here a sand castle with a washed out moat, there two little depressions where his butt had sat in the sand.

The path went on for a mile, the tracks like two interwoven stories; boy story and dog story. The stories told me a thing I could not grasp. Words written in sand, some of the letters wrong. I started running. Then I came to the end. The tracks stopped. There I found Bear's clothes in a pile. The footprints led to the pile but not away from it. I could not grasp the meaning of the story. I sat in the sand, my mind a muddle. I thought of the nasty stuff that Karla had said. I understood her frustration for the first time. I saw that she needed challenge. Her life with me had led nowhere. She was a lousy mother, she said, which was not true. She accused me of complacence and unresponsiveness, and that stung. Then she asked me if I loved her and that was the worst. I wonder if one can love but the love not be received. Is it possible? Does cause really lead to effect? Had I failed to grasp Karla's story just as now I failed to grasp Bear's?

It was brilliant on the water. Images burned into me. The tide was going out. I picked up the clothes — they were wet — and I walked back to the motel.

Karla stared at the clothes when I came in. I told her how the tracks went down the beach and stopped. I told her the story I did not understand. She picked up the clothes and brushed the sand from them. He never folds his stuff, she said. Bear had been pestering Karla once, demanding her attention, wanting to know why she would not play with him. She told him she was thinking and to leave her alone. Talk to me, Bear persisted, I talk to you when I'm thinking. Cause or effect, Karla thought.

She grabbed the keys and ran out to the van and was in it driving before I could stop her. I ran after her and when I got to the beach, I saw the bus down the beach driving in the sand. I went back and phoned for a tow truck from the motel owner's place. Then he and I ran down the beach. . . .

The bus made it most of the way but was up to the hubs where it finally stuck. We caught Karla in time to drag her out of the surf. She fought and screamed. She knocked the motel owner's teeth out with one fist and punched me in the balls with the other. I sat on top of her to keep her from going back in. She would have drowned herself.

Bear is gone. I was not unlike him. Searching for the cool rush of air from a bicycle tire. Uncomprehending and bold. Bear waded into the surf, thinking he could see the Ship-pan. He fell and the ocean current, like a ghostly underwater hand, took him away. Zeph would have plunged in after him and followed him out. Dogs have fierce loyalties, stronger than those of humans. They are loyal to the death. So Zeph went into the water after our little Bear, his brave head struggling to keep up.

I am cold. Deep, unshakable cold has seized my bones. It is as though the icy Pacific has closed over me, and sweeps me to sea. Cause, I wonder, or effect?

J.

TEN

I

November 1983
Flight

Dear Mother,

Forgive me. I have decided to give Mohan a chance to clear the slate before he dies. I will do as Piara says and make peace with the old man before his sorry life ends.

Jaswant

Gurjit was at the airport. He looked Sijjer up and down. "You are pissed drunk," he said, "and you look a mess."

He knew that Gurjit was being merciful. Not mentioned were unheeded messages and the telephone unanswered. Not mentioned was a trip Gurjit made shortly after Bear's death. He had arrived in Vancouver to find that Sijjer had disappeared for the five days of his stay.

Gurjit's place was a large studio in a block of warehouses. It was brightly lit, freshly painted in shades of eggshell. The sleeping area was an open corner with two simple cots covered by *dhuris*. The rest of it was organized according to function. In one corner a darkroom and print dryer, in another, a drafting table and easel. The easel supported an unfinished oil painting of a hollow-cheeked Punjabi girl. In another corner were two large desks with manuscripts stacked near a typewriter. On a shelf above them stood Gurjit's five black books from his journey. A skylight admitted a broad beam of afternoon sun which illuminated the worn black covers of the books.

The afternoon light gave way to shadows. Sijjer sat on a cot across from Gurjit and watched his brother pull off his high leather boots.

"What do you need, Jassy? Coffee, a shower?"

"When do we see him?

"Tomorrow. I told him you were coming."

"You see him a lot?"

"Lately, yeah. He doesn't have long. I don't know. Strange how I suddenly wanted to be close to him."

"Yeah. That's sort of why I came."

Gurjit stood restlessly. His movements were charged with grace and power and his face shone. He towered over his younger brother, who sat still and quiet in a deepening shadow.

"How come you never answered my letters or calls. I wrote every week. Did you get the letters, Jassy?"

"I don't remember," said Sijjer.

"I know it's hard sometimes to let someone help, but don't forget we're brothers, alright? When everything is gone, you'll always have one person left, and that's your brother. Don't forget that. You'll be doing both of us a disservice if you forget that. I've been worried about you, man. You never wrote or called, so I dropped everything to come out there . . . what happened to you, Jassy? Where was Karla?"

"She'd moved out for a while."

"You mean she came back?"

"She's back . . . sort of."

Gurjit sighed. He went into the darkroom and put on coffee. When he returned Sijjer was between the blankets, his face to the wall.

Sijjer feigned sleep, knowing that Gurjit would go out. He listened to him moving about, then the lights went down and the door clicked softly shut. He arose and retrieved a bottle from his bag, sat back on the cot and took a long pull.

It was dark. A faint ray of light filtered through the skylight and touched the black books. A clock ticked near the cot.

There was no good reason for not having answered Gurjit's messages. No reason he could think of why he had slipped away to stay at a hotel when he discovered that Gurjit was coming to town. He knew from long experience the futility of hiding anything from his brother. For five days he had stayed drunk in the downtown hotel, the days smashing together like wrecks in a freeway car accident. He remembered little, but one impression had stayed with him. From the room of the hotel there had been a clear view of the mountains across Burrard Inlet. Drunk, he saw for the first time what they were. He recognized the two distinct formations known as the Lions. The Lions lay on their bellies, facing each other across a chasm, their heads raised. Drunk, he saw that they had been watching him from their vantage point. Watched him and pondered fate. They knew all. They were possessed of a quiet mastery of the ages and their judgement was disinterested.

After that week Sijjer found that, wherever he was in Vancouver, his eye was drawn to the Lions.

II

He went with Gurjit to the hospital early the next morning. Outside the room they were met by Mohan's bride. She was baggy- eyed and had sheaths of gray in her hair. She was not as fat as she had been in happier times.

"He has been waiting," she said and they followed her into the room.

Mohan lay on his back flat and without a pillow. His legs were stretched straight and looked as unbending as two sticks of wood. His hair was feathery and pure white and no longer stood up, his skin waxy and sallow. Around him hung the sweet odour of rotting fruit.

The old man stared with wide eyes at his sons, then he shifted his body slowly and with great effort lifted himself to half-sitting. Mohan's bride bustled to crank the bed up behind him.

"So, you," he said. He waved his bride and Gurjit out of the room. "So, you. You see how your father has lost his strength, ah. This is the beginning of death. Soon I will be nothing. My strength will be taken away somewhere and put to a better use, that is the way of it. Everyone eventually has their strength taken away . . . "

Mohan seemed to see irony in this, for he chuckled. Then the chuckle transformed into a slow, steady cough, like a truck engine being cranked over without firing.

At length the coughing ceased. "When you get to this point, all you have is the past, did you know that? Even if you spent your whole life living for the moment or looking into the future, when you get here, all you have is the past. Nothing else. Present and future are gone. You look back and see it all, the mistakes, the bad stuff and you see it means nothing. Nothing! All of it meant nothing!"

This time, when the coughing began, the truck engine suddenly caught and Mohan went into a red-faced spasm.

Sijjer hit the nurse's call switch by the bed, but Mohan's hand shot up and snapped it off.

"You're always such a crier," he growled. "Always trying to get someone's attention, you. I hate that in people. Can't do anything without getting someone's attention. I wanted to ignore you. I wanted to teach you a lesson because I saw it in you. It looks like I failed. You are still a crier. A baby."

"I manage alright."

Sijjer went to the window and sat on the sill. Outside it was a warm fall day. Indian summer, was the name for it. He had always found that term embarassing. Like Indian giver. Even after he knew enough to see they meant the other Indians, he was still conscious of it. Anomaly. That's what he was.

Mohan had been coughing, but now he stopped and

regarded Sijjer in his old hawkish way.

"A man has expectations of his sons. Expects his sons to be men. Gurjit became a man."

"Meaning I'm something else."

"You are a baby. A talking, crying baby, full of excuses always."

"Excuses. I don't need to make excuses to you. You're the one who needs an excuse here . . . ah, forget it. I didn't come all the way here to argue with you."

Mohan looked out the window now, vacantly, his mind abstracting.

"Why then? Why exactly did you come? What is the meaning of coming to see a man in his last days, when his strength has been taken and he's full of the past? There's a reason, there must be. I know you. I know you because you were once my son and I hoped that you would become a man. But then, but then . . . then there was the girl, wasn't there? Then we saw. Then . . . it was then that you showed me that I had made a mistake. That I had mistaken a dog for my son. Yes, a dog . . . "

"What girl?"

"What girl? What girl, he says. The one you destroyed, or don't you recall? The one you threw into hell. I would think you would at least remember her, or is that part of your joke, that you ruined her, threw her away, then forgot about her." Mohan's voice rose now, and took on a keening tone which Sijjer had not heard before.

"Don't remember her then. Forget her if you can. What girl? he asks. You make me sick. She went crazy, did you know that? Did you know that you did that to her? Sweet she was, innocent! Young! She had to be strapped to a bed and given drugs with a needle. They made her mind a blank. You say so easily, what girl? As though it were nothing. Trivia. A thing of trivia. She tried to kill herself. She tried to throw herself off a forty-storey building! What girl! The one you destroyed because you are not a man but a skulking dog. Only a dog chases something just to bark at it and kill it for stupid fun. Only a dog! You promised to marry that girl. We brought her here from Punjab so she could marry you. We took her away from her mother when she wasn't yet eighteen. Then what? You threw her away as though she were just a bit of dirt. You threw her away like a dog would a bone. Sure, forget her. You buried her like a bone, you *kotu*, you dog!"

Sijjer could only stare. It dawned him that the girl was Manjit. He forgotten about her, just as Mohan had said. He had never wondered what had become of those shy eyes. She had run from Mohan's house and that was the last of it. He'd seen her running, her face folded in some profound humiliation that he did not understand.

Or was it the last time? Was it she standing in the snow on a cold winter day, her feet bare? Was it she, her head in a *chuni*, lying in the lake? Was it not she struggling through an anonymous street, her baggy *silwar kemiz* tripping her in the wind?

Sijjer shook his head to shake away the nightmares. "I hardly knew her," he said, but his voice had no strength. "I never promised anything."

"You betrayed her."

"I did not. I refuse to take responsibility for that. How was I to know she was brought here all the way from . . . why didn't she go back then . . . " His mind crowded up with the awful enormity.

"Refuse, pah! Forget. Refuse. Forget and refuse all you want, no one cares. It makes no difference. I'm telling you facts. I don't ask for excuses. The fact is I have only one son. You are not my son. Just a man I know. Just a dog . . . and everything, everything you have done will come back on you, you will see someday. We could not face our community after what you did, did you know that? We were disgraced, our named dragged in the mud. I could no longer hold my head up in public . . . "

"This is ridiculous," Sijjer broke in." Whose fault is it that you read into my intentions? No one asked me. You built the whole thing in your mind. For God's sake, I never even spoke to the girl. Now I came here because I believed you wanted to settle our differences. I came here to make up with you after all these years, and you lie there and throw accusations . . . ridiculous accusations at that! Don't you think it's time to make a little peace with me, Papa? What is this about the girl? I'm your own flesh and blood after all, not her."

"Who ever told you I wanted you here?" Mohan snarled. "I know of only one person who would do that. Piara, that idiot of idiots. Piara, am I right? He is as soft and stupid as a woman.

"You want forgiveness. I know you want forgiveness. You long for it, but you don't deserve it. Hah, I know how badly you want to be forgiven, just like a dog. I will die and nothing will be forgiven, what do you think of that? You humiliated me. You destroyed that young girl. Why? Why? All because of some stranger, some *gori* woman. Some white thing you found. You are no more my son, you hear! You are fatherless, a bastard! A bastard for people to kick! I have one son, only one . . . " Mohan broke down into a spasm of coughing which stopped him from going on.

Sijjer turned to leave. But he stopped at the door and waited for the coughing to subside. "How can you talk to me of destroying people after what you did to my mother . . . "

Mohan's lips made a little round circle as though he had been slapped on the mouth. His eyes bulged in surprise. "Get out," he croaked.

"And, just for the record, I want you to know that I heard all about it. All about your father and brothers and why you left Punjab. I know all about you. I understand what makes you tick, old man." Then he went out.

In the corridor Mohan's bride had her *chuni* pulled across her face. She let go a sob and rushed into the room in Sijjer's wake. Sijjer and Gurjit walked away.

Gurjit said, "She's been by his bed five weeks solid."

"He must command loyalty, our father."

III

Mohan died less than a month later, his heart giving way under the burden of his disease. Gurjit phoned, making plans for the cremation, but Sijjer balked at this.

"It's our last duty to him, Jassy. We've got to clean his body and all that. Piara will be there to help out. Why don't you come down with him?"

"I don't know."

"What do you mean?"

"I don't know if I'll come. I have to think it over."

"There's nothing to think about here, man. It's just one of those things you do and get over with. No matter what kind of trouble you had with him, he was still your father . . . "

As Gurjit's ire rose Sijjer hung up. He went outside and stood in the rain. He waited until the ringing of the phone ceased before he came in again.

It was noon and the light of day revealed the squalor of the house. Tapestries lay twisted and dirty on the floor of the living room. Bottles and glasses and newspapers littered the place. Finding it intolerable, Sijjer dumped bottles and glasses in the sink, then shook out the tapestries and spread them out. Then he suddenly stopped and sank into a chair, leaving the job unfinished.

Karla had moved out yet again. Alone he was beset by a sense of isolation so stark it was as though he had been doused in ice water. He went to Karla's study and sniffed for her pungent scent. The scent was stale. A photograph of the stone giants of the Easter Islands had fallen from its place. He picked it up and hung it. He opened the doors to the sundeck and stood in the light. The sun's rays were cold. The chill brought on the desire for a drink, but there was not a bottle to be found, and, at that moment, the ring of a child's voice echoed in the street. To drink in the light of day, while children played in the sun, seemed a terrible wrong.

He had once imagined the act of setting alight Mohan's byre, had seen himself with a flaming torch under an open sky, the wood casting up thick white smoke, the flames engulfing Mohan's face. It was not like that, of course. The image was from Prito's description of cremations in India. There would not be a byre of logs in Toronto, of course. It would be some kind of gas machine. The remains were enclosed in a casket, enclosed again in an oven. In a concrete dungeon, not under open sky.

To the north the Lions reflected a dappled light through winter clouds. They were pure in their whiteness, sheathed in fresh snow and ice. Pure and immutable. . . .

PART TWO

ELEVEN

Ditchdiggers

I

1984

Dear Mother,

In the beginning there was simply the sound of Bear's breathing. It was loud and disturbed, the way it was when he had a fever. It emanates from the walls of his room. I am afraid to rise when the walls breathe. I remain frozen in my bed and wait for morning. Some time later I hear the distinct sound of paws clicking on the kitchen floor, the lapping of water, the jingle of a dog's tags as he scratches.

Now I hear a scream. At first it was barely audible, distant, unreal for its constancy. But as it became louder, I came to know that it is stifled and muffled but very near. It is from Karla, this scream. It is something powerful that is stifled, so the stifler is powerful indeed.

If these sensations were only dreams. For days I believed they were. But they are ghosts and, as you know, I am a light sleeper.

You once said I reminded you of a egg about to hatch. . . .

Karla leaves me periodically, only to return. She cannot stand to be in this house. Our relationship has become strange.

J.

In the lab there is little in the manner of human warmth. The photographs of wild animals posted up by a desperate young undergraduate serve only to accentuate the sterility. Function and analysis reign, reducing the place to a machine. During the day the machinery buzzes and clicks with the constancy and efficiency of insects. But at the end of the day, unmanned incubators, spectrographs, freezers and computers revert to a wakeful state in which their red eyes make them predatory. These predators never blink. It makes an uneasy peace.

In this ambience Sijjer reclines in his office, which is a glass-enclosed corner of the lab. He watches the snow blow down outside. The December darkness is relieved by a skin of snow on the landscape; his eye follows the smooth hills and lawns of the campus. He dreams of the sea. . . .

Now Karla appears. She moves along the bench touching tubes and instruments as deftly as a magician, then stands at the door of Sijjer's office, one hand on one hip. Her elven look has been transformed by grief; her hair has lost its golden dust. She is soft, like a wounded and fragile creature of the forest.

"Caught in the act," he says, holding up a beaker of whisky. "I am so surprised to see you here."

"I just wandered out."

"You walked? You must be frozen." He offers the beaker, but she ignores this gesture.

"It's not so far when you have the time. I'm moving out. I thought I should let you know this time."

She thrusts her hands in her duffel coat and turns to go, then hesitates, drawn back it seems. "Do you often sit drinking here. I mean, in this darkness, in this . . . soulless place."

"Drinking gives one the best sense of life's abundance. You probably don't know that."

"You drink to escape life's abundance," she counters.

The dream of the sea, of a glossy, waveless waterscape, dissipates. He sits up and watches Karla.

"Please have a drink."

"No."

"You are so beautiful when you hate me."

"I don't hate you. I feel bad that you're wrecking yourself."

"Not quite true. My work is wrecking me. I'm not wrecking me. I'm trapped in a maze of deathly questions. I'm struggling in a current of moribund analyses. You know where all this scientific inquiry leads?"

"Where does it lead?"

"To hell and death in that order. I have been given a research grant on hell."

"Then quit. You're not doing anyone favours by staying. And besides I hate hearing this kind of talk."

"At least let me drive you home. I mean your new home."

Karla shrugs. As they drive through the falling snow, it is as though the apocalypse has come. Sijjer sees no electric lights, no signs of the civilized world. He and Karla are the last on earth, searching unhappily through the wilderness. "It's like a dream, Karla. We're at the beginning."

Karla's new place is as dark and white as the snowy blackness outside, the rooms bare of decorations or comforts. Naked floors and walls. A fireplace. On one wall a daguerrotype of a wrinkled native woman, half the subject in deep shadow like a halfmoon. There is the scent of spruce at first, then the thick smell of wet wood burning as Karla makes the fire.

"You never ask why I leave or come back," Karla says.

"Alright, why did you let me bring you here?"

"That's not the same . . . "

"It's because of the dark, isn't it. You can't stand the dark. You can't stand darkness and you can't stand empty rooms. Even I know that about you. And because you're cold. You know what I've been doing these past months. I go through your clothes dresser every night when I get home. I have an idea I can tell how long you'll be away by how many pairs of panties you leave behind. So far the longest you've been away is two weeks – you left only four panties . . . So why do you keep coming back?"

"Does it disturb you so much?"

"You have to decide one way or the other. It's nothing to me." He says this, but it catches in his throat so that she cocks her head and looks at him.

"Last time it was bad dreams," says Karla. "I walked by an old folks home one night. It's near a field overlooking the bay. I thought I heard people inside, crying and talking. I sat outside on the grass and listened to them. It was very beautiful in the open fields and down below you could see the ships floating like toys in a bath. But then that night I had a nightmare. I was an old woman. They tied me to the bed and my arms and legs were too weak to fight. I protested but no one understood my language. They were very gentle, the attendants, and they told me I was too old to look after myself. Then they beat me and, you know . . . took me. It was humiliating more than anything, without any power . . .

"Another time Sterns told me a story about something that happened to her. I don't know why she tells me these things. She thinks you and I should divorce. Divorced people always say that. Safety in numbers. Safety in the failure. When she looks back on her marriage, she says it's like remembering one day, but a long day. A strange long day in which she wasn't herself. She doesn't remember the reasons she had for making certain decisions, but she remembers all the details clearly. She doesn't remember why she got married in the first place, nor why she got divorced. But she says her long day ended in night, with doors slamming, accusations thrown around like spears. Then she was left all alone with half the bookcase, the pots and pans, the television instead of the stereo, the sofa instead of the dining table. She laughs about it now, but I don't think she laughed then.

"After that day there was, of course, night. The night that followed that long day was the first part of being alone. There was this shocked solitude to deal with. There was endless silence. Her friends, even the other tenants in her apartment building seemed to vanish. She would listen for the quiet lapping of the waves on the beach, and the trees whispering. Through the window she could see the black outlines of trees and sometimes the white froth of a wave. There were lights across the bay but they were distant. She felt haunted then, just as I did. And you do.

"Then one time she awoke in the dark, freezing cold, her blanket fallen away. She reached for her husband and remembered that she was alone. Then she went to the kitchen and found an intruder forcing the window. When she turned on the light, they just stared at each other, frozen. Recognized something about each other. Vulnerability. Solitude. His face was white and drawn, she said, like one of those Japanese actors. And he kept on coming even after she had turned on the lights. She had to stab him with a kitchen knife. Five times. Blood on all the windows in the morning.

"So I moved back after she told me that."

"I didn't know you were scared, Karla."

"You can stay awhile. If you want to."

Karla is silent. She kneels before the fire, which throws wild shadows against the walls. Her eyes are lambent green and calm.

He has been sitting back from the light watching the fire rise, and now he leans forward to warm himself. His creature-hand walks where it will. It clutches her sweater, then encircles her waist searching for warmth. It climbs her ribs, counting them, then touches the bottom of the hill of her breast. As this creature finds the warmths of her body he remains cold.

By the fire it is bright, but cold. As Karla lifts her skirt, silence is imposed, and the face of her naked vulva shines in the firelight.

This is the real mystery: this frost that grips him as he makes love to his wife.

II

February 1984

Dear Mother,

I have quit scientific research. I have been working at it for months now without belief, without spirit. The only questions

I have asked throughout this dark time is 'why?' without aim. So an aimless 'why?' to experiments, a 'why' to the observation process, a 'why' to the analysis of results. Why science? Why research? I have not answered this, so I have quit.

After a week I looked through the newspapers and found that my skills are as narrow and concentrated as a laser beam. The only job I qualified for outside of science is as a labourer. Tomorrow I start my first shift laying pipe for a private contractor.

Karla has moved out and taken all but one pair of her panties with her. I do not expect her back for the next month. She frightened me badly before she left. I woke in the middle of the night to her screaming. Her mouth was closed yet she screamed. As though she were trying to scream underwater. Around her head were dancing fuzzy spots of light, like bubbles.

J.

He bought the steel-toed boots after the first day, and gloves after the second. Sijjer's back ached and his thoughts dulled after five days of shoveling. His first week he became intimately acquainted with the handle of his shovel, learned its tolerances and strengths, where it was fickle or dependable. During the second week, after the old water pipe had been removed, they invited him into the bottom of the ten-foot pit to shore up the new pipe with wet gravel.

It was February and the sky had vanished behind a moving mass of cloud. The men shuddered in the chill wind and tempers were short. The foreman threatened to fire Sijjer because he was slow and took frequent rests. But Sijjer did not care. The fatigue emptied his mind and in this he found relief. . . .

They laid in the water line and prepared to enter through a new manhole. The foreman passed a sledge hammer down to Sijjer. Sijjer heaved it against the thick slab of concrete and it bounced off. He then struck ten blows with all his might. The concrete surface remained unscathed. At the lip of the ditch the foreman lit a cigarette and smoked as he watched the sledgehammer bounce on the concrete. Then he tossed the butt into the pit and walked away in disgust. Sijjer lay the heavy hammer aside to catch his breath.

"He'll fire you, man." Conrad Grey poked his head over the rim of the manhole and hung there observing Sijjer's repose. "Then you'll have to walk around for a week looking for work and then you'll find yourself doing exactly the same thing, only somewhere worse, and you'll have lost a week of wage and you'll kick yourself."

"Yeah," Sijjer answered. He took up the sledgehammer and tapped the concrete half-heartedly.

"You look kind of green at that hammer," commented Grey. He hauled himself out of the manhole and climbed into the ditch. "Watch now," he said, taking the sledgehammer from Sijjer. "You see, you let the weight of the hammer work for you. You sort of raise her up, then you just start her off in the right direction, give her a little pump, then let her work for you. You just guide her down. You do it like a dance, the way your heart works. Every heartbeat, you give a little juice, see . . . "

Grey swung the hammer with his body, moving with it so that in one fluid motion the steel head bore down in a long concentrated arc. With the second blow a chip flew. After ten the surface crumbled.

"Now you try. You need to, ah . . . summon up some juice. You know, some force . . . " He said this with a distinct tone of doubt.

Now when Sijjer took up the sledgehammer, it followed his lead. His arms ached after twenty strokes and he stopped to rest.

"All you got to do now is get some new arms." said Grey, and with that he went away.

Grey was flawed by a marked limp, but he was tall and rangy, his features cut as smoothly as surf-carved stone, his eyes clear and steady. Now and again he stopped what he was doing to advise Sijjer in a solemn way.

Sijjer had not spoken to any of the men before this. The crew kept a distance from him, sensing that he was not like them, that he came from another sphere of work where he did not employ his back and hands, and sensing too the cold air that pooled around him. At first Sijjer thought that Grey was curious, or that he felt akin as an outsider on the crew. But it became clear that Grey was not really an outsider here, after all. He was quiet around the crew, but the men respected him for his strength and sense. So Sijjer was left to conclude that it was curiosity that made the other man take an interest.

He was told to ferry the lengths of pipe down the line to where the men were laying it in the deep, sodden trench. No one came forward to share in this work. Sijjer waited, knowing he could not carry the pipe alone. The foreman looked down the line at him, scowling, and spoke into the ditch. Heads popped up and they looked at Sijjer. He went to the stack of pipe, picked up an end and held it there. Then Grey hopped out of the ditch, hunkered down the line and silently took up the other end of the pipe. They carried it back up, passed it down to the silent men.

"Thought you were tamping in the ditch there, Grey," said the foreman. But he said nothing more as Grey went on carrying the pipe.

Sijjer stopped as they took hold of the next length. "I don't really need your help, Grey. They can fire me if they don't like me. If they want to play games . . . I couldn't care less about it."

"I couldn't care less neither. How about that?" said Grey.

"Well, what I'm saying is, you don't have to jeopardize yourself here . . . I don't need charity from you."

Grey looked at him a moment, stopped by this. But he laughed then, as if Sijjer had told him a familiar old joke. "Partners," he said. "You never had a partner in your work, did you. See, it's an important part of life. Partners help each other. I'm helping you today. Someday you'll have to help me. Without that we wouldn't have a chance in hell. That's what it's all about. If no one ever helped the other guy, well we'd be as heartless as any of these sons of bitches."

"Who?"

"All these city folks you see here. The folks that just work their whole life so they can get money so they can buy stuff and live all wrapped up in themselves. They get proud and think what they have is everything they need. They start thinking they're all alone. Individuals. Individuals! They think their house or food or car is everything, I guess. I never knew people were like that until I came back here to the city."

Sijjer simply picked up his pipe. In all his life he had never known real friendship with another man. He had his brother Gurjit, and he had spurned even that contact of late.

So Sijjer was not fired in the end and neither was Grey and they worked together as partners regularly after that. Then a mass of Arctic air moved over the city, and the job ended. The men went their separate ways.

He drove one day in the apocalyptic darkness of February. On the street leading to his house he glimpsed a yellow luminescent ball bolting in the beam of the headlights. The van swerved and slid and came to rest in the middle of Sterns' front lawn. He could see the object now, clearly a dog, clearly Zeph, urinating on a tree.

"Zeph, here boy. Come on home, Zeph-boy." he called. But Zeph did not come. He harkened to another call and bounced away through rising drifts of snow. Sijjer scuffed across the lawns to his door.

A stubborn chill began in his shoes in the wet snow, wicked into his bones and spread. He searched for a bottle he was sure was there, found it with a single inch of a drink left, and this was not enough. In the darkness of the living room he sat with a blanket around his shoulders and watched the flicker of gold outside, of the virtual Zeph charging around the house.

He remembered warmth. A bonfire on a beach. Fire fueled by log sculptures of driftwood dragged over the sand by the fire-makers. Cascades of sparks over the water and the fire-makers dancing in a primal celebration of warmth.

Warmth, precious warmth. But even then he had not participated.

TWELVE

Conrad Grey

I

Grey saw two kinds of cloud from where he lay; there were dark wisps which streamed finely at the roof of sky, and beneath that, puffy wheels that rolled on invisible ramps. The high wisps reminded him of the hair of his Anne, the way it spread across the sheets like threads of fine black silk. Seeing her hair in the clouds this way, he could feel and smell his sweet Anne. And she was sweeter now that he was gone.

He realized he was gone already.

He wondered if she would know to come to this dusty, abandoned house where he lay on his back on the floor. For two hours he had waited, watching the afternoon clouds stream across the pale northern sky and watching the street. Maybe she would not know, he thought. 'Maybe she already knows I'm gone.'

The sky grew paler; it was getting late. In his mind he tracked back and took leave, touching the places and people he knew. He tracked to Bernard, his mining partner, then went through a day of his working life, touching on the men of the crew, touching the machines and the tools he had worked with and would not use again. He touched the rock formations in the drifts where he had walked hundreds of times; he took leave, even, of the rock. Then he tracked homeward, cutting through bush, through the swamp and the fields, touching it all. He came to the building where he lived with his Anne and here he parted with her and heard her flute and her ringing voice. He said farewell to his Anne, letting go of her. Then it was time to be gone.

But Grey heard a sound and stood up as delicately as he could with his barred mining boots and heavy oilers. He deftly caught at his lamp as it swung out. Someone tried the window, then he saw it was Anne and he wrenched the window open himself and hauled her through it.

"Connie Grey, you wild man. What the hell did you do? Did you know the police . . . I guess you do know . . . " She was out of breath, looking at him as if he were a stranger.

"I have to be moving," he said. "What did you bring for me?"

"They made a complete wreck of the place. These two RCMP guys. Well, if you're leaving, I suppose everyone knows where you're going, don't they?"

"Don't worry about that. Sit down for a second, will you."

Grey scouted out the window and saw a car moving slowly up the block.

"What will you do, Connie? What's going to happen to you?" she whispered. "You're this . . . this wild man. There's no place for a wild man like you on this earth. No one will understand you . . . "

"Don't worry about that. I guess you heard some of it by now."

"Everyone's talking about it. They say . . . "

"Let's just forget all about that stuff, Anne. There's no time. It's mostly talk, just like always. I've got to leave here. I'm going to try to keep in touch somehow. Now what did you bring?"

He changed into the clothes she brought out. She handed him two twenty dollar bills, saying, "That's all we had at home . . . "

Together they watched a police car move down the street and turn the corner.

"You won't be coming back here, I guess," said Anne. "I might as well just go back to Winnipeg."

"I messed things up pretty badly, didn't I?"

"You are completely wild! I'm so confused about everything. I thought I knew you."

"You'll forget about all this mess in a while."

Grey half-expected her to start crying then, and it stabbed him to see that she laughed instead.

"You really are wild . . . " She clung to his shoulders for a moment, but, in a way, he was already gone, limp-running through the alleys to the highway.

He came to a dimly lit cafe at the edge of town but stopped outside. He lit a cigarette and smoked it down as customers came and went. It was eleven o'clock and the sky was still a washed-out pale blue.

In the cafe a sleepy yellow woman leaned on the cash register and watched a small television propped before her. In one corner an old-timer wearing an animal skin cap hunched vacantly over a cup of coffee. . . .

"Hey, Benj," called the woman to the old-timer. "You get this. We're in the news again. Thompson's in the news! Someone clobbered a miner. I even know him!" She turned to Grey. "You hear about that?"

"It's all through town," said Grey. "I knew the guy by sight. Radki."

"Radki, that's right. I heard about him too. I got two boys in T1 and my old man in T2 and they've told me a few things, you know. They told me about some of those sons of bitches down there. You might know my boys. They're about your age . . . "

"Yeah, yeah," said Grey. He ordered three orders of back bacon and toast and wrapped them in a paper bag and stuffed them into his small rucksack with a couple of apples. Then he went out the door without looking the woman in the eye again.

A police car was parked on the only highway leading from town so Grey backtracked to the railway yard. He followed the line some way down, then concealed himself in the bush.

He settled back under the pale sky to wait for a train. He

closed his eyes and saw Radki on his knees with his helmet fallen to one side. Radki looked as though he were praying. He saw the scaling bar flash into the little sphere of light from his lamp, dropping like an owl to strike and vanish in the dark.

II

On the long ride west Grey cast his eye upon the giant beauty of the land. Through the open door of the freight car he saw the vast wheat fields giving way to rolling scrubland and later, the foothills. The mountains towered up, cut by misty valleys which the train ran through and through in the way a fitful sleeper moves in and out of dreams. Between the valleys each snowy peak, each leaf and drop of water thrown from the glacial run-off was sharply resolved in the strong mountain light.

In the freight car it was cold and Grey huddled in a sheet of plastic. He slept and woke, slept again and woke starving in a trance of light. Then he was jerked awake as the train came at last into the city. He smelled the unmistakable rankness of the sea and the trance was broken.

He had come to Vancouver as a matter of instinct. A homing instinct, for this was his place of birth. With his arrival he had no need of further plans; he had come home. Now as the train slowed, his recollections of his early childhood were vivid. His home had been near the port, a stone's throw from the waters' edge. From it the high ridge of mountains on the other side of the strait could be seen. There was a fish cannery nearby, but he recalled the house as an airy cottage on a bluff. He remembered the salty spray of the sea and the way it cooled his sun-baked face. Nearby was a park filled with immense forests and wild geese which waddled though forest meadows ablaze with flowers. In the mornings he was wakened by the bellow of ships leaving the harbour, the house yellow with rich sunlight. In the trees the birds shrilled. He remembered the warmth of the kitchen and that his mother prepared thick porridge on winter mornings. A small, blue flame played under the boiling pot. Everything was clean, he remembered, and smelled of spruce.

Grey had no doubt that he would find the old place the way he had left it twenty-seven years before, even as the train bumped across a level crossing and entered the railyard by the port. It was dark. He jumped down and followed the tracks back out to where the yard opened onto a street which smelled sharply of rotting fish. It was small and dull here, after the magnificance of the mountains. He followed the street along to an unlit pier and clambered over the fence and ventured down to the water. Here at last was the ocean. It lapped sluggishly at the rotted footings of the old pier. As the morning light increased a rusty barge came into view. Scum appeared in which dead fish, some weeds, a beer can and a limp condom floated together. A large rat watched Grey from a hole in the wood.

He spat into the water and moved off the pier. He headed up the hill towards the centre of town, through the midst of office towers and down deserted concourses. He trekked in an arc through the city as it awakened, saw workers descend from buses and Chinese vendors setting up their stalls. Drunks staggered in the morning light. Three hours later he was back near where he had started having made a complete circle through the city core.

This was the Lower Eastside – a warren of flophouses and taverns and garbage-strewn alleyways and fumey streets. It looked to Grey like a dilapidated version of Thompson. But he was not disappointed with this, nor with the sea nor the city which did not match his dream. Instead his dream painlessly died as the new fantasy, that of Thompson, flourished in its place.

III

Grey considered his first day in Vancouver as a sign of good things to come. He settled himself into the Balmoral Tavern, ordered a jug of beer and waited and watched. Within an hour he had met half a dozen men and women, two of whom were Metis brothers by the name of Dupray. He drank with them through the evening and ended crashing down in their place that night and staying on there.

The Duprays were an odd crew. The elder, Ramond,

claimed he was a construction foreman, but Grey could find him every afternoon at the Balmoral, tilting glasses of beer. After a week Ray admitted he did not work, that he was a house burglar, specializing, he said, in TVs and clocks. The TVs he sold as fast as he stole and these provided his livelihood. But the basement was crammed with clocks of every kind. Dupray explained it to Grey one morning and showed off the clocks as proudly as an art collector in his gallery.

"They all work," he told Grey. "I make sure each one of 'em works good."

"What are they for?"

"Keeping time. I like having lots of time around. It's good for you, in the long run."

Grey chuckled at this but stopped when he saw that the other man looked thoughtfully off without a trace of humour in his face.

"And," said Dupray, ponderous, "They're like having an insurance policy, see. They're worth a lot of dough, these clocks . . . you try buying one."

Willy, the younger brother, did not speak or respond in any way to anyone but Ramond. Willy was simple-minded and ate huge quantities of any edible stuff including garbage. He spent hours in front of the television, his hand fiddling his penis until Ray made him zip up. Willy refused to go into the basement, fearing the click and hum of the clocks.

In this strange milieu Grey was content to keep to himself. He searched for work. He searched for his old house near the harbour. It was hard to locate, that house. Rather than brightly painted, airy cottages by the sea, he found only tiny woodframe bungalows, overgrown and rundown, windows broken, siding rotted. They were indistinguishable in their squalor and nothing like his cherished image.

He did not know why he looked for the place. Sometimes he asked himself that question, but went on searching without answering it.

He had an upper storey room in Dupray's house which overlooked the street. There was an great oak tree outside the window, and when the breeze came up, the trunk moaned and the leaves spoke. Grey's mind drifted. He had a need to come to terms. Events had run ahead of him. Lying on the old mattress his chest grew heavy with anticipation, yet the future was an impenetrable cloud.

III

Childhood was in shards. A large cracked fragment, yellow with age: moving images of sisters and Aunt Jeanine, mother. Another piece, unplaceable and small: the toothless grin of the singing fireman. And there was the other large shard, clearer, harsh with the smell of pine oil: the foster care of Mrs. William.

It was winter. Someone was saying the word foster over and over, and all he could think of was frost. Darlene and Melie dressed him up in three pairs of pants that day so that he could hardly bend his knees much less run. The outside pants were corduroy and when he walked, they made a zip-zipping sound that he hated. Then his sisters were gone, his mother was gone and he was with strangers. They were kind and talked to him softly, not to say anything it seemed, but only to make soft cooing sounds for him. He did not understand the idea that he was to be taken care of by strangers. He asked after his sisters but no one answered him in a way that made sense.

There was some time, a few days or a few months, in the large pink room that belonged to the tall man and his wife and son. But that ended when he ate the white pills. They brought him to hospital after that and only once came to see him. He was not surprised that they left him there. He had done something wrong, knowingly. He understood that much.

He wanted Darlene and Melie. He asked who was taking care of Cookie the dog.

He was brought to another house. The William home was spotless and quiet, dominated by the sombre hues of antique furniture and the incessant tocking of a grandfather clock. It smelled of pine oil and wax and soap. The curtains were drawn to protect the old wood.

The woman William was pink-eyed, wan and old, if not in years then in demeanor. She had wire-rimmed glasses, wispy greying hair and an apron permanently affixed to her dress. The only aspect of her that was not faded and old were her shoes which were mannish, black and shiny.

She directed a sealed-lipped, shy smile at Grey the first weeks, and she was nervous from wanting to embrace him and not doing it. Her hands darted towards him, touching his hair, tracing the space around his shoulders, following with tight-smiling attentiveness his every movement. Then afterwards she gave in to the urge and would crush him to her as if he were clothing. He quickly learned to go limp and to turn his head away to catch a breath.

Her eyes were pink from crying. She had done this before Grey came into the house and she did it while Grey was there. No one knew why. Her husband thought she cried because she was unable to bear children and thought it would stop when Grey came. Then, after Grey was there, he thought she cried because of Grey. William stopped consoling her at some point early on. When he heard her suppressed sob, he reached into the refrigerator for a beer, poured it with great deliberation, then finished it in a single draught.

The man William was sparse, veiny and knobby-kneed. He rolled his sleeves to the elbow and wore a bamboo ring around his bicep. From his years of working on the greenchains his hands were huge and powerful. He left the raising of the child to his wife along with all else domestic. "The house is woman's land," said William, "and you and me are just the guests." William deferred to the law of women, the code that was not put to words but which Grey was expected to know by William's example. Beer drunken from a glass, not a bottle. Boots removed in the vestibule. Rude or unnecessary noise was punishable by the silent withholding of food.

All this Grey took in but did not heed. He survived the hugs and ignored the darkness of the house. Bravely he countenanced the railed bed they made him lie in at night.

He waited for his sisters to come. By the front window he stood, peering around the edge of the curtain, watching the streets and waiting. When, after a long time, they still had not found him, he climbed from his bed and left the William's house, his bare feet slapping the cool night pavement. But he became aware that he was being stalked. Beside him a dark, low shape slid, ready to pounce. He the hunter, was being hunted. The hunter was a car, the black Oldsmobile belonging to the man William. Then he was limp in the woman William's arms as she cried into his hair.

The escape seemed to draw the man William's attention to Grey. He peered at the boy over a glass of beer one evening, sizing him, perhaps as he would a piece of fir.

"C'mon out to the garage, boy."

Grey did not know the garage. He had concentrated on knowing the house, the woman, and knowing the waiting feeling that went on and on, fighting with the dying of his hope. The garage was the building in the back, a place where the man William went away to hide. Now he peered at the inside things of the garage and he felt very small. It was man's domain, the hard-worded, strong-smelling thing that he had seen at home. There were naked, bent women on the walls. To one side, low and sleek, lay the black Oldsmobile which had captured him in the night. The car was fearsome, an enemy. It made sense to Grey that it lay here, an animal in its lair. There were other things which he put his eyes upon but did not think about: a wall full of drawings of tools, each drawing filled with the tool itself, a rack of fishing rods, a propellered motor in a barrel of oily water. And the man William.

William stared at Grey for a moment, and Grey looked away. William was nervous. He picked up a pair of pliers and dropped it on his foot. Cursing badly, he hopped, then sharply looked at the boy. He fiddled with some fishing tackle and stuck a hook into his finger.

"Just don't stand and stare like a dummy, for Chrissakes," the man William yelled. "You never learned manners?" He collected himself, looking towards the house. "Listen, son, don't you like tools? Hammer, nails, stuff like that. Look here at all this stuff. Boys got to learn about that. Someday you gotta get yourself a job, just like me."

He handed Grey a hammer and a handful of long, bright nails. This Grey accepted gratefully, then shoved the nails into his pocket. With the hammer he banged the floor and a piece of wood, wanting William to ignore him. William looked at him and grunted. Grey hammered down a ridge of cement on the floor, working his way along. He came to the Oldsmobile. The chrome gleamed in his face. It was alive, grinning, waiting to scoop him up if he ran. He tapped the chrome quietly with the hammer, out of sight of William. Then he took out a nail and tried it against the black paint. He ran down the side of the car then, the nails dug into the side of it, and ran straight into William's large hand.

William lifted him by the back of the shirt and shook him. The veins in his neck bulged as he tried to speak but could not. "You dirty bastard," he finally choked out and tossed Grey, like a dirty rag, into a basket of other dirty rags.

"I told her I was going to help raise a kid, and, goddamn it, that's what I'm gonna do, no matter what kind of little bastard he is. I know he hates me. But for her sake, I'm gonna do this . . . " As he talked he fished in a box and extracted a dog chain and a lock. William dragged Grey out of the basket and clipped the chain around his neck and snapped the lock onto it. The other end he tied to a post in the middle of the floor, far from the Oldsmobile.

He went to school. There was glue which stuck to his fingers and dried there, and there was the alphabet and numbers which made him sick to look at. By the end of the year the teacher had told Mrs. William that her son would fail grade one. Mrs. William tried to teach him at home. She made him repeat the letters and then made him write the letters and numbers out. It always came out wrong. Backwards 'j's and 'p's mixed up for 'q's. The numbers were worse. Nothing she did made it easier. It gave him headaches and nausea. His hands would shake with tension and pain.

But Mrs. William kept trying to teach Grey. She bought him books with big pictures and letters in them which Grey tore up one morning when the headache made him furious.

"He's retarded," William pronounced from the bottom of his beer mug.

"Then you teach him. Teach him something he can use out there."

The man William took Grey by the arm and led him down the steps to the garage. "Teach him something useful. Can't teach him nothing 'cause he's tied up in the middle of the floor. She's gonna find that out and then where'll I be." William mumbled on to himself and Grey listened and was calm. "Listen, you. Don't get in no more trouble. You been punished long enough, I guess, but you got to promise to keep your paws off the car. You hear?"

It was a clear winter day and the garage was chilly. William brought out the leash, but left it in plain view on the work bench, coiled up. He handed Grey a saw and a two-by-four and placed him on a bench at the opposite end of the garage from the Olds.

"Try to make yourself a boat with that."

Grey sawed at the wood for a moment. He watched William tinker with the outboard motor. Gas and oil spilled from the guts of the thing making a splendour of colour in a spot of sun. Grey put his foot into it and the colours flashed irridescent green and purple. . . .

The man William smoked down his cigarette and dropped the butt in the drain. The flames leapt up with a woof that sounded like a blanket beat by the wind. Grey jumped clear of his puddle, action preceding thought by the second it takes for flames to sprint across a pool of gasoline. Then for one instant he stopped frozen in the flame-lit glare of the man William. The flames surrounded the car. Man and boy plunged out of the door.

From the house, from the woman William's lap, Grey watched the firemen work. When they went away, the garage was a skeleton and the black Oldsmobile was a smoking hulk.

Grey expected to be thrashed or killed. Even though he could not remember doing anything wrong, he knew he was guilty of something. He had been caught saving himself, caught in the snare of William's eyes. But if William blamed Grey, he kept it to himself. He had the remains of the garage cleared away, and never spoke of it again. With great solemnity he clipped a leash to Grey's neck whenever they were alone. Together the two set off on fishing trips in a dinghy, foster father at the tiller and foster son tethered and locked to the transom.

With the garage gone the house changed. The pervasive silence gave way to William's mutterings. William took over the kitchen during long bouts of beer drinking which were conducted straight from the bottle and with his shoes on and with the television blaring on the table before him. The curtains were open to the world, the subdued tocking of the clock drowned out. There were times when William's big hand came at Grey to knock him sprawling like a pup onto the floor and times when the mutterings turned to a drunken snarl. After a year Mrs. William was reduced to a wraith, her hair springing from her bun at all angles, her apron wrinkled. When William lost his job they decided to move.

There ensued a long drive in a new Oldsmobile. Grey clung to the back seat and watched the road spew out behind, wondering how long it would take him to to walk all that way back. He never doubted that someday he would.

THIRTEEN

I

Grey knew that no one knew where he had gone. So his hopes for rescue painfully died over the months. But in the north there were others like himself. There was no separating him from the Cree, the Desoto, the Blackfoot children. Grey was never lonely, but he stayed alone. He remembered who he was, a hunter, stalking, sharpening his skills. He successfully ignored the education they tried to force upon him and lived out in the air when he could. Home was a bed and table. Home was the old white couple who were not a part of him.

So he grew in the north, in the land of day seasons and night seasons, under the gyrations of the north lights, the celebrations of spirit gods.

One day he was no longer a child. It dawned upon him suddenly as he beheld an object, a car. It was a convertible, so new the tread of the tires was still tar black, the chrome a perfect mirror. A thing of beauty to most teenagers. But to Grey, fifteen years old, it was a devil alit in the middle of

Thompson, Manitoba. He hated it, as much as anyone can hate a machine.

Yet there it was, gleaming at him, and there he was, suddenly realizing he was no longer a child. Hands in his jeans, cigarette unlit and dangling, he stared at the thing for some time before he saw the cigarette lighter in the dash.

He often remembered that day, for the light was clear. In his memory he looked at his shadow on the wall and saw that it was full and tall. In the memory he went in for the lighter of the car, challenging the gleaming evil of it. Then, further insolence, he tried the seat. In memory the owner appeared, baying like a dog as Grey, finding the key in place, fired the ignition. Eight cylinders roaring to life, and he was gone. Rubber in second gear, slewing around a corner, bucking down the perma-frost-heaved highway. The spring air, heated by a sun as big as the horizon, boiled around him. The possibilities offered by the sensational life, of speed drunkeness, spring, the new boldness of manhood, were as apparent as the spring sun. And in memory a girl materialized in the seat beside him. Young, breasted, she drove with him through the spring day until the sapphire twilight deepened; then they returned to town, and he crashed the car by the wrecking yard and left it.

Later the man William followed the trail of woman's clothing from the front door of the house to the chair beside Grey's bed. He then sat wearily, crossed one leg over the other and shook his head. William was by then a bitter, tight-lipped widower of sixty, who often appeared drunk when sober which was not often. He would have entered the room unnoticed were it not for the profane stream of utterings which issued from him, drunk or sober.

"You liddle sonuvabitch," drawled William.

The girl slid under the covers overcome by an attack of giggles.

"Go away," said Grey.

"You fend fer yerself, eh. That's all you ever knew. Fend fer yerself. What the hell do you care for anyone? Allays such a quiet fella, you. What did you care if she lived or died? She was nothin' to you but dirt under yer feet . . . "

"Go away."

"How d'you suppose you got to sleep here under this roof and all? How d'you figger you got the best of the best while other kids . . . "

"I live here, William. Now piss off."

"By the grace of my late wife, God rest her soul. You liddle sonuvabitch. You never cared fer her at all. You gave her nuthin' in return. She loved you, saved yer life, and what. You pushed her away like she was nuthin'. Just like a snake or a lizard or somethin', you. YOU KILLED HER, YOU BASTARD."

"You're pissed, William. Go sleep it off."

"You killed her, you bastard," said William quietly, "You could of give her something back but no, her heart broke and she died. And I just want you to know the only reason I stood for havin' a cold-blooded lizard in my house was because of her. Now it looks like you're man enough, so you can get the hell out."

William stood, stared at Grey in his bed. In memory then, this was Grey's last triumph on his glorious day of manhood. He moved out of William's home and found a room in the miners' residence.

That was how he began working at T3. He pushed a broom in the minehead for two years before he was sent underground.

II

The room in the Dupray house was shaded and calm.

Grey revelled in the fact that he occupied his own private room with a mattress on a dry floor, felt positively blessed that outside his window was a grand old oak. His housemates were as odd and entertaining as any friends he had ever made and he was quickly fond of Dupray, despite his idiosyncrasies. He had to chuckle to hear Dupray bellowing with laughter at Willy, or see his bull-necked, cat-muscled stealth.

Ramond Dupray was proud and self-sufficient, generous and crooked. In a leather holster on his hip was a sharp buckknife which he bragged of wielding. He had taken a helpless foundling off of the street and adopted him as brother. He opened his home to a string of strangers and expected little in return. Dupray felt a kinship with Grey, in part because he sensed that he was in trouble with the law, but also because his cleanly carven face, brooding eyes and long silences reminded him of the best of Dupray's own Metis people. In Grey, Dupray sensed a deep vein of incorruptibility that he respected.

"I'm gonna fix you up, you lazy cuss" Dupray said, coming into the room. It was raining outside, big drops slapping the leaves of the oak tree. "Get up, you beautiful son of a bitch, I got you a job."

The job was midnight to morning, as a watchman on a construction site in North Vancouver. But Dupray did not drive to the job site that night, turning in at the dockyard instead.

It was dark and foggy. They drove east along the waterfront until they were at the end of the harbour, then Dupray got out of the car and searched among the box cars. He called Grey over. An ancient Indian woman huddled by the wheel of a boxcar, her shoulders wrapped in a blanket. A scruffy terrier growled by her side. Before her a tiny fire fluttered out periodically yet never failed to flicker to life again to give off no more than a suggestion of light and heat.

Dupray squatted across the fire from her, and she looked up suddenly as if from sleep. Then she smiled and withdrew a handful of gleaming bones from the folds of the blanket.

"Those there are worth more than any money could buy," Dupray whispered. He pulled Grey forward for the old woman to see. This set her to muttering.

"What's she say?"

"I don't understand much of that old lingo she talks. I only learned a few words. Something about a ghost."

Dupray held out a fistful of quarters for her and she took these into her blanket and lay the bones out on the ground. She pushed certain ones around with others making them clack as though made of stone. She sang out words in her language and prodded the bones, trying different ways. Finally she scooped them up and sighed with fatigue. She closed her eyes and muttered a few words before falling asleep.

"There," said Dupray, "we're done."

"Done what?"

"Well, the old woman says you got to watch out. She says a

storm following you around."

"What's that supposed to mean?" asked Grey.

"I don't know. We have to think it over, I guess. You can't always tell what she means at first."

Grey started his job the next night. In the rain he walked a naked concrete slab, guarding piles of wood and steel and bricks. The site was near the docks and big marine rats scampered on the high tension wires overhead.

He slept in the mornings and worked seven nights a week. Sometimes the job foreman or an engineer or the owner the of site came by and honked their horns to make sure he was awake. But otherwise the place was silent. Dupray dropped by a few times at odd hours, but then these visits ceased and Grey was alone. The building grew each week; like a Frankenstein monster it had new parts added on, then it seemed to wait, looming in the dark to be brought to life. First six floors, then eight, then fourteen floors high. Then it was so high that on foggy nights he could no longer see the light bulb that burned atop the crane tower.

In the dark Grey clambered to the top, up scaffolding and ladders so that he could look out over the dark waters of the inlet. The dark climbing reminded him of the pit and the last long climb he had made in his escape.

Then one autumn night, when the moon was bright, he looked down from the top floor and saw a pickup truck pull into the yard and park by a pile of steel reinforcement. A stranger got out and began loading the steel, a piece at a time. He made no effort to conceal himself. The steel bars clanged into the bed of the truck.

"Hey, you!" Grey yelled from the fourteenth floor. The stranger looked around, then continued loading.

Without thinking Grey picked up the nearest thing that came to hand, a fist-sized chunk of broken concrete, and let it fly. With a shock he heard, rather than saw, it hit the man. Then all was silent but for the purring of the truck motor.

It seemed to take a year for him to work his way down from the roof. By the time he was on the slab and crossing it in the bright moonlight, he felt a tiny stab of pain in his bad leg. It went away when he saw the would-be thief. He lay beside the truck, conscious and wide-eyed. He too was Indian and wore a braid with beads in it.

"You got me," he said as Grey came up. He kept his eyes on the moon.

"I was aiming for the truck, you know, but that's what you get for . . . Are you hurt bad?"

"I'm hurt, you don't have to be a doctor to see I'm hurt, so just shut up, okay?"

"Sure, you're hurt. You can expect that if . . . "

"Just do me a big favour and shut up, will you? No one shuts up when I tell them to, that's a major problem. You better call the police and tell them you got me."

It had never occurred to Grey that he might have to deal with the police in this job. "Don't I know you?" he said.

"Maybe."

"Why don't you get up, so I can see your face better."

"Think I'd be here if I could have got up?" said the thief.

Grey went to the slab and brought back a flashlight he kept hidden there. He played it over the legs of the thief and shone it in his face.

"You're okay. Now get up."

"In the back. It hit me in the back, whatever it was."

Grey suspected he was about to be jumped. So he put the flashlight aside and suddenly hauled the thief over on his side. The man fainted.

The moon glowed. The shadows of the concrete forms were sharp against the sky. Silver light glowed on the face of the stranger.

Grey dragged him onto the pile of steel bars in the back of the pickup. It was several hours before daylight yet, so he remained calm. The solution to his problem would come. He thought first of leaving the truck near the police station, thief and all, but he did not know where that was. So he drove the truck around the block and stopped when he heard a groan from the back. The stranger was awake, propped against the cab and staring at the moon. His face was ghastly pale yet serene in the silver light. Grey hung out the window on crossed arms.

"Hey, what's your name?"

"Kenny. Kenneth."

"Look here, Kenneth, you got yourself in a mess out here tonight. We're both in a mess, in fact, seeing as the police are out. What do you figure I should do with you?"

"I think my back's busted."

"What?"

"I can't feel my legs no more." Kenneth's eyes watered and he started to cry softly. "I can't walk."

Grey turned his head away. After a moment he said gently, as if to a child, "No point in crying about it, is there, man? I mean it's just what happened. I didn't mean . . . "

"Just shut up, will you?"

"I was just doing my job. I wasn't even aiming . . . "

Grey drove again, not knowing what else to say. His breath had left him when Kenneth had said his back was broken. He thought for a moment he would vomit, then he wanted to bolt, but he did neither and drove. He wondered what would become of Kenneth and thought that he would not ever like to hear more about him. He drove slowly, his mind working through a dismal process. He wondered who Kenneth was, whether he had family and where they were. He wondered what people his ancestors belonged to. The pick-up cruised aimlessly along the vacant, lamplit streets of North Vancouver, and in this bleek landscape Grey felt as alien and ill-prepared as a naked man in a snowstorm. The hospital appeared suddenly. It was a small hospital, a series of low, modern wings, but there was a red-lit 'EMERG' sign before a set of automatic doors. Kenneth seemed to wake up. He peered sorrowfully at the lights as Grey stopped the truck down the street.

"You gotta take me in there, you know, I can't make it," choked Kenneth when he saw where they were. "Look, I can't walk from here."

"Shit," said Grey. He hauled Kenneth out of the truck and carefully dragged him along until they were on the ramp to the sliding doors. Inside they saw unbroken whiteness: white walls and furniture, even the nurses and receptionists were dressed in white, all white. It looked as cold as death inside the hospital. Kenneth clung like a child to Grey's shirt.

"Don't leave me in there," he begged. "I'll give you anything. Listen, brother, so help me, I'll tell them all about you. I'll tell them you're in trouble with the police. They'll come after you. They'll know where to find you. Please, please, don't leave me here."

"What do you mean, don't leave me? What do you want me to do, man?"

"You gotta come in. I'm scared . . . they'll kill me in there."

"Shit," said Grey. He tried unsuccessfully to disengage his shirt from Kenneth's fingers. "What are you scared of?"

"I was in when I was a kid. I was real sick."

"So. You're a man now."

"Oh no, I'm not. Everyone used to say it. I'm not really a man at all. I'm still a kid. Even my mother used to say it. I never grew up, she would say. Please don't leave me in there."

"Shit," Grey muttered.

"Indians die in hospitals, don't you know that? We're, like, killed by all that modern stuff. It doesn't work on us."

The doors slid back and they blinked in the coldness of the interior. The nurse looked at Kenneth and buzzed for a stretcher. The young Indian had begun to sob and he clung to Grey with both hands. But he let go when they loaded him onto the stretcher.

"Next of kin?" asked the nurse. Kenneth appealed with big, liquid eyes, but Grey stared him down.

"None," said Kenneth. Then, they wheeled him away and Grey slipped out into the dewy pre-dawn.

He never returned to the job site, driving the pickup truck that night across the bridge, high over the inlet. In the last minutes before dawn he found a place by the fish canneries to leave the truck and hiked homeward. It was purely accident then that Grey found the home of his childhood.

He had explored in the neighbourhood behind the cannery enough times that he was familiar with all of the houses by then.

Three or four times through the garbage-strewn alleys and deserted streets and he knew it all. But at this early hour he saw an elderly woman ahead of him, a bright plastic bag dangling from each arm, pushing her way through the broken gate of a house which he'd thought was condemned. There was something in her walk, a peculiar tilting of her heavy body from side to side like an old, broken-springed bus, that made him stop in his tracks and squint at her in puzzlement. He knew that walk.

Grey passed by the house once and looked back from the end of the street. He felt the blood rush in his ears. He could see now the patches where the old yellow paint had not worn away and the small window over the alley where he used to peer out. He hopped the fence and went to the door. But there he hesitated. What would he say? Had he seen his mother?

Rather than knock he stepped off the stoop and peeked through a window. He hardly recognized anything. Shockingly, a room which he vaguely remembered as being his mother's bedroom and which he remembered as bright-lit and spacious was, in fact, as cramped and dim a room as any he had ever slept in. Dupray's house seemed like a mansion in comparison. The placed possessed a rotten reek, even on the outside. Through another window he saw the kitchen. A television sat atop the stove which he had fondly remembered as issuing dancing blue flames on winter days.

His curiosity about the identity of the familiar figure waned. He took one last sniff of the decayed house and walked away.

FOURTEEN

Karla Mistral

I

Karla would always see her little Bear in other children. She reconciled herself to the fluttering in her breast, the chill in her womb. In her mind her son lived and grew. Six months after his death she saw him in winter clothes, his hair needing a cut, and after a year she saw him grown taller and become serious.

She could not breathe. Her lungs had lost the power of absorbency, or her breathing muscles had given up. She struggled, wrought with compensatory sighs. She opened windows, thinking the oxygen had gone out of the air, gasping at minute contaminants. Her once upright shoulders were pulled in by emptiness.

Her parents arrived. Her father was weak and foggy-eyed, sapped by Karla's ordeal. To see him was to see the passage of time, and a mirror of her own aging. If he faded, she wondered, then what became of mortals?

Sharon Sterns suggested that Karla pray at the seashore. There had to be a reckoning, said Sterns. There had not been a a memorial service because Karla had refused to allow it. She stayed away from the sea. Bear was not dead, as far as she knew. In the absence of his body the term 'lost' had an open-endedness to which she clung. Sterns recommended a doctor for the breathing problem. The doctor prescribed Valium.

After parents, after Sterns and the doctor, Karla was alone, forced to breathe, forced to listen to Sijjer's fit breaths. She became annoyed, then jealous. She imagined that he stole the air from her. He was insensitive. His greed was boundless. So she moved her sleeping place from the shared bedroom to her study, but still heard, or rather felt, his inhalations.

She moved out, ostensibly because her husband had become a drunk, but in fact because he deprived her of air.

II

Karla's father exuded a fog that shimmered like polished metal. As a child she assumed everyone saw it. She called him 'Shiny Papa' early on, and they thought that clever, not knowing what she saw. By the time she was old enough to know that it was visible only to her, Karla knew not to speak of it.

She was close to her father. As a teenager she visited Shiny Papa at his office. She knew his teaching schedule by heart and paced his paper-cluttered warren while they talked. They debated the medicinal practices of Stone Age Indonesians, or the impact of the latest Soviet Five Year Plan. Controversies between father and daughter raged for hours, fouling Professor Mistral's teaching schedule. He seemed to prefer arguing a point with his young daughter to the offerings of the academic world. Later, at home, the thread of the discussion was taken up over dinner, and on weekends as the two sailed their skiff on the lake.

Her world was of one in those days: her Shiny Papa. She had no need for boyfriends or the tiny-minded stuff of television. He was a storyteller of extraordinary proportions and a talented debater. His mind was rich and at its best in her presence. His lispy baritone rose and fell like the skiff on the lake as he infused life into long dead pharoahs, and sensitivity into the fiercest of the Viking warriors. Tragedy, romance and sin, ecstasy and the profane: nothing compared to the adventure he offered.

But she lost this rapport when she married, and Shiny Papa tarnished. The shininess became thin and he aged, not gracefully but with a sudden falling down of flesh, hair, skin, as though the metallic fog were a glue that held him together. Karla told Sijjer how she imagined her father alone, his curiosity and inventiveness given away to silent contemplation. She worried that he had no one to talk to. When she saw him he looked doddery.

She wondered if she had betrayed him. There had never been another man for her. Who would need anyone when one had a father who shone?

But she already knew he was fallible. She knew precisely how he aged.

In the mornings, awakening to the musk of stagnation and disappointment: his wife's breath. His wife: her face, wrinkled and bitter, even in rest. She's a withered leaf, a shard, and he blames no one for it but himself.

Mornings he drags himself from bed with piercing behind the eyeballs, the result, not of late-night study, nor of exploring the skies with his old refractor, but of too many brandies badly drunk, and staring like a zombie at the television.

Mornings he stands before the bathroom mirror, scratching his scalp to send a flurry of dandruff onto liver-spotted shoulders. Such keen intellect once resided in that face! The grey stubble he scrapes from his jaws, no longer out of vanity, but simply out of habit. First cigarette while he shaves, second while he strains his bowels.

O Shiny Papa! Karla knew it all. She could not visit him for a time because she saw. But when she became pregnant, she was drawn back to his warren of an office. She thought she could bring him to life! She wanted the old dialogue to spark into fireworks, welcome for the new universe incubating inside her.

So one day after a long absence Karla returned. She went in to his office without knocking, the way she had always done. Before her sat Shiny Papa, flipping through a stack of glossy, pornographic magazines, his cigarette hanging unlit from his mouth.

During the time of suffocation she dwelled on Shiny Papa though, nostalgic.

There was a place that belonged to a long dead colleague of Shiny Papa. It was a hunting cabin built years before. Shiny Papa had taken her there once as a child, and the two had spent weeks canoeing the lake and exploring the forest. When she was older, he brought her there to ski on the logging trails. Those had been magical moments that she never forgot. Indeed, she found her way back to the place after she moved to the coast. She found the cabin standing but untouched since her last visit with her father years before. So she made a point of returning twice a year, once in summer and once in winter to ski. She had brought Sijjer there once only, when they first moved to Vancouver, but he had not seen the magic of the place.

She spent three weeks there after Bear disappeared, dreaming of her father. She stayed another month to regain her strength. In the mountains, in the presence of her dreams, air and light breathed through her and she was free.

III

She saw the colours around others. Bear, a gluey corona of tangerine that travelled between him and the dog Zeph. Sterns, yellow sparkles against the green of leaves. And there was that which had the power to shock her – the electric blue flare of Conrad Grey. When she saw him drunken at her door with Sijjer, she had jumped back reflexively to make space.

Sijjer, an intermittent veneer of gold.

Originally it had been he who had made her forget Shiny Papa for a moment. She was attracted by Sijjer's vulnerability and his curiosity. He offered her a hope of a new adventure. Now he was to blame. She went away and returned to him, expectant. His process was not the same as Shiny Papa's. Sijjer aged by drying himself up, withering with alcohol, giving in. The heart fled out of him, leaving his eyes vacant, the gold veneer disappeared.

In the period after the loss of Bear Karla was unsure on her own. Despite Sijjer's obvious weakness, she waited for him to show a sign of faith. When this did not happen, she realized that it was more likely that it was up to her to muster faith, not Sijjer.

She chose morning to speak to him, when the light was bright.

"You're not working today." She tried to sound concerned.

"I haven't worked in five weeks," he answered. Sijjer smelled ethanolic, even though it was eight-thirty in the morning. "Are we out of money or something? I imagine we'll run out at some point. Don't know what I'll do then . . . "

"Listen, I think we need to get out of the house for a while. It's not good . . . here."

Sijjer sat at the table and looked at her for the first time.

"Is that coffee I smell? And toast?"

"I'm making breakfast. You don't seem capable of putting a bite of food into you. Why didn't you ever learn to take care of yourself?"

"I did. Well. I was taking care of different things. Not food, I suppose. I was taking care of my mental attitude."

She put out scrambled eggs and toast, saw herself doing it, but did not take joy or satisfaction in it. Feeding him made her slightly nauseaous, in fact. She persisted, fighting it.

"I think we should go away."

"Yes. You said that. Holidays? Vacation? I'm already on vacation. Haven't you noticed?"

"I'm serious. To the cabin. "

He stared at his eggs, unsure of their function. "The cabin? Oh yes, that. Why now?"

"I thought it might be a way of . . . breaking out of it."

"I see," said Sijjer, not seeing.

He agreed to go with her. That was not in doubt from the beginning.

But it felt wrong. She had expressed faith, or at least thought she had done so, and it had soured in her stomach as she did it, as though she had eaten poison.

She had once expected adventure from him. Now she had poison. . . .

The cabin was nestled high in the Selkirks, an eight-hour drive from Vancouver. They hardly spoke during the drive, the poison burning in her stomach, her breathing laboured. She listened to her lungs protesting life.

They had to hike in from the road along an old deer path to reach the cabin. Winter lingered under the trees and the snow was deep. In places where the spring sun shone through, there was bog and frigid run-off streams. By the time they reached the cabin they were soaked to the thighs.

It was one room with a pair of windows overlooking the deep lake that extended the length of the valley. There was a short porch and log steps down to a path which led to the lakeshore. Karla kept the canoe concealed in the brush near the lake, concealed even though the nearest habitation was miles away. In the fall there were a few hunters. At one time there were loggers, but the logging operation which had stripped bald the faces of two of the surrounding mountains had ended a few years before.

She opened the place and they changed into dry clothes. The cabin was dry, the wood ready where Karla had stacked it last summer. Other than a few mouse turds, it was clean. She lit the fire and stove. . . .

Sijjer did not speak or offer help. He stood about on the porch staring into the forest, then wandered a short distance in the clearing outside the cabin, lost.

He who had offered adventure now needed a place to hide. Karla looked out the window at him, sensed her faith ebbing.

She noticed that the roof of the outhouse had collapsed. She had expected that and had brought a bundle of shakes from the car.

As evening drew on the forest became quiet. Karla heated soup, left a portion in the pot for him. She cleaned up and tried to relax by the glow of the stove.

It was her place. But Sijjer's presence interfered. She could not remember what to do next. She wanted to be alone suddenly. She had made a mistake in bringing him here. She pulled on her boots and plunged through the snow to the lake side.

The lake ice was unfathomable in the darkness. The coldness and the space were calming. If she had a choice, she would die here, she thought. She would lie down on the ice and watch night steal over the mountain tops. The sky would drop her veil to reveal the nakedness of the stars, chilling and distant. No one would know. She would simply go the way of the other forest beings.

Above the lake she saw the flash of a meteor. The streak was blue like lightning. It brought Grey to her mind. He with the lightning blue. Karla wanted to forget about Grey, whoever he was. She was haunted by the light and the flicker in his eyes. It had captured her the way any fire-watcher is caught, gazing into its depths to see fire's mystery.

What was he but another adventure?

She followed her footprints back to the cabin. It was warm inside. Sijjer sat by the door, wrapped in a blanket. Lost.

Karla stoked the fire and paced the room. She stopped and heard the distant cry of a wolf echoing in the valley. She was tired. Tomorrow she would try again to muster faith.

IV

In the morning she awoke to a crack of the ice on the lake breaking up. The morning was bright and the sun was above the mountain ridge.

Karla lit the fire. Sijjer was asleep in the chair. She pulled the blanket over his shoulders and again felt the strange poison at work. She crawled back into her bed and listened to the ice cracking. When the cabin was warm, she drew her skis down from the rafters and waxed them by the fire. She knew there would be spring ice on the trail. She packed cheese and bread, a thermos of tea for her breakfast. Then, skis and poles over her shoulder, she set out before Sijjer had stirred.

She hiked into the woods and upwards. Half an hour later she came to virgin snow on a sloping ridge, and she snapped up her old bindings and skied. The ridge made a spine between two mountains along which an old logging road ran. It ended in a bald, logged-out mountain face. . . .

It was icy on the shaded part of the trail, then she hit sun and the sliff-sliffing of her skis became muffled. The sky was huge and deep blue beyond the dazzling snows of the crest. There were delicate tickings: the music of the spring melt and of the movements of the small animals. A rabbit thumped far below on dry ground. A surprised squirrel scrambled in the boughs of a tree. Birds yakked at the sun.

Karla sweated and felt the cool air through her woolen trousers. Her nylon shell flapped like a flag. How grand were these sensations! The brilliant colours of sky and snow and forest, the cool air, the fecund scent of melt and spring. This was the adventure she lived for! Definition and colour and texture. The poison was washed clean by this. . . .

She thought of Sijjer with genuine pity for a moment, for the first time wondering how he had suffered the death of Bear. Her thoughts were clearer away from him.

She worked uphill for an hour, then stopped on a sunny rock to eat. Her heart boiled as gently as a kettle on an open fire. Rivulets of sweat tickled her skin. The sun was hot on her face. She felt her pores releasing the poison from her blood. In the sun and the air, she could find the faith she sought.

She fastened her skis and returned to the road. She noticed a series of big potholes in the snow to one side of the road and stopped and examined them. They were animal tracks, but she had no idea of the animal. The tracks seemed too big for any animal that she could imagine, but then the tracks were old, had melted to indistinction and frozen again. Further on, in the shade one print had not frozen. It was padded, had long claws. Lion? Bear? But they were asleep this time of year. Bears hibernated, at least. She was not certain of cougars. She mulled on this, trying to recall. Perhaps it had been awakened by a rockfall or an intruder. She recalled a name: Ursus horribilis. There were said to be grizzlies in the area, but she had never seen one. She considered turning back, in case she met the animal. But that was no way to act. It would feel like a retreat in the face of her own forest, her own heart. And Sijjer was there . . . She moved slowly along the road and listened to the forest. The birds shrilled, the streams bubbled under the snow, an owl hooted. The tracks ran parallel to the road, then she saw a huge, frozen turd. She stared at it, trying to imagine the beast that had made it. She could not. The tracks veered into the brush beyond that, among a trail of broken branches. Whatever it was, it had sought the warmth of the valley below.

Karla continued up the spine to the crest of the bald mountain. She puffed up the last steep incline and found herself in a snow field high over the lake. In one sweeping gaze she took in the five peaks around the lake, the length of the lake itself, and far beyond, the wind-blasted granite and ice of the Rockies.

This was a thing to live for, this essence. The bounty of the earth unfolded under this mountain. If Sijjer would open his eyes and see this essence, he would have faith.

Karla clomped around on her skis to begin the descent back down the spine. There before her, as if by a trick of light, stood a bear. It stood less than twenty paces away, huge, unreal to her. Karla rubbed her eyes. It was as though a ten-foot screen had dropped from the sky with the portrait of this creature upon it. It was a full-grown male. *Ursus horribilis*, his fur shaggy and grey. He was close enough that she saw clearly the long claws and where one of his ears was torn in half. She had never seen an animal so huge. He moved now, sat back on his haunches and sniffed at the air as though lost. His dim pig eyes sought her. Karla's nylon jacket snapped in the wind. All else was still.

Instinct told her to run, but fear froze her. She concentrated on calm. She listened and watched and began to thaw. She thought of unfastening her skis. Tears welled into her eyes as she bent over. She was aware of the bear moving towards her, but she forced herself not to look. She devoted her concentration to the task of unfastening her bindings, yet this was not simple. What should have taken seconds, stretched into minutes. Her fingers were not only numb, but weak. The bindings would not come unbound. By the time her feet were touched by the shadow of the slowly advancing bear, neither ski was off. She tried to straighten again but her knees went rubbery and she sat back with a thump onto the shafts of her skis. The skis, jolted forward, began to move down the gentle grade towards ursus. He was close enough to smell.

She breathed, heard each separate sound of the breaths coming out of her. Protesting, belaboured breath. Inside she screamed. Her eyes closed, and she ceased to watch and listen except to watch and listen to herself. So she did not see ursus step aside as she slid within inches of him in her curious seated arrangement, her poles dragging behind.

When her eyes opened, Karla was well down the sloping spine, moving smoothly along in the wheel depression of the road. Startled, she immediately lost her balance and toppled. She skidded to a stop. On the hill above she saw the grizzly ambling away, profiled against the violet sky. He stopped once to look behind him, and in that instant she saw, as clearly as she had seen the bounty of the earth, blue lightning which rose from him like smoke, just in the way it had from Conrad Grey. Then he vanished over the snowy crest.

FIFTEEN

I

February 10, 1985

Dear Mother,

'First your mind goes, then you die.'

Gurjit said that. He was always full of small wisdoms. Dear Mother, there is a lion's claw inside me. It was playful at first, tickling my guts, warning me. But it has lately turned hungry and is ripping, day and night, deep within my chest. Is this hallucination, or is it death?

My question is this: what is death, but the essence of the great changes?

Changes, despite me. Lately this house has come under the influence of the incessant changes. Outside it has grown brighter and the chilly grip has loosened. It is spring. The earth moving into the next phase of its great circle. Nothing stops for death. Not life, not the earth. Changes steamrolling on. Clear light and open skies have moved in as if to celebrate this celestial change. To the north the white shawls of the mountains have been withdrawn. The Lions are visible again, perched astride the earth and the sea like twin gods.

One god of change, one god of death.

II

February 16, 1985

Dear Mother,

Tomorrow I visit Uncle Piara. I have ignored Piara and Naseeb these years. It seems there has always been the aroma of masala frying and sound of rotis being clapped from hand to hand as Naseeb prepares a meal. She sends rotis ballooning up on the stove the way you used to do. She greets me with a shy hug. Somewhere she has hidden a fresh pot of yoghurt wrapped in a blanket and she always hums the same tune from a 1940s Hindi movie. When I arrive, Piara will be lazily stocking shelves or leaning over a National Enquirer *at the counter. They have always been old, as long as I can remember. They have always been kind and caring, expecting nothing in return. Unobtrusively, humbly, Piara and Naseeb have found the key to quiet joy.*

I have never appreciated this, really.

love, J.

"O Jassy," sighed Piara, wrapping his arms around Sijjer. "Jassy, Jassy," he said, "how come you never showed up in Toronto to fire up your Papa? We missed you, boy."

"I'm sorry, Uncle. I couldn't make it."

"Ah, well, you know I'm always glad in my heart to see you. You're like my son in a way. But even so . . . it makes problems."

"Problems?"

"Sure. You know, you went and did something kind of crazy

there, Jassy." Piara looked at Jassy then and a line of worry creased his face. "Maybe you don't even know what you did. See, when you let down your own flesh-and-blood family, people notice. There's after-effects. Everyone gets sore. I know how you were feeling and all. I know the story. But a lot of people, they don't really understand that – they don't see why you didn't go back there to fire up your dead father. You left Gurjit all alone with that big job. A lot of people don't see it. Your Auntie Naseeb for one. She just can't see it. She says she's through with you now – don't want to see you no more. And this kind of thing makes the whole family look real odd, you know. Our people, well, you should know how touchy we are about what folks in the community think."

Sijjer sniffed the aroma of spices wafting from the kitchen and his heart sank. The upsetting thought struck him that Naseeb might forever spurn him. Changes had crept up on him.

"I can't really explain why I didn't go. Maybe some day I'll be able to explain to her. I don't know."

"Sure, boy. Sure. I already been working on that. Trying to get her to understand. But she says you are so wrapped up in your own problems it's made you blind. She says selfishness is an evil. Come on. Let's walk."

Piara led the way out of the store and along the road that ascended the base of the mountain.

"See, Jassy, it's part of life. Some things you got to do, even if it don't feel right. That's what we mean by tradition, see. One important tradition is that, if your Pa dies, you got to go and wash him down so he burns clean. You and your brother supposed to dress in some nice clothes and shave him so he looks respectable. You handle that cold body and it makes the fact of death sink in. It's a ritual tradition. It's what holds people together when the going gets rough, see."

"I don't have any traditions. They vanished along with my mother. I have myself now, and as you say, my own problems. Nothing else."

"A parent never recovers from the loss of a child . . . " Piara said gently. "I know that. But you still got your wife. And you got a brother. You know I had to help Gurjit do all those rituals, but he missed you. In fact, he cried, you know. He cried because you didn't come. It's tough to see a big strong man like Gurjit go down crying that way."

"Gurjit cried?"

"Yessir, real water."

They walked under the shadow of the looming mountains. Above, the forests were dense, the life in them as vivid and tense as fire. Sijjer saw the forest's cool, dark corridors. He could not see the Lions, but they were close, towering somewhere above. Omniscient.

"You know, even though some of the things you done aren't really right and everything, you can still depend on me, Jassy. That is if you ever need to."

Sijjer looked at his uncle's shoes. They were cheap plasticky-looking things which Piara had tied once and left them tied so that the backs were busted down and flopped with each step.

"My wife left me."

"I see," said Piara, not properly impressed. "So what you going to do now?"

"I don't know. All I can think about is how I'd like to start all over again. Everything. My whole life, from the beginning . . . "

"That's not possible, boy. That's not life."

"I know," Sijjer sighed. "But maybe I should at least start my marriage over. Death hangs over Karla and I. It tortures us to be together. I think little Bear's spirit has never left our house. I need to move and change or I'll die. Maybe I'll get a divorce. Maybe even get an arranged marriage, like you and Naseeb.

Piara stopped walking and turned to him with irritation. "What are you saying? Is this some kind of joke? You just told me you gave up on our traditions. You know how it seems to me? It seems to me you cut yourself off. You never shared your grief with others, never ever went to the Gurdwara to pray for your lost boy. You never asked support of your own kin and blood. Not even your brother? So who do you expect would find you a wife? Who would help you with that? That's a community affair. But you don't get something for nothing. You got no community. You're independent. Who would arrange anything for you? And besides, you don't just give up on the person you've shared your life with. You don't just give up on your wife because of grief. Haven't you learned anything in your life, boy? Haven't you learned you got to take care of people? Sometimes they drift away and you got to go out and bring them back."

III

March 2, 1985

Dear Mother,

I dreamed last night that Karla was back. In the dream I woke up and went to the bathroom and she was there, perched on the throne as regally as a cat. She was smiling, happy, full of elven spark. She was the spritely, sweet elf I once knew. Then I awoke and for a while I was sure I was with her. I heard her voice distinctly and I saw her sitting at the end of the bed. . . .

She lamented about something she had done as a child, about how she had hurt her mother's feelings and didn't mean it, and all the time she looked at me with her eyes clear and bright. I sat up listening in my bed, not asleep, not dreaming. Then she was gone leaving behind an afterglow of dancing lights. They were like fireflies. I noticed that after that happened, the breathing I've endured each night, the breathing that comes from the walls, stopped.

love, Jassy.

Over the inlet the massif on which the Lions sat gleamed in the spring sun. Astride the earth and sea, the Lions were splendid and potent.

Sijjer went away from Piara's feeling as cold and thoughtless as a stone. He had been thinking of possibilities before, ways of escaping, which is how he came to mention an arranged marriage. But now he was a rudderless boat, towed along in a strange current.

He saw Conrad Grey as he walked through Gastown searching for a likely bar. Grey was panhandling for his supper money on a street corner. Embarrassed by this, Sijjer tried to slip by unnoticed, but Grey hailed him.

"Interruption of cashflow," Grey smiled gently and turned out his pockets. He showed not a trace of humiliation in this.

Sijjer took him to a grill in Gastown where his friend put away two steaks, a dish of fried squid and a hamburger, all washed down by half a dozen glasses of beer.

"Don't you ever get hungry?" Grey asked him.

"I can't remember the last time I was really hungry."

"No matter what happens to me, I always make sure I put away a good meal. When I've got the money . . . "

"I would have helped you out before if I'd known."

"I was okay before. Now is now. Tell the truth I need cash pretty bad."

Sijjer looked at him, then looked into his drink. He tossed back the double scotch and ordered another.

"When you drink like that," said Grey, "you ought to eat."

They moved from Leo's after some hours, down the street to the Lamplighter, where a rock band played and a man whom Grey identified as a junkie skipped rope on the dance floor amidst a crowd of dancers. The junkie had an old man's head attached to the body of a scrawny child.

Sijjer became drunk. His elbow leaned on the bar and his hand propped up his head. The elbow slipped on the surface so that his head jerked down every few minutes as he watched the incredible gyrations of the drug addict. He turned and attempted to explain to Grey what had happened to him that day, but the story bogged down in details. In a complicated sentence, he said that he had always been a loner and always would be, but Grey hardly listened. His attention was elsewhere and anyway nothing could be heard over the band. So Sijjer drifted into a reverie about the junkie, wondering about his world. Did he face solitude, and the stone- cold stillness of the heart? He imagined that even the junkie's world included moments of sensation, colour, and ecstasy. The thought occured to him that he was dead. That he had drowned along with his son. That he never had a spirit. Before him the junkie danced like a wizened child, dancing in one of a billion minute worlds. Each world was a possibility, a niche in which spirits flourished, slept, burrowed on until the end.

The bar was loud and full. Grey was talking to a woman with magnificent tresses which swung to her hips. He turned and looked at Sijjer.

"What?"

"You're in love," Sijjer croaked.

They left the Lamplighter, hit the Anchor and ended up at Number Five Orange. This last had strippers who entered the stage by sliding down a chrome post through a hole in the ceiling. They were young, pert girls, and they looked at the audience with eyes haughty. Sijjer imagined the dancers as little children, colt-legged and flower-faced, winsome and shy. They moved to the floor and proceeded to gyrate like serpents and spread their legs like women in the labour of love.

More drinks were ordered and drunk and with each Sijjer's heavy trenchcoat drew his head lower. He pulled out his wallet and paid over and over again. Grey moved around the bar talking to patrons and dancers, his face a blur in the crowd. Then a car materialized and they were out, blowing through the chill air of the night, someone driving like a teenager, revving the motor, thudding on brakes, gas and gears.

Sijjer passed out.

He awoke on a cold, dewy bench in the West End. It was not yet dawn, the sky the colour of dirty pewter. White mist hung over the grass and trees and it was very still.

Sijjer swung himself to a sitting position and saw that Grey sat a few feet away on the ground. He was awake, smoking a cigarrette and sipping from a new bottle of cognac.

"You alright?" Grey asked him.

The chill swept through Sijjer's bones, causing him to shudder violently.

"Try this," Grey offered.

The cognac steadied him out. He wrapped the trenchcoat tightly around his shoulders.

"Bad night," chuckled Grey. "Complete with weirdos. I've never seen such a bunch of . . . bah, weirdos. Who were those guys? I can't stomach perverts like that. I'd just as soon run them into the sea."

"What guys?"

"You were lucky. You passed out before it got too weird. Ha! How we ended up with them is something I can't figure out. Pissed-drunk! It's what happens when you get pissed! Every time I get pissed I end up with bugs and queers!" He laughed easily.

Grey looked well, as though he had gotten a comfortable sleep, had awoken in excellent humour and breakfasted. His eyes were rested and shiny. He told Sijjer he had not yet slept.

"I've been watching the morning come around. I love watching the night go slipping down under like that. I could watch it every time and I still would love it the same."

"That's the time when people die. The body has a rhythm and the body temperature – the metabolism – drops to a low just before dawn. Circadian. The daily death," said Sijjer as he got up.

"That makes sense to me. Die right along with the night. Not a bad time to go at all."

"Do you believe man has a spirit?"

"Don't you? How else you going to account for the fact we do stuff without using our brain?" Grey laughed.

The cognac warmed Sijjer but fractured the dawn into a nystagmus of separate visions. He sensed the earth reeling over towards the sun like a great sailing ship righting itself in a vast sea. Grey's face appeared in dark, then light, then dark, as clouds jerked across the sky. Stray rays of light lit distant mountain peaks, suddenly revealing the huge faces of the Lions.

"Look at that. They've got eyes," he said.

"For sure they got eyes. Ears too. You ought to see them up close. Scare the shit out of you."

"What do you mean?"

"You mean you never climbed up there? You can go right up there where you're looking. Right between the eyes if you want to. There's ice up there. And the air's nice and clean. No noise. I get sick of all this crap we have to breath in every day. I saw a guy dying in the street one day, his lungs all jammed up . . . "

"You smoke . . . "

"That's different. There's dirty smoke and clean smoke. You get sick from dirty smoke."

"Well, I don't know anything about climbing," said Sijjer.

"All the more reason you should do it, man. You see, it's just a matter of will. You just will yourself up. Will yourself not to fail. It's all a matter of will."

By the time the morning traffic commenced the cognac bottle was empty. Grey said he had to get out of the noise so they tramped eastward across the city, first following the waterfront, then the rail line, and finally the urine-stained sidewalks of East Hastings.

Exhausted, Sijjer lurched on legs of badly jointed steel, on feet of concrete. He clunked along the sidewalk, concrete on concrete. He followed Grey, drifting like a small boat pulled by the current. They were in places that Sijjer had never seen. Flophouses, cinemas featuring Chinese pornography, a butcher specializing in horsemeat. Again he had the sense of apocalyptic ruin. Decay and rot following the incessant change.

Then they were out of that and into a quiet pocket of residences, street signs with Chinese script, and finally a run-down house which had been last painted white but which was now dun and sepia and moss green. Tall weeds ruled the yard and two shells of cars perched on blocks on either side.

Sijjer followed Grey inside, watched him gulp raw wieners from the fridge, then moved into an empty room where he half-sat, half-lay on a mattress. The room was dark and quiet, and he fell into a soaring flight of a sleep, gliding down into a dream.

He swam in the wake of a rowboat in which a naked woman rowed. The waters were languid and murky, and when his body thrust forward and up through it, he glimpsed the interior of the boat. The woman's legs were open, her long throat and back were arched. He glimpsed the moistened, red petals of her vulva in the clot of hair. Her lean belly rippled. As he doubled his efforts to make the boat, it moved out of reach. Eventually he gave up and watched it recede in the distance. With this came a nagging sense of remorse. He had not tried hard enough. The boat had slipped away because he was inattentive. Desire had flagged.

In a mood of myopia Sijjer awoke for the second time that day. He was plagued by a persistent erection, and he was as drunk as when he had gone to sleep. For a long moment he studied his surroundings. The cracked, stained walls, cloudy window, the musty mattress were as alien to him as the bottom of the sea. Submerged he was in a foreign sea, his movements and thoughts hanging before him like underwater creatures. He was aroused, but his penis was no more a part of him than a shark or a killer whale. The sensation and awareness of his sex was independent and animal.

As it dawned on him where he was, his hand floated to his hip pocket. His wallet was gone.

This was disturbing. He had let himself be robbed. Where was Grey?

Sijjer brought himself slowly to his feet. Somewhere televisions blared out in voices of cartoon characters. He stepped into the cathode-tube twilight of a parlour and counted six televisions. In front of the televisions sat a hulking figure, with eyes glazed. Sijjer came close.

"Hello."

The figure did not budge.

"Do you know Grey?" Sijjer stood before the televisions.

"Don't scare him, for Christ sake," said Grey from the kitchen door. "He don't talk anyway."

In the kitchen Grey was as Sijjer had left him, eating at the broken wooden table. Now he had a large portion of chicken before him which he ripped into with dog teeth, and a quart of milk which he gulped from the carton. Another bottle, this one of vodka, adorned the table like a fresh flower.

"I got us some food." He tossed Sijjer's wallet onto the table. "I figured you'd be hungry and I didn't want to wake you up. You were snoring like a bear."

Sijjer resisted the urge to seize his wallet. He sat down at the table and gingerly took a piece of chicken in his fingers.

Where they sat they finished the bottle of vodka, mixing it with water, and then, towards the end of it, not mixing it. They went out, moving through the slick Eastside streets, through a vale of neon and headlights and street walkers. They returned to the bars at the lower end of Gastown and resumed the rounds of the previous day.

In each new bar Grey collected a drunken pal or two. In one place they were derisive of Sijjer, someone muttering "Paki" and someone else referring to him as "raghead." Sijjer could not react, but Grey put his elbow to the throat of a man in the corner, as casually as Sijjer would have shaken his hand. Then they went on, Grey giving a one-sentence low-down on the different characters they encountered. This one attempted suicide by fire, that one was recently out of the pen, another was a pimp.

Sijjer remained submerged in the strange sea bottom in which he had found himself upon waking. He swam in darkness, surrounded by silent depth. The city played in slow motion, lit by unearthly neon glare, glittering with rain. Dazed, vaguely titillated, he pulled forth his credit card when called upon, and drank. Stripjoints, prostitutes, rubbies, johns, police. A fight commenced; there was an accident. He stumbled over the stump of an amputee.

They two sat in an empty silent street. The crystal was broken on Sijjer's watch, the hands stuck at twenty past two. The watch had broken when the bars had been closed twenty minutes.

"So who lives here," asked Grey.

Sijjer looked up and saw Karla's apartment. From the window came the peculiar warm flickering that could only be fire. He led the way up.

Karla peered over the chain-latch then opened the door.

Sijjer stood at the door, waving his hand down the hall a little, and holding himself against the deep-sea current. He came into the fold of warmth and yellow light, suddenly chilled and then deathfully weary.

"God, you smell horrible."

He could see now that Karla had just awoken. She wore a robe and her hair fell about her face in strands. Her long eyes blinked slowly at him. It was late. The time had come for explanation.

"I lost the car . . . " he began, surprising himself.

"You what?"

"We started out . . . this is Grey . . . Connie Grey. We started out harmlessly enough in a restaurant . . . didn't we Connie?" This was said as a sort of joke, but nobody laughed. "I just wanted to tell you, you can come home now, it's been long enough . . . "

Grey looked pointedly at Sijjer, then disappeared into the bathroom.

"Who is that man, Jassy?"

"He's a friend. Friend of mine. Perfectly alright."

"It's not alright. This is not your home. What are you doing to yourself . . . going around with characters like . . . "

Sijjer caught a glimpse of Grey moving from the bathroom towards the kitchen fridge. Karla went on for a few minutes with a whispered lecture about lack of respect for her choices, but Sijjer was aware only of Grey, opening a carton of juice, throwing together a sandwich.

"I better go," said Grey. Sandwich in hand, he weaved his way by and was gone, his limp echoing in the stairwell.

"Who was that?" Karla asked herself quietly. She went away. Sijjer heard her running a bath for him, then she came back to him.

"I want to sleep. There's a blanket on the cot."

"Wait a minute. I want to explain something," he said. She waited but he could not say more. It was not because there was not more to say. About Grey, about Piara, about the pain in his chest, about having the will to climb perhaps, but he was arrested in this. He was not standing still for one thing. He meant to be standing still but there was movement. He drifted upward as though his buoyancy belt had come loose. But no, he was sideways, drifting, now downwards.

He lurched into her, his hands seeking the top of her robe just as they would seek the edge of any precipice, then he gained this edge and her breasts, ruby-tipped and tawny, sprang forth at him. Karla staggered backwards and fell, Sijjer on top of her trying to find the key to her warmth, searching for the lock and the door. He wrestled between her legs a moment, then became suddenly still.

"Get off," she said coldly.

He buoyed up slowly and was standing again, still moving as before, then sitting with a bang as the back of his legs hit a chair.

Karla in her nudity was smooth and flushed. She rose slowly, as though injured, then drew on her robe.

For a moment Sijjer saw the arched neck of the rower in the boat and glimpsed the sweet rose petal of love. It retreated from him, as in his dream.

SIXTEEN

I

When Grey first came to Sijjer's house, he was aware that he was an intruder on a very private tragedy. The evidence of the loss of the boy-child and the wife's absence were stained into the walls, incensing the empty rooms.

"You ought to let some light in here," he murmured, but restrained himself from reaching for the closed curtains. He had an aversion to closed curtains.

The second time he came to the house, he noticed that Sijjer, half-drunk, was himself an intruder in the funereal atmosphere, and Grey went through the place opening curtains and windows.

The third time he went uninvited, hoping to borrow some cash. Karla was there. He had not seen her since the night he and Sijjer had crashed in on her place. The atmosphere was tense, but the oppressive darkness was gone.

"I never can tell how long she'll stay," Sijjer confided. "She gets fed up and runs like a kitten in cold rain."

Karla came into the room and the men were quiet. She looked from Sijjer to Grey and back.

"You've invited a friend. You should have told me."

"I just dropped by," said Grey. "No one invited me."

When Grey spoke, Karla blushed and her eyes avoided him. Grey saw this and was embarassed.

"Connie noticed it seems brighter when you're back in our home," said Sijjer.

"Our house," said Karla. "House, not home."

The fourth time Grey went to the Sijjer's, he had no good reason to go. The truth, if he would admit it, was that he went to see Karla's blush and the way her eyes avoided his. The excuse was that he was repaying Sijjer his loan.

Karla was home alone. She invited Grey in, but he saw the blush beneath her golden bangs. She reminded him of someone from his past.

"Are you hungry," she asked. "You always look hungry."

"I almost always am."

"I made soup."

They ate together, her eyes avoiding him and not wanting to, the way a self-conscious child might do, eyes glued to soup bowl. They did not speak until the soup was finished, then Grey heard himself say something, almost not recognising what he had said. It came out involuntarily, pure and strange.

"You're beautiful."

Karla swallowed and began to speak. She looked at him, then stood suddenly and said, "You had better leave now. You can't stay here."

II

So Grey knew she was in love with him. He wanted that and did not want it too. Sijjer, he considered a friend, but not a friend on equal footing. Sijjer was a friend who needed help, not competition.

But Karla was in his thoughts, and later, his dreams. She was wounded, like her husband, yet in her it was fascinating, magnetic.

He made himself not return to their house for a long time. Grey stuck to his quarter, Gastown, feeling a power flowing within. He had little money, but confidence surged, so he spent.

One spring evening he watched a derelict ship, a rubbie, fight a current of people on his course up the sidewalk. Someone elbowed the rubbie aside and he flopped against a wall bonelessly, spun as in a gale and fought a grand battle to regain his course. Grey thought of William.

"Hell," he said aloud. "That is a living hell." He went and gave the old man a cigarette.

It amazed him that after the years of nursing a hatred for William, the hatred had turned, transformed he knew not how, into pity.

Grey smoked his cigarette down and tossed it twinkling into the darkening street. The spring night was descending with the strains of music and the scents of flowers and perfume. Lovers arm-in-arm, brushed by him. He walked feeling a power light and fleet, a prairie grass fire burning in him. He thought of Karla's blush and knew this power came from her, yet he felt impotent keeping himself from her. He hunkered down the street, heavy on one leg, light on his bad one, feeling a nucleus of pain in his thigh, feeling the glowing promise of fertility and warmth in the air. He was blessed with the the power, light and fleet, of love.

On the next corner Grey stopped walking for he saw the old medicine woman from the railyard. She looked out of place, cross-legged in the doorway of a shop, her terrier guarding the flame which flickered weakly by her side. She chanted from within the folds of her blanket. Passers-by had gathered, curious. She shook herself out of her trance, threw back her blanket and looked straight at Grey. She hailed him. But Grey did not know her language. He went quickly on his way, down the streets to the bars.

In the Lamplighter he drank so that the power subsided to a heartbeat. He picked up a scent in the air and spotted the girl engaged in the arms of a man in an expensive suit. A band was playing on stage, playing "Darkness, Darkness" so loudly that Grey could not hear his own voice ordering himself beer. The girl, whose name was Francie, freed herself and came to him when she noticed him talking to a waitress.

"I thought you were meeting me at seven," she said to Grey.

"Here we are."

"You." She put her arms around his neck and caught hold of his cascade of black hair. "I don't know why the hell I fall for beautiful men. They always keep you hanging."

"Who was that?" Grey nodded in the direction of the expensive suit.

"Just some jerk. Let's get outta here."

She led the way out of the Lamplighter. Her walk, her high breasts, her shining legs drew stares. They strolled through the evening full of the peculiar scent of fresh oranges.

"You a Pisces by any chance?"

"Yeah," said Grey. He had no idea what he was.

"I thought so. I can always tell a Pisces right off. Cool and smart. You got mysteries there in your eyes, man, right where everyone can see them. I'm a sucker for a mystery man. You know what sign I am?"

"Uh . . . the sheep?"

"Sheep? . . . oh Aries. Nope. Aquarius. Connie, tell me one of them mysteries you carry around with you. Tell me something good."

Grey laughed. They were in a steamy-windowed wonton kitchen on Main Street. He ordered curried beef and wonton soup, steamed rice and fish broth. He took his time, feeling his power.

"Okay, I want some peace. Somewhere beautiful to live. Steady loving from a good woman . . . kind of boring, huh? Just the basic things any guy's after."

"That's nice. I like it. I'm the same really. Know what my dream is? A place of my own on the beach with the sound of the surf down below and a good stereo playing the Stones. Big waterfront windows over the ocean so I can watch the ships going by and storms coming in. A job in a nice clean strip joint, main act, a fridge full of Perrier and maybe a nice little convertible Ferrari. Oh yeah, and a solid man, just like you want a solid lady."

"Sounds like a lot."

"Yeah? Well, my girlfriend Lorna, she got all of it, all except the place on the beach. You watch me. I'll be there sooner or later."

She was not very bright, Grey decided. She wore too much makeup and she ate too fast. They had seen each other in the bars over the weeks and he knew nothing about her really.

He went along with her to a party in a penthouse overlooking the bay. From the balcony Grey saw the ocean he had once envisioned. There was neither fog nor scum from here. The water was a black mirror that reflected the lights of the city close to shore. Further out in the harbour it was a black void broken by the constellations of ships' lights. This was the ocean he had dreamed of.

Grey took a beer and found a corner from which he could see the bay and ships. But he was not at peace. He was stirred by the pureness of the power, but it was as out of place here as the medicine woman on Water Street. A woman nearby gaped openly at his crotch. She wore tight, glossy clothing. Grey gradually became aware of a corrupted lust on display in the place, an exploited and tired desire. It was well known, this lust, too well known. It was a tired old play and everyone at the party had a role. Francie returned with a woman whose shirt Grey could see through. A cross hung delicately between her breasts.

"This is him," said Francie by way of introduction.

"Wow," said the woman, "You must be six-foot-four."

"Six-two."

"You better watch yourself, Sweetheart. They will eat you alive."

Grey wanted to leave. The power, light and fleet, was cowed by the frank and tired lust. A couple who had been necking as they danced, began undressing each other. The man exposed the woman's breasts and fondled her nipples. She groped in his pants. Then a second woman joined in and pulled the rest of their clothes off. A small crowd hunched over a round glass table snorting lines of cocaine. Francie had disappeared.

Grey moved slowly through the crush towards the door where he was confronted by a small man with heavily pomaded black hair and a complete outfit of black, shiny leather. He was youthfully slender yet stiff too, as though his body were made of light, breakable balsam. The man blocked Grey's way, eyeing him intently. Just then Francie appeared.

"This is John Pound, Connie. He's the host."

"And she is a cocktease," said Pound.

"Shut up, Johnny. What are you saying?"

Grey would have flattened him then, but Francie moved between them.

"It's my party," Pound shrugged."You say what you want at your parties, remember? Anyway, nobody thought it was rude. Why don't you have a drink, Brother?" Grey shrugged, turned around and went to the kitchen where he took a twenty-sixer of gin which he found on the table. He removed his jacket, tied one sleeve and slid the bottle into it. Then he got himself a beer. Pound was waiting at the kitchen door.

"You care to try some coke?"

Grey shook his head.

"Uppers, downers, grass?"

Grey stared at Pound. "I'm fine like I am."

"You bet you are." Pound looked him over again in a way that made Grey decide he was queer. He thought he should have hit him while he had the excuse.

"What's with you?" Grey asked him.

"Hey, I know people in every kind of situation, Brother. Every kind." Pound smiled broadly. He smelled richly of talcum, aftershave or deodorant, perfumed from head to groin in it. "You remind me of someone I used to know, that's all. See, Brother, nothing to it." Pound laughed. "Nothing with me. Nothing at all. Hey, I want to show you something. Come on . . . I won't eat you."

He led the way down the hall. It was a big double penthouse and all the rooms but one had glass doors onto a terrace. Pound went into the windowless room and switched on the lights to reveal a gallery of photographs. The photographs were of Native Indian men, some of the subjects old, most young. Some of the younger ones were nude under studio lights.

"Sort of a collection," said Pound.

Grey knew the men in the photos. They were trappers, men of the woods, fishermen and vagrants, drunks and criminals, artists with beautiful vests, one in a suit who looked like a lawyer or politician, one in ceremonial garb and mask. And they were hunters. In their eyes, in their tense stances, they watched and stalked.

But again, the hunters were hunted. Hunted by this little wooden man. Grey had seen this in a movie. In the movie an Englishman had the heads of animals mounted in macabre testimony to mastery and dominance.

"You recognise these fellows?" Pound laughed. "No, seriously, I'd love to shoot your portrait. I pay fifty bucks for it. We can do it right now."

"Why?"

"Why not?"

Grey felt a dangerous blade of rage moving within him. The power of was transforming into something deadly. Under his fist the balsam wood would splinter into a thousand pieces.

"Nah, what the hell," he sighed and kept his hands in his pockets. He walked out of the gallery feeling sick.

He stayed at the party for a while longer, fighting it now, not knowing how to fight it, knowing he had to. He hated this place. He went into one of the bedrooms where he had spotted a compact tape recorder, slipped this into the empty sleeve of his jacket and left alone.

He followed the alleys and sidestreets, walking, thinking, summoning the power, light and fleet. But now he felt only the corrupted desire to possess instead, and he was alone.

In one of the maze of alleys of Chinatown he came across Willy, Dupray's brother, his head popping in a trash bin. Willy was bone-thin and smelled like he was rotting. His face and hands were black with dirt, his hair matted and rank. He froze when he saw Grey.

Another kind of hell, thought Grey. Poor Willy, demented beyond hope, was lost. He tried to coax Willy to come out of the garbage and home, but he ran away panic-stricken.

III

Willy was lost, resorting to his old habit of eating out of garbage bins because Dupray had stopped feeding him at home. Dupray had stopped feeding Willy the day he had come home with a case of whisky and gone to his room.

Dupray was down to the last bottle of the case. This was significant because he had told himself that when the whisky was gone he would pull himself together. He screwed the cap on the half-empty bottle, stuffed it under the mattress and stood unsteadily. The room smelled bad. There was nothing in it but the steel bed, the mattress, whisky bottles and Dupray himself. From outside the closed door came the multitude of voices from the televisions.

Dupray opened the door and glared at Willy's slumped figure silhouetted in the light from the screens. He emerged from the staleness of the room and stood near Willy for a minute watching him. Willy stank, the world stank. Willy did not move, stupefied by the televisions. Dupray quietly kicked one of the televisions over onto its back where it continued broadcasting a commercial about catfood. Then he kicked it again, hard, so that the picture died to a spark.

With the moral support of the last bottle of whisky on the seat beside him, Dupray went downtown to face his world. If he had not gone out, he might have beat on Willy and, even low-down and drunken, he consciously avoided that. Willy was his blood-brother after all; Dupray had nicked their thumbs and pressed them together. It was a blood pledge.

It was a soft spring evening filled with a scent which Dupray identified as rotting fish. He drove his old Valiant down Hastings Street, sniffing the air and squinting at the lights. Then, as if out of the air, there materialized unmistakable blonde plaits of hair swinging along Water Street. She was swallowed a minute later by the cavernous opening of the Lamplighter, which happened to be Dupray's destination. Now he parked, considered his options for a few seconds, said "Fuck it," loudly and was about to go ahead into the bar despite her when she emerged again. She was with Grey and he had his arm around her. As Dupray watched them, she reached up and bit Grey on the neck.

"Son of a bitch," said Dupray. He was numb. He pulled the car out and glided slowly back home.

"Son of a bitch," he said as he lay down the last hand of whisky. "A guy's down and every son of a bitch comes along and boots his arse. You take people in and they turn around and kick you in the pills . . . " He lay talking like that and sipping from the bottle. Then he stood and walked around, talking, saying, "What's a guy supposed to do?" and so forth. Willy, with animal instinct, slipped out the back door into the alley in search of food, and so avoided a confrontation with Dupray who began to wander, talking, throughout the house. Dupray went to Grey's room, kicked through his meagre possessions and wandered back through the parlour where the dead television lay, and then downstairs among the clocks and back up again, bottle dangling from his hand.

Dupray heard a sound and moved into the parlour. He reeled around twice and flipped open his buckknife. He flicked at the air, shadow-duelling, reliving a recent fight, dancing the steps with his opponent, then recalling the white face of fear, the shaking of the hand when Dupray kicked him against the wall and carefully pressed his blade home. He danced, feeling the light tremble of the knife as it went into the living flesh. The white face had transformed into the face of a child done wrong, embarassed at the letting of his blood.

Dupray had fought often with his knife and won. There was a thing in his eyes and in his build that challenged men. He was big and brash and now he was mad with rage.

So he danced, shadow-duelling, stabbing at shadows, waiting for Grey.

She was not Dupray's usual thing, the blond plaits. She was a hooker, or so he assumed, which was not unusual, but she had gotten his number somehow, which was unusual.

Dupray danced and stabbed, remembering and raging.

She had been cold, then saucy as he pursued her. She had

told him he was disgusting. "What do I need? A million bucks?" he had cajoled. But this teasing was not good, for she had the upper hand. She sat near him at the Columbia and mocked him in front of the men who respected him. Mocked him in front of the street that he ruled! Some of the men snickered. She switched her head back and forth the way an angry cat switches its tail, and she looked at everyone with hot eyes. Everyone but him, of course. How she mocked him! "Go on, Ray, give her your million. What you waiting for?" someone put in. They laughed outright. He kept thinking how he would keep his head, but he did not do that, thinking "Smart bitch, smart-assed little bitch." He made a fool of himself, but he could not stop after a point. . . .

Dupray danced, sweating, saw her long neck as it curved up and exposed itself to Grey.

She had come around to him after weeks, months. She started to see that he ruled the bars, that he had respect. After he showed off another pretty thing he knew, then she came around entirely. Could not help but come around then. So then he relaxed, made her laugh, even though all the while she made his breath catch in his chest as though he were a teenage boy on a first date.

Dupray shuffled and swigged from the last hand of the last bottle. He shuffled but it was really a dance of the knife and he knew all the steps. He raged at her and at Grey.

He raged remembering the scent of woman sex, the way it was spread around in that flat of hers with big rooms empty but for a bed and a telephone. She was evicted from that flat, for hooking. Evicted and came in out of the pouring rain that night and Dupray was in the Lamplighter alone, and she alone coming in with her hair like sopping silk cloth plastered down her back, her trunk and a suitcase with her. "What the hell happened?" "Forget it," she spat, but no he could not forget it seeing her eyes were red and swollen. He bought her a brandy and she let him, and when he told her to move in with him for a while until she got back on her feet, she said yes.

Now there was the flicker of a shadow and he balanced the knife on his palm; now he crouched and now he sprang. In the shadow-duel the glint of the blade flashed like a single bared tooth.

He should have known it would not work. He remembered now that he did know. His house was no place for a woman! He knew she would hate the newspaper curtains, the gigantic bag of garbage in the kitchen, floors which had never ever been washed. The six televisions in the parlour and Willy stuck to them . . . Willy! He had known what she would think of Willy! But he was drunk, drugged on her and so ignored what he knew. He put her in a hotel overnight and spent the next ten hours flying like a mad bird through the house trying to reverse the effects of years of using the place as a warren, not a house. He fashioned curtains from bedsheets, bought a rug to cover the blackened floor, washed walls, painted and patched, bought pots, pans and dishes, moved out a mountain of garbage, even tried to change Willy. Like a crazed bird he was, stoned, out of his mind on her. Expended every cent and every ounce of energy he had, picked her up and brought her back, hauling her massive trunk and suit- cases into the house. And so she had come in, cast a gaze around the room, taking in Willy and the televisions. And she simply froze in the doorway, saying, 'oh God, is this where you live,' then stepping backwards out of the door, turning, running away down the sidewalk, probably running all the way back to town.

Dupray stopped his dance. He did not see her for a month. Then he saw her one night at the Lamplighter, as smart and cute as ever, her haughty head switching back and forth like a cat's tail. She was with a man and they looked over at Dupray and laughed.

Now he knew. He had seen Grey with her.

Dupray flicked his knife in the darkness of the room. "She don't like him . . . where'd he get money to go fucking around. I gave him that money, didn't I . . . " Dupray sliced the air with his knife. Then abruptly he re-holstered the weapon and went to his room, dug through a pile of clothes and found his jacket. It was balled up and in the dark he could not make out the sleeves. He got one arm in one sleeve but the other caught and he cursed and stamped angrily, then became still as the front door opened. Grey's tall form was in the doorway silhouetted, then the lights went on.

Grey laughed. "You're a mean sight," Grey said.

"Piss-arse. Don't laugh at me, Piss-arse."

Grey shrugged. "Where's the whisky?" He went into the bathroom and closed the door behind him.

"Piss-arse!" Dupray shouted. He fought some more with the jacket, finally disengaging it and throwing it onto the floor. "Where you been, Piss-arse?"

"Out." Grey chuckled from the bathroom.

Dupray hung about outside the door, mumbling threats and clenching and opening his big hands. "I told you not to laugh." He crashed against the bathroom door with his full weight but the door was not latched. It banged aside easily. Grey glanced at him and zipped up his pants. He leaned against the wall.

"Something wrong?"

"Yeah, there's plenty fucking wrong. Tell me, Piss-arse, who got you work and put you up and fed you when you were down? Hey? Who showed you the ropes? Damn pretty-boy-piss-arse . . . "

Grey looked blank.

"What'd I ever ask you to do in return, hey, pretty-boy?"

Grey shook his head. "Look, I'll leave. Only you never told me I was bugging you, man."

"Buggin' me? You see this?" Dupray flipped out the knife and flashed the blade open in one move. "You know I could cut you so damn bad right now . . ."

"So what?"

"Yer a damn Pretty-boy-piss-arse."

Grey went to the sink and threw cold water on his face. If Dupray had not drunk the last hand he would have seen Grey's body, how every fibre of every muscle was waiting for a movement from Dupray's knife. But Dupray had finished the whisky and he still saw the blonde plaits.

"Tell me, Piss-arse. What makes you so special? That face of yours? That pretty-boy face? Tell me what a pretty-boy like you does to be able to tail around town like he owned it." Dupray waved the dull steel in front of him like a conductor with a baton. "A guy goes along through his life expecting things to get better as it goes. You always expect change comin' around the corner. A streak of luck maybe, or a girl. Then a guy gets through that part and sees all that hope was kids' stuff. You start gettin' on into your thirties and you look around. Most men that age, their luck came around already. They got somethin' by then. A car. Wife and kids. A house. But what do I got here? A couple of losers sharin' a busted down slum. And what do you got? You got your pretty face, don't you? Everytime I try and GET somethin' . . . goddamn. Always some son of a bitch standin' in my way. Tried to get an education, you know that? I tried and tried and I couldn't make it. There was always some smart little fucker would make me look bad, some cute little bastard was always up there where I wanted to be . . . I tried harder than anybody — all I wanted was a fair shot. But I wasn't smart and I know I ain't pretty. Jesus, I used to kick the shit out of those smart kids though . . . "

"Put the shank away before you cut yourself, Ray." Grey took a towel down and rubbed his neck.

"I never saw the justice in it. Some guys. they're born with rich folks. Some guys got brains and some got looks . . . but you look at that poor bastard Willy. What's he got? No brains, can't even talk. What's he supposed to do? No folks except me. A face like a pig. All he's good for is fiddling with his withered little dick and hopin' for the best. All them blessed sons of God out there scramble around for money and jobs and women while poor Willy eats garbage. What's that? Don't he deserve somethin' better? Ain't he a man? And you know what? Them cocksuckers take every scrap of everything they can get their greedy hands on. The hell with guys like Willy, they say. There's only a certain amount to go around, right, and the thing is, if you let 'em, they'll take it all . . . " Dupray trailed this off as he brought his drunken focus back on Grey. He flicked the knife in the air, slashing at shadows. He began his sinuous dance once more.

"You going to stick that in me or what? I'm getting hungry," said Grey.

The knife wavered back and forth. "I could do it, you know that. You kinda remind me of them kids I used to beat on in school." The knife came up to eye level and Grey looked down the long, thin line of it.

"Okay, cut me then."

Dupray's knife moved. Grey reached around behind his back and tore away the doweling from the towel rack. He cracked it down on Dupray's wrist and the knife clattered to the floor.

Dupray backed out of the bathroom and slumped on a chair. "You hurt my arm, asshole. I think it's busted." He held up his wrist and stared at it dully.

Grey came out and leaned the doweling against the wall. "What are you waving a knife at me for anyway? I thought we were friends. I don't know what's eating you."

Dupray rubbed his arm and let Grey see the bruise. "It's that chick you're with. She drives me crazy. You can have her. I'm finished with her."

"Aw, Ray," said Grey. "You mean that blonde. She's not worth this. She's nothing to me. Nothing." He shrugged and went to the fridge and opened it. "It looks like a mouse went through here."

Then the doweling came down on Grey's head the first time, felling him. When it hit him again, he blacked out, which was just as well because then Dupray kept hitting him, breaking his face.

When Grey came to, one side of his face was hot and numb and one eye was closed. His vision was hazed and his lungs seared with each breath. Hacking, he pushed himself up on one elbow and saw that the haze was smoke and under the smoke there were flames. A crate in the parlour, the new rug, the bedsheet curtains, and, as he watched, the walls themselves, became flames. Grey crawled to the back door, stood and banged it open. He felt blood running on his neck and face. Firetrucks wailed up the street, red and sparkling like toys. Then a police car, then two, sailed in like hawks.

When Grey saw the police, he ran in the opposite direction until he stumbled and fell into a bush. There he lay watching the fire burn until daylight.

IV

The fifth time Grey went to Sijjer's house, he did not think of his reasons for going. He stood in the doorway fingering a fragment of tooth in his mouth, down-looking, bleeding, waiting for Karla's shocked paralysis to pass. When it did, she silently led him by the arm into the house and lay him down on a sofa.

"You poor man, you poor, poor man. Who did this to you?"

Grey shook his head. He wanted to sleep. He sat very still as Karla brought water and towels and gently bathed his face. As sleep overcame him he heard Sijjer's voice in the distance and felt love's power, fast and fleet as fire, burning in his chest.

SEVENTEEN

The Hunter

I

Dear Mother,

What becomes of the dead? Do they simply cease to exist? If so, then how can the non-existent cause pain? How can the non-extistent perpetrate calamity after calamity among the extant? I think about my son constantly. In my heart I believe he exists somewhere still.

In the confusion of our failing marriage another factor has intruded. My friend Conrad Grey has taken refuge in my house. He is a harsh reality of unknown proportions. Beaten within an inch of his life, an excellent candidate for aggressive plastic surgery, he lies like a spectre of violence, of ruin, and he stalks us. Since he arrived, Karla has remained at home nursing his wounds. She will not look him in the eye, so drawn is she. The hum of this attraction is as loud as a set of wet high power lines. To say I am jealous would be an over-simplification. I am transfixed and murderous at the same time. He never speaks to her for she simply responds to him and there is little need for words. I am a side issue, the unwitting cuckold.

In a way it's beautiful though, the way my poor Karla has warmed like a plant awakening after an icy winter. You see, it is I who am her winter.

J.

II

"You need a doctor, you know. Nothing will come right this way. The bones are broken."

She removes the bandages from his nose and jaw and gently cleans the wounds. He catches her hands and puts them aside.

"I can doctor myself," he says. He puts his hands to his nose and with abrupt pressures moulds himself, straightening a flattened nose, attempting fruitlessly to push together a cracked jaw.

III

Grey awoke in the dark, and for an instant smelled smoke and heard fire crackling around him. Then he lay back remembering what had happened. He delicately explored his face with his hands, then his hands went to his pockets and came up with a broken cigarette which he placed between his lips and lit. "Shit," he murmured, "can't taste the tobacco." He smoked it and lay with his eyes open, thinking.

Broken and vulnerable as he was, he felt good and strong. The power had resurged, light, kinetic, like a lightning ball in summer. Yet it was confused by the urge to possess Karla under Sijjer's roof. And he thought of what had happened in Dupray's house, thinking that he had expected something like this but had not known the shape in which it would come. He had gotten out alive, and in that lay his luck. It could have ended in the burning house. It would have been that easy.

He had expected it because it was a logical consequence of what had happened up north, even though, now as he lay broken and truthful, he saw that he had put off thinking of the mine. He had put it off the way a man might avoid an enemy until he is forced into confrontation. He was forced to look at it now. In the still of the night it lay bared. So he thought of Radki and as he did so his leg began to tingle. The old pain which had been asleep all these months that he had avoided his enemy, now grew.

He cast around in the darkness for Sijjer's bottle of whisky. He hobbled to his feet and poked around on a table, then a shelf, then he tried a cupboard. He knocked a vase over and it fell to the floor with a hollow crash. A moment later the lights came on and Sijjer appeared.

"What's happening?"

"I needed a shot. Couldn't find the fuckin' lights."

Sijjer went to his room and retrieved the bottle.

"Old injury in my leg. It acts up once in a while." Grey took his drink and sat heavily. "What time is it?"

"Five-thirty."

"You always up this early?" Grey asked. Sijjer was fully dressed.

"I don't sleep very well."

"That's no good. You need sleep. Looks dangerous the way you are. You don't sleep, you die. I learned that a long time ago. Still learning it. You can't forget the basics. Did you ever think of that?"

"What basics?"

"Survival. Basics of survival. Animal basics. Plant basics. The things you need to keep you from getting iced by some idiot with a buckknife. Example: protecting what's yours."

Sijjer poured himself out a glass of whisky and sat. "Go on."

"That's all. When a man don't protect his ground, it's because he's forgotten the basics. It's because he's lost his spirit."

"You're mocking me, Grey."

"Mocking? I don't mock."

"You think I've lost my spirit? I come from a rich culture, you know that? Thousands of years old."

"You know it's funny about the white man. He thinks that man has a spirit and animals don't have any spirit. But the red man thinks just the opposite. He thinks that animals have the most important spirits of all and man has to commune with them. And the funniest part of all is people live in white society for a while and they lose any spirit they had to begin with. "

"What are you saying?"

"Nothing. I just noticed that that's what happens that's all."

"You're saying I'm a white man from living in their society all my life. That's pretty self-righteous of you, considering."

"Yeah, yeah."

Sijjer glared at Grey, then threw back his drink and poured another.

Grey held out his hand for a refill, oblivious or at least uninterested in Sijjer's glare.

"Everyone takes up a certain space," Grey said. "You go around in this space and that's yours. That's your most basic ground. You never think about it until somebody comes along and hangs their ass into it, then you have to do something about it. Men do it. Dogs do it. You don't sleep, you get stuff in your blood. Your view of things goes to pieces. Nope, if you don't have your strength, you don't have your spirit, you're not much good."

"Is that what happened to you? You've never bothered explaining how you got smashed up."

"Let my guard down. Didn't read the situation. Maybe . . . maybe my spirit's shot. Jesus, I can't even taste the whisky. Tell me, you want me to leave your house?"

Sijjer did not answer. He surveyed the wreckage of Grey's face. Along one jawline was a gaping laceration that oozed plasma. The high crown of the nose was smashed flat so that Grey's breath whistled through it. Both eyes were closed to slits. The lips were a pulp, the front teeth a line of irregular stubs. It seemed to Sijjer that Grey had worn a mask, and the mask had been ripped crudely away. Without the mask there was no longer an appearance of humanity. Only flesh and blood. This was a revelation about the human condition, like seeing a corpse for the first time.

Grey smiled into space, the slash on his jaw oozing. They did not speak for some time. Finally Grey said, "You want to hear what happened. I'll tell you. I got six steel pins in my leg. Can't walk as good as I used to. They said I was lucky to have this leg at all. You got anymore of this whisky or you going back to bed?"

Sijjer took out another bottle.

"I worked in a mine up north. Nickel mine. Underground, a mile or so down in the Canadian Shield. Down there everyone works in pairs. You and your partner are supposed to watch out for each other. But, I never had a partner. Not for a long time."

"Seems like a while since I rode down in the Cage, down to fifty-four hundred level. I did that for almost nine years all in all. The Cage is this big room that drops like a stone into the hole. You see this blur of rock going by. You suit up each day in your oilers and boots and all, then drop like a stone into the ground. You would think the cable was cut and the Cage was just falling free. But it would bounce to a stop, then you'd be in it: the smell of cement and gunpowder, working all day in the dark – you get used to it. You get used to the wet and the rumble of blasting in the levels above. At the end of the shift you get the steam in the shower rooms – huge shower rooms pouring down hot water. That's your reward. I remember every light and smell. You get your battery and lamp, get your orders from the foreman, and you slog through the dark, through puddles and mud. Sometimes drill, sometimes build dams of wood or walkways. But one thing was, Connie Grey always worked on his own without a partner.

"They always said I was 'odd man out,' you know, but it was because I was the only Indian on the crew. Hell, I never minded it much. I didn't care. I got used to working alone. I never had to train some greenhorn and go through all that. The bosses never came around and bothered me. I'd work how I wanted to work, take my time, take a break when I wanted it. I'd sit back and have a smoke and it was quiet. If I sat in the dark and quiet long enough, I used to hear a growling noise that came from the walls of the stope. When I first heard it, I knew the rock was alive. Like an animal it was. I thought differently about the rock after that. If I listened hard, I heard the earth breathing, slow and steady.

"The other men, they were probably relieved that I worked alone and never complained. They gave me the choice of tools

– drill bits and stuff like that. Had my pick of the drills. They always gave me my space and my peace, as long as I was out of the way, down some hole where they couldn't see me.

"But then Bernard came along and that all changed. The foreman came up to me one day in the minehead and says, 'Hey, I got you a partner, Grey.' He was kind of sheepish when he said it, staring at his boots and the like. The foreman was a jerk. He used to boast how he was Dief's bodyguard back in '59. No one believed him. Anyway, I get in the Cage that day and there's Bernard. Bright yellow, spotless oilers, shiny helmet, new black boots and his ear protectors and safety glasses on before we even left the surface. God, the men laughed at him. He was so strange looking. He was kind of small and he had this wrinkled up face like a Chinaman. He was Desoto Indian. Pure. That first day I reached over and pulled off his earmuffs. 'Later,' I said to him and he just nodded like a moron.

"He never said anything – not a word – for the longest time. I guess he knew I was pissed off at having my lonely routine broken up. He was dead silent the whole time we were together. Each morning he'd get in the Cage with his boots and oilers and helmet cleaned and shined. Down there, underground, it's like a big mud pond in most places. You get so dirty that even after a day anyone would be completely black with oil and grit. Nobody thought of cleaning their gear except Bernard. The men started calling him 'Mr. Clean' and they made as if he was a fairy. He was one of those natural targets if you know what I mean. It never takes people long to zero in on targets in people like Bernard.

"So we worked on together, him and me, without his saying a word. He followed along what I showed him to do and he was a good worker. We got acquainted through the work, without talking. Went on like that for weeks. Then one day we were hiking some pipe through this stope full of water and Bernard stepped into this place and sank in this hole. Right up to his chest in ooze. When he got himself out he was a mess, and shook himself like a cat that's walked in a snowdrift. 'One ting I hate is de dirt,' he says to me. The way he talked, his accent and all, got me laughing, and Bernard started laughing and after that we were friends.

"Maybe I'd been saving up, or maybe it was because he was different. Or maybe it was just that we were alone all day in the dark. Whatever it was, it got me talking to Bernard things I never had any need to talk about. He listened. He had this sense of humour and laughed at all kinds of stuff I never knew was funny. We got on well, Bernard and me. We got so that we worked together as smoothly as a couple of dancers. After a while I noticed things about him. Weird little things. He was strong as an ox. Stronger than anyone I'd ever met. Way stronger than me. He could lift a bundle of steel bits on one shoulder with hardly a grunt. Those bits must have weighed, I don't know, two or three hundred pounds. No one carried the bits around in bundles the way he did. He could work an eight-foot scaling bar with one hand which wasn't normal. He wasn't showing off, it was just natural. I looked him over in the showers, tried to see where all that power was and I could never figure it. He was so small, small shoulders and a body plain, with no muscles to look at. His strength was inside somewhere – it had to have been inside. They talk of guts of steel a few times. Gut strength. Maybe that's what he had.

"One day we were taking apart a catwalk up over a pile of blasted ore. There was a pipeline full of sandfill on the catwalk. Engineers' mistake, they said. It was a tricky job, walking along a two foot plank, forty feet over a pile of rock splinters. We had to take apart the pipe, carry it down the catwalk, then pull the catwalk apart behind us, unhooking the hang-bars from the ceiling of the dome. My nerves were bad that day – too much drinking, too little sleep. Most dangerous time, just as I was telling you. I remember I looked down from the catwalk and saw the pit of the stope, a black pit with its rock walls gleaming like a thousand eyes were looking out at you. It was living rock. Sweating, panting rock. I saw it move, always out of the corner of my eye I'd see it . . . and that time I swear the rock moved. I thought: man, if you fall, it will be like falling into the teeth of a hungry wolf. I remember I thought that.

"Next thing I know, me and Bernard are on either end of a pipe full of cement and sand, and I'm staggering with it, forty feet over the teeth of this wolf, and I trip. I don't know how exactly. Maybe I slipped. Went right over the edge of the catwalk, missed the safety ropes clean. But I hung on to that pipe, swung out over the pit, thinking I would fall any second and wondering why in hell me and the pipe weren't going anywhere. Then the pipe started sliding back up onto the catwalk with me on the end dangling. I looked up and there was Bernard, got the pipe by his fingertips and hauling it back on top. Still don't see how he did it. It doesn't make much sense. When my lamp flashed over his face, I could see he wore his calm, Chinaman expression and he wasn't sweating a drop. He saved my life."

Sijjer poured out more whisky and Grey tossed his back to kill the pain in his leg.

"Old Bernard," Grey said, "I started thinking he was magical and I would be safe as long as he was my partner. Men get maimed or killed all the time in the stopes. But I felt safe.

"He was born in one of those nowhere reservations in the middle of the scrub. Down some dirt road at the end of a highway. It was called Fish Lake or Fish Point or something. You see these places acrosss the prairies: a bunch of shacks stuck out somewhere, where some band tries to hang together and make a go of hunting and fishing. They're always dirt poor, at least every one I've ever seen. This Fish Lake was typical, I guess. All old folks and the little kids. The young ones take off as soon as they can.

"Bernard was thirteen when he headed for Winnipeg hoping to get a job or an education or something to get him off the reservation. He had no idea of anything probably. Ended up sleeping in abandoned warehouses or the shelters and surviving by his wits in the street. Couldn't get a job, of course. Some of the kids were hookers or thieves or whatever. Lost aimless kids, lost spirits. The usual thing for native kids in a Canadian city, right?

"After a couple of years of roughing it, he started thinking the reservation didn't look so bad after all. He made up his mind to go back, but first he had his city buddies to say so long too. They got into some tavern. It was one of those sixty below Manitoba winter nights. After the place closed they had a long way to walk and they only had jean jackets and worn out boots.

Bunch of kids drunk. Set out on their way, freezing right through even though they'd drunk about a hundred beers each, when all of sudden this car stops, this brand new Mercury, and the driver's just out the taverns himself and knows he can't make it home. So he gets Bernard to drive for him. So they go sailing along very pleased and warm in this car, sliding over the ice and ploughing into snowbanks, joyriding, I guess. Only then they sideswiped a parked police cruiser along the way and there was this chase. Anyway, the end of the it came when Bernard lost control and flipped the car. The owner of the car busted his back, paralyzed for life. And somehow, even though Bernard was a minor and was asked to drive, the owner sued him for a quarter million dollars and it stuck. They put him in jail for some reason or other."

"How a kid gets through that and grows up to have a sense of humour, I'll never know. But Bernard wasn't usual, like I said. He told me that the moment of that accident was one of the important moments in his life. He could not forget the way the car slid and how they rolled and the windshield crumbled like ice. He said he had a vision at that moment. Like he saw the future and the past and present together as one. Said it was like going from one world into a new one. I never knew what he meant by it. But the accident changed him. He got a job after he got out of the House, then he got married and had kids, all within a year. He started to pay his debt.

"And he discovered he had a new sense — what he called 'the signals.' He said something like, 'Dose signal around, eh. You don't got to read 'em, dey're dere.' That's how he talked. He told me if he'd had the signals before, he never would have had the accident. 'De body is like an eye. Like tird eye.' That's how he said it. He felt his body could see things that his brain didn't know about.

"I didn't believe in it. Half the time I thought Bernard was nuts. Well maybe part of the time I didn't know what he was. I tried to figure out what he meant. A light would get into his eyes, a light from deep. Spirit light. And when he talked about the signals, the light would glow.

"We stayed away from the other miners. The miners ate together in the lunchroom, a vault cut into the side of the main access to our level of the mine. It was a long narrow room with two long benches running the length. At the door end was the place where you tagged in and out at the beginning and end of shift. And there was the shift boss's desk. The men used to crowd around the heated end with the foreman. But Bernard and me would eat our lunch at the other end of the room where we could have peace. See, some of the men on the crew went a bit haywire when Bernard joined on. Before him they sort of ignored me. But when Bernard came they would shut up when I walked by and they gave me these looks. I knew they talked about us but I didn't care. The foreman started calling us 'youse two,' instead of using my name. Sounding like youse two so-and-so if you know what I mean.

"Maybe they thought Bernard was a fag. He had this funny, dancing walk and he had his Chinaman face, wrinkled up. His head was shaved down every couple of weeks by his wife. He was dead silent around the men. I guess it made them uncomfortable that he was so different and so unashamed about it. Then they saw that him and me became friends and, well . . . they started hating me too.

"That was why the 'squaw' stories started. They were stories about Indian girls – in the stories they were 'squaws.' Indecent stories about what the miners dreamed of doing, or really did. A mixture, I guess. Two or three would tell how ten of them gangbanged this one or made this one drink piss, or how they shoved a bottle up this one. I'd heard it all before but the white miners never said these things right in front of me. You hear stuff like this in the poolhalls and taverns all over the north. But these men wanted to get to us. They had started hating us. So they told these stories and watched us to for a reaction. That was the game. We were the game.

"I ignored them, let them make asses out of themselves. But poor old Bernard couldn't ignore it. He'd hear a story about the torture of a young, drunk girl by a bunch of leering, drooling white men and he'd stop eating his lunch. His sandwich would go dry in his mouth and he could not swallow. A glaze would come over his eyes. Of course, the men noticed it. They loved it. They loved their game. I'd say to him, 'Don't let it bug you, man,' but he'd say, 'Don't let what bug me?' as if he hadn't heard a thing. This went on for weeks.

"Then one day this miner named Judd Norman started telling a story about a guy Bernard knew. It was straight lies. About how this Indian sat outside his girlfriend's place for a week waiting for her to come out, then, when she finally did come out, he raped her and they had to use fire extinguishers to get him off. Not much of a story, except that Judd Norman used the name of the guy. Norman juiced it up, went into details about his sticking a golfball in her ass while they were doing it. I don't remember what else. It wasn't the worst story but Bernard had enough. He stood up after listening in his glazed-eyes way. Walked up to Judd Norman, stood right in front of him and said, 'You lying bastard' and then slapped Judd Norman's face so hard I heard his neck crack. Norman was too stunned to do anything. The whole crew was silent and still. The foreman finally cleared his throat and said quietly, 'Now none of that,' and that was that.

"Maybe Bernard shouldn't have done it, I don't know," said Grey. "But the damn squaw stories were done with, that was one thing.

"But the foreman seemed to think there was a score to be settled, so after that he took us off the drill, even though we both had driller's papers, and put us doing shit work. He got us digging around for old timber in pools full of lye that eats the skin off you. Then he had us on 'cleanup,' digging mud out of ditches. You could do that job forever because when you dig out a ditch the mud runs back into it. Underground there's no place to drain. We were on that mess for weeks. He used to stand over us and watch.

"Then we were finally back on the drill and I thought the treatment was over. But he put us drilling in this awful, crumbling ground with rocks raining on our heads. A couple of times we quit drilling and jumped clear because we heard the ground popping. We pried down slabs of loose rock with scaling bars. One time I started up my drill and Bernard came and turned my valves off and handed me a cigarette. 'Breaktime,' he said, which was funny since we had just finished breaktime. But I could see that he was serious and had that light in his eyes like two extra lamps he was carrying. So we took another smoke break, this time a long one that went up to lunchtime. When we came back from lunch a chunk of rock the size of a Cadillac was sitting on my drill. Wrecked the drill. Bernard just winked. 'Gotta watch out,' he said and tapped his chest. 'Keep yer eye on dem signals.' I guess there was something to it.

"Then he took off. Bernard up and quit without telling a soul. No explanation. I went to his place and it was empty, the whole family disappeared without a trace. I never saw him again." Grey touched his face gingerly. "I was hurt, I guess, and pissed off at him, but I never got a chance to tell him. Never saw him again.

"Maybe it was because of the signals. Who knows? He wasn't usual, like I said. He had his strange sense. Anyway, it got tough after. I tried to fall back into my old routine, but I'd gotten used to Bernard being there. And then there were the men. They were dead against me now."

IV

Grey slept poorly after Bernard quit. He went to work with leaden legs and eyes bleary from the blazing of nightmares which broke up his sleep. The dreams were simple, of the mine, of accidents: of falling or suffocating or being crushed.

One day he slogged along the main drift, drill on one shoulder, bag of tools slung over the other. A train moved up and slowly by him, the axles creaking. It was the end of a long day of coldness and loneliness, and he was awash in tedium and fatigue. Never had the work been so oppressive, never had the caverns been so silent. He reflected on Bernard with flashes of anger and sadness. He could not look at a distant moving light without a small burst of hope that it was Bernard returned. So he was not watching the train. He felt a twitch though and turned in time to see that a steel rod hanging from an ore car had jammed into the wall of the drift behind him. As the train rolled forward it arched back like a sapling. Grey threw himself down as the steel snapped forward and lashed the air where he had stood.

He was wet and shaken. He wanted to scream or smash something, but his only company was the distant reflection of the motorman's lamp.

That day a miner died. He fell down a vertical dump shaft, two thousand feet to the ore crusher at the bottom of the pit. There was a safety line near the dump shaft opening which had been clipped to his belt as he had worked, but the belt itself had come unhooked. Grey saw them bring in the miner's remains, nothing more than a bloody pile of rags wrapped around a wrench.

The men refused to operate the dump shaft door the next day, so Grey was assigned to it. He found the dead man's belt still clipped to the safety line. He unhooked it and clipped his own belt to it. The dump shaft door was a slab of steel controlled by pneumatic armatures. It opened and closed with a hiss and a slam of steel on rock. Grey opened the door as the ore cars moved up, then he operated the dumper, flipping the ore cars so that they emptied into the dumpshaft.

He was certain that he had foreseen the death. As he worked he pieced it together so that it made sense. He imagined that the rod that sprang at him from the passing ore car, had unhooked the dead man's belt.

Grey peered into the yawning chasm. It was black beyond the edge of the beam from his lamp. He heard the low growl of the rock. All the way down, he thought, the falling miner would have heard the sound. All the way his lamp would have flashed on the face of the living rock.

V

Stope Captain Joe Radki had stayed in the background during the baiting of Bernard. He had not ever spoken to Grey in the years that Grey had been on the crew. He had watched everything. He came down to the end of the bench one day and sat across from Grey and set to chewing on his sandwich thoughtfully as he stared at the tips of Grey's boots.

"You know, I got a theory," Radki drawled. "I got this theory about your people. I been workin' up north here for almost fourteen years now and I seen a lot of your people. Hangin' around in taverns mostly. Most of 'em don't care much for work. I watched you and your little friend there, Mr. Clean, and how youse operated down here in the mine. And I got this theory that you and your friend and the whole lot of you Indians are gutless as worms."

Grey looked up. He looked at Radki's granite grey eyes, but they were fixed on the ground.

"Maybe there was a time when it was different. That's what some folks say. But it don't matter much. You look at your modern Indian, like that little pansy of a partner you had, and you just have to laugh."

"Fuck off," said Grey plainly.

Radki stopped eating and wiped his mouth on his sleeve. He was a good-looking man up close, Grey realized. Tall and hard-muscled like Grey. And he had a way of smirking while he talked and looking off in the distance out of the rock-like eyes.

"Hey, I'm bein' serious here," Radki was saying. "I'd really like to meet a real gutsy Indian, one with fire in him instead of just whisky. I mean what about that Mr. Clean. Kind of interestin', really. How he ran off there like a little girl. Couldn't take the heat. What is that? No gumption, I guess. I seen lots of Indians like that . . . "

Grey stared.

"When you plannin' to skip outta here, Grey? When you going to run off after that faggot friend of yours."

Grey tossed his coffee in Radki's face. Then he walked out of the room and down the drift to the stope.

The next day Grey was assigned to Radki's stope on Radki's request.

The stope captain came and pushed his face into Grey's. He did not look off as he spoke now. He face was very white and his breath smelled of chewing tobacco and meat. "You get ready, Grey. You be ready to work your red butt off."

Grey knew enough about Radki to know that he wanted revenge. What he did not see was why he had been provoked.

This worried him. He had known cruel people enough in his life, but he still did not understand. How hatred and calculating cruelty thrived. He knew to play along, work in Radki's stope and collect his bonus wages, which was a change. This stope was the highest producer in the mine afterall. He decided to wait, thinking he had no choice.

On the first day he set up his drill near the other men. It was in the main area of drilling in the vein and the ground was solid. Grey worked fast and kept an eye on Radki whenever he was near. The second day the stope captain sent him into a hole where there was water seepage. Water spattered onto Grey as he drilled. He did not mind this, content to think that this was the other man's revenge. As he worked, he whistled beneath the crashing noise of the drill.

The third day Radki took Grey out of the watery hole, even though the job was not complete. He motioned for him to follow with his drill. Grey picked up his gear and went along. Radki spat streams of tobacco as they walked. The spit looked golden as it passed through the ray of the lamp. From behind Radki looked like a cowboy. Swagger and holster. Except that his holster carried a crescent wrench instead of a gun.

They passed the main stope and kept on for a mile down an exploration cut with no rails in it. Finally they turned in where the water and air pipes came to an end. Radki stooped through a small hole that opened into a high dome.

"Set up here," said Radki with a grin.

Grey shone his light into the ceiling, knowing what he would see. The roof was cracked and broken and pieces of rock had fallen, either trapped by an incomplete protective wire mesh, or on the floor in heaps. The ground was unstable and dangerous. Grey set down his drill and shrugged. . . .

"Don't drill too noisy either, or we'll have to blast the whole thing out again."

Grey shook his head and studied the ceiling.

"Hah," said Radki. "What's that supposed to mean? You too chicken to say you won't drill or what? Some smart friggin' rockhead you are."

"I never said I wouldn't drill," said Grey. "Only the hose

they got here won't reach from the main."

Radki checked this with a frown.

"That's no sweat. I'll bring the extension." Radki's voice boomed between the rock walls. He moved off, leaving Grey to set up his drill.

Grey scaled down loose rock, prodding here and there, systematically going over the whole dome. The ground was very bad.

Radki returned with a big coil of yellow hose on his back. He hooked it into the air main and to Grey's hose. He looked up at the ceiling the way Grey was doing at that moment and he grumbled something profane about engineers.

Grey set up his drill. He turned the valves and the explosive sound rebounded in the enclosed chamber. Then there was a distinct popping sound and Grey turned the drill off and moved away from the rock face. Radki stood by the mouth of the cavern, his light pointed up.

"It's pretty crumbly in here," Grey said quietly.

Radki said nothing.

The ground breathed a wet, salt-granity smell and it was still. Then it seemed to hold its breath and wait. Grey stepped up to the rock face and turned the valve on his drill. He drilled a shallow hole, then fifteen minutes later withdrew the bit and turned to see Radki's lamp still by the cavern mouth. He set up again and sank another hole, then began a third. Partway through the third hole there was a sound like a gunshot and the ground began to fall. It fell behind Grey and he spun and dropped the drill. Then a piece of rock hit his helmet and Grey fell backwards over the drill, the beam from his helmet glancing crazily off moving, falling rock and mesh as the mesh broke away and came down.

It became quiet. Grey lay on his drill wishing he were unconscious. He could not move and his light was gone. He felt the broken rock around him steaming and puffing, growling frantically. A cloud of ammonia drifted in over the broken rock stinging the inside of his nose. It was absolutely dark. The rock breathed and shifted around him.

After a long time lights appeared, seven or eight of them, pointing over the rock and up at the dome ceiling, searching, then shining in Greys' face. They pried him loose with scaling bars and then a fiery pain was unleashed in Grey's leg and swept up his spine.

"I lay up in hospital for months. They broke my leg over a few times, stuck some steel rods in it and some plates. The doctors said my leg was smashed practically flat. Said I was lucky to keep it. I got used to the feeling after a few months. I got acquainted with the pain. I could tell when it would start up, knew exactly where it hid out. It would start as a little burning hole and then, sort of catch fire. I used to shake with pain, man, and the nurse said my face would go as white as flour.

"During that time in hospital I was low down thinking about Bernard and Radki. Maybe Radki never expected me to drill in that bad ground, or maybe he knew I would. I couldn't get his stinking face out of my mind for months. I lay there hoping my leg would get better enough so I could get back underground."

"You're must be crazy. Not only that but you're a fool, which is worse," Sijjer stated quietly.

"You don't see, do you? It was between me and Radki. Radki stepped over my line, into my space, man. No one can protect that but me. It was up to me to shove him out. People do that all the time.

"I finally got back on my feet. Took almost a year. Six months of treatment in Winnipeg before my leg worked. That red-hot pain kept me down. The only good thing that came of it was I met a girl. College type. She used to play flute during my therapy and, you know, I think it helped."

"Her name was Anne. She was a music student, Cree, and she worked part time at the hospital playing her flute to gimps like me. By the time I was ready to leave to go back north, I guess she was kind of hooked on me. She was a bit wild. Young, pretty thing. She made life pretty good for a while. She could cook these real fancy meals. French, Chinese, Italian. Tell these pretty little stories she'd make up while she rubbed down my leg. She'll be a good mother one day, that Anne. Even wanted a kid with me, at least she used to talk about it. Makes a guy feel good to hear a woman talk that way. We started making plans together. Only time in my life I had real plans, even if I didn't quite believe in it.

"So they put me back to work in the minehead at first, doing general maintenance. Then I was on another level before I asked for a transfer back to my old crew. I know what you're thinking. Why the hell would I go back on the same crew after all that happened? Don't know exactly why. But I do know that, when I finally got into the cage with them that morning, I felt like I'd been thrown down a deep shaft and been climbing out of it for a year.

"I never thought much of what the crew would be like when I went back. It was strange. They started out acting real friendly to me, like I was a long-lost hero and we'd been pals the whole time. Men who'd never said a word to me before came and sat beside me in the lunchroom, clapped me on the back and made jokes about hospital nurses and stuff. The foreman treated me like I was his son. Gave me the best drilling jobs, hired on this young guy to be my partner.

"I stayed pretty cool. Didn't believe in it. I guess maybe I was thinking about Bernard even if the crew seemed to have forgotten about him. I got the feeling that the men were doing all this pally shit for each other, really. So I kept cool.

"Radki was still there. He didn't act like the other men, Radki. He kept his distance. If I looked at him, he had to look away. It took me a while to see he was scared sick. He reminded me of a dog that walked onto another dog's territory. You know, the way they stand stock still and look away while the other dog sniffs them. He was skittish, Radki was. And he had a right to be too, because every time I saw Radki, I swear, my muscles would go into spasms and my leg would howl. Sometimes I would shake and start to sweat if I saw the man. My vision would go blurry. I had to control it.

"But the leg was getting better all the time. It never went back to normal, but, aside from the pains I got when Radki was around, it felt better and better. Before the accident I used to walk to the minehead before my shift. It was two miles or so and I'd cut into the bush, through some muskeg where I'd sometimes see deer or moose. I used to love that. In the winter I'd follow the train tracks home in the dark. After the accident I couldn't do that for a long time. I'd have to limp along the road and hope for a ride."

VI

Grey stood on the shoulder of the road peering into the woods. It was a late-spring dawn and the light and colour was seeping into the bush. He saw the textures of brown and grey transform to a wash of colour, then the colours become vivid. He counted the different species of bog flowers.

Often he was arrested this way, by the light and colour of living things. The accident had changed his vision. He had lain under the rock, his lamp smashed out and he had waited in absolute black darkness. With his one free hand he had touched his eyes to make sure that they were intact, then he had pressed them to see the red flare from the pressure. Only this reassured him that he was not blinded and there was not a ray of light to be seen. He felt the rock around him, sweating and breathing. It seemed to soak up light.

Then the lamps of the rescuers had appeared, pouring out light that was like liquid gold. It had hurt his eyes and warmed him. He had seen particles of gold rays, spraying onto the rock.

After that ordinary light could catch him up. He saw its power. He saw traces of it in what most people call pitch black. He saw how it died at night and grew in the morning, pulling the colours from the tiny northern flowers. He saw textures and grain and the shimmering world of reflection.

A car pulled up beside him.

"Hey, get in, yer gonna be late." Grey tore himself away from the light. He climbed into the car not looking at the driver, lost still in his vision. Then the car picked up speed and he looked over and saw that the driver was Radki.

Radki had never stopped before, nor had Grey wanted him to. Now his muscles began to coil and twitch.

"How's that leg?" said Radki.

Grey opened his mouth to speak, but no sound came and he checked his impulse, his bloody ones, and smiled tightly. He was determined to stay cool.

"Well, it looks pretty good anyway. I heard they did an A-1 job on you. Doctors can do one hell of a patch job these days, eh? Why I got this uncle whose heart stopped on him one day, just like that. But they started that sucker up again and now he's lyin' in a hospital in Regina. Been lyin' there for eight years now, hooked up to all sorts of machines. Alive though."

They pulled up to the minehead and Radki parked. Grey hopped out quickly, but Radki trotted to stay with him.

"Hey, look partner." He caught Grey by the arm. "Hey look, I'm sorry about what happened. I know I'm part to blame for it, so let's forget it, okay?"

Grey took the hand away but stood his ground and stared the other man in the eye. They were the same height, eye to eye.

Radki shifted back a fraction of an inch. He flushed red but held his gaze.

"Look man," he laughed, "this kind of stuff happens all the time. You ought to know that. You work underground, you get hurt. Hey, I been hurt. Look at this hand. See that? What the hell you lookin' at me like that for? People gotta be careful. It could have been me in there, Grey. Could have been any of the guys. Would they blame me? 'Course they wouldn't. 'Course not." He clapped Grey on the shoulder and suddenly looked relaxed, like his old brash self. "Take it easy, huh. Maybe we'll see you in my stope again some day." Then Radki shook himself and winked at Grey before going into the minehead.

Grey's breath caught as he drew on his oilers and boots. His leg trembled as if it were cold. He sat down on the bench and stared at the leg. Radki was not afraid anymore. He had been afraid but he had confronted Grey outright and beaten his fear. Now he was the old Radki, and this was wrong. The score had not been settled yet. It was far from settled, he realized. He remembered waiting for Radki to even up the score after he had thrown coffee in his face. He remembered how he had watched for for the other man to come, not knowing what to expect. Now Radki had been waiting, he realized, and he had let him down.

Grey went to the cage and it dropped in to the dark rock

and bounced to a stop at fifty-four. He watched Radki, who looked back once and winked. In the lunchroom Grey went through the motions as though he were dreaming. The foreman gave him his assignment, his new partner asked him what to do. Grey went through it all sleepwalking, and when he woke up he was drilling, drilling a hole far deeper than it should have been.

He shut off the drill and left the new man alone. He went down the drift to the stope. He went in and searched until he saw Radki and Radki saw him. Then Grey went back to his place and drilled. He was not thinking now, simply going through the motions of work.

It went on for another day like that. Working in a dream, the trembling of the leg. Going to Radki's stope once or twice more, then going back. Sometimes Grey did not hear when he was spoken to. Sometimes he drilled in one place for twice as long as he was supposed to.

Beneath thought, Grey was the hunter. In his dreams, the dreams beneath thought, there was a track and a spoor.

Later he went to Radki's stope again but did not find him. Then he heard a horn and realized they were about to blast. The men were setting down their drills and heading out of the stope. A scoop tram howled by, lights glaring. Grey switched off his lamp and stood in a recess near the stope entrance. The men passed him by without seeing him. Then the stope became quiet but for a whistle blowing deep within it. Grey switched his lamp on and moved towards the whistle. When he found the man on watch clearing the stope for the blast, Grey turned off his lamp again and sat against a wall. The watch moved by him, light shining and whistle blowing. Grey waited until the light moved down to the drift. He then headed into the depths of the stope with his light still off. He went steadily and did not stumble. He moved towards the blast area by instinct until he saw two lamps huddled over the charges. Grey knew it was Radki and the powderman. That was the rule: the stope captain and the powderman set the charge, everyone else cleared out. The two beams moved towards him, then went round a corner. Grey heard the brash voice of Radki rebuking the powderman; then the powderman went off to check one last time that the stope was empty. Radki lit a fuse and headed in the opposite direction. He walked along with his lamp held in his hand, shining it on the rock face, checking the men's work. He turned suddenly when he heard Grey's step behind him. He shone the lamp in Grey's face.

"Your lamp's out, Grey," said Radki.

"Battery," said Grey softly. He came up close but could not see his face because Radki shone the beam in his eyes.

"This is a blast area. Didn't you hear the signal?"

Grey shook his head and shoved Radki backwards onto a mound of rock. Radki lay on the ground, not moving a muscle. Grey could hear his breathing. It seemed to fill the stope. It was taken up by the living rock so that the whole place breathed as one. The lamp shone in Grey's eyes.

"You're not scared anymore," said Grey. "Or are you?"

"The hell I am." hissed Radki, "the hell I am." Grey booted the light out of Radki's hand and switched on his own light. There was a dull thud followed by the rumble of falling rock as the first set of charges went.

"The hell I'm scared of a gutless shit like you," Radki forced a laugh, but he lay stock still. The second set of charges sounded like a crack of thunder and the falling rock made a deafening roar that drowned his voice. His lips moved silently. Grey never knew how the scaling bar came into his hands. He did not know he was carrying it until it came down dull and heavy on Radki's back as he tried to stand. Then the gut-coiling, muscle-twitching, painful, pent-up rage came spitting forth like a rabid cat and it took the scaling bar from Grey. It made the bar come down harder on the stope captain's back, then on his helmet, knocking it away. Radki tried to stand but sank to his knees as though he were praying. The third and fourth charges were roaring near by, the gunpowder and rockdust billowing down the cavern.

When it began clearing off and the echo of the last blast died away, Grey was sitting, his arms spent. The scaling bar had disappeared beyond the fringe of light and Radki lay face down, his skull crushed. Grey's anger was gone and he felt strangely sleepy. He looked at the other man's head without comprehension at first; he had to reconstruct what had happened as he sat. He only remembered hitting Radki once.

"Son of a bitch," Grey muttered.

His mind went on, processing the situation. He did not freeze. There were now two ways out. He could either try to hide the body and go back to the lunchroom, hoping that no one would notice Radki missing until the next shift. Or he could run. Running meant finding the air vent and emergency shaft, then climbing fifty-four hundred feet to surface. Going to the lunch room meant pretending nothing had happened and depending on chance. It also meant dragging the body around and Grey knew he could not do that. There was some evil in doing that. He knew before he touched it that Radki's body would be as heavy as nickel ore, and that it would cause him trouble. So Grey ran.

Because of the blasting the men were in the lunchroom by now, so Grey was alone to find the air vent. He went straight to it and started to climb the ladder. He climbed steadily and made himself go slowly. He counted out one hundred steps, then stopped for the count of twenty, then went on. After two hundred steps sweat dripped down his legs into his boots. After another two hundred he missed his footing and had to hug the rungs to his chest while he gathered himself. He went on, heart pounding, breath rasping, the sweat running in a river. The shaft narrowed in places to a point where his back scraped the wall, then it widened, then narrowed again for a long way. For the first time underground Grey had the sensation of utter vulnerability. He imagined the earth, the rock, holding its breath as he passed through it. If it were to shudder or shift, he would be squashed like an ant. The earth was alive. The rock was alive. It panted and quivered around him. It watched him with a million eyes as he passed through its bosom. He muttered words of supplication and gratitude. He apologized for what he had done. He cursed his anger and he cursed Radki. And when he cursed Radki, pain bolted up through his bad leg like a reply. He clung to the rungs and clenched his eyes shut. Then he went on, one hand, one boot, one hand, one boot. Resting every fifty steps, then every ten. Far above he saw a small point of light as beckoning and elusive as a star. He focused on the rungs then, five steps, then rest . . .

Grey emerged in the building housing the fan. The place was deserted. He had no idea of how long he had climbed but it was dark outside. He slipped into the yard and crawled under the fence into the woods. Through the melting snow he hobbled homeward, then he changed his mind and broke into Bernard's abandoned bungalow.

IV

"You killed him," said Sijjer.

"Yes," said Grey. "You understand? I killed the son of a bitch."

Sijjer sat back into his chair and tried not to stare at Grey. How strange he looked, his humanity torn away, his humanity exposed. It was bone and blood and . . .

"Spirit," said Grey. "I killed him because I still got my spirit. That's why I did it. There is no law of spirits. There's no spirit cop that tells you what you can't do. It's when you've lost your spirit that you don't know what to do. Then you have to listen to something outside."

"You killed him," said Sijjer quietly.

Grey shrugged.

A few minutes later Grey fell into a profound sleep. His breath whistled unevenly through his broken nose.

Sijjer walked through his house slowly touching his possessions, looking at the contents of his home and trying to view it anew. In Karla's room he watched her sleep, pondering. On her wall in the half light were photographs of Easter Island. The monstrous faces of the statues lay sideways, half-buried and decrepit like fallen gods.

Perhaps he had missed the point all this time. How had he defined himself? Where was his spirit? Where was his guide? Sijjer stared at the faces of the gods. People had carved these stones because it had helped order the world, making it sensible. But Sijjer saw that he had no gods, no stones, and his world made no sense at all.

EIGHTEEN

Punjab

I

Dear Mother,

What are the real truths of existence? Flesh and blood? Death? Pia wrote, "The naked fact of life is death. Life simply awaits death, then dies."

J.

Sijjer had not yet slept. Karla was out of sight, locked into her room, and Grey was motionless on the couch, his face a deathly mask. The house was silent, as if having weathered a storm.

There was a frightening implacability to the telling of Grey's story. Yet there was a glimmer of integrity which shone through the criminality of it like a gold medallion in a smoky flame. He suddenly hated Grey, goaded by his presence and unable to translate his messages into meanings. Perhaps he simply told a tall tale. It struck Sijjer that he was out of his depth. He grasped words not meanings. It dawned on him that he had never really understood Pia. 'Life awaits death.' They were mere words.

As Sijjer left the house, it began to shower. He headed for a bar, Leo's, and sat watching the rain which looked like a silver powder falling to earth.

The bar was empty and Sijjer felt ill. He thought of trying to vomit. A pain had settled in his chest during the night. He imagined cancer. Metastasis. Growth and death. He died, even as he lived.

One awaits death, then one dies.

He stumbled into the late afternoon rush hour, found the VW bus near the tracks and drove, reeling, into traffic. He drove southward, out of the city.

The windshield wipers flapped away the silver rain powder. It was warm, and in the suburbs children played in the rain. The silver powder collected in oily pools. In one place small, tanned boys ran in a line through puddles, sending silver flying between their bare legs. They wore torn jean shorts and lifted their arms as if to fly. Waters from the mountains surged in the river below a bridge he crossed. At the end of the bridge ambulance lights flashed in the silver mist. A cyclist lay on the road in peaceful slumber, his bicycle crushed beside him. . . .

One awaits death . . .

He drove furiously, reeling in his seat, drunken, the pain in his belly expanding, shrinking and expanding as if in mimickry of his heart.

There were farms, then forests growing up to the road's edge. Finally, a sudden break in the trees and in a place far from the city, was a half-acre of pavement, or half acre of grass, and a building of raw, rain-darkened concrete. High on the concrete were sloping skylights and at the top, a coppery onion dome. A single splash of red ribbon broke the dull, munitions-bunker solidness of the structure. Over the door was the inscription in Gurmukhi.

He pulled into the empty parking lot and scuffled through a blast of blown rain to the steps.

The heavy wooden doors were unlocked. In a vestibule, was a low table with a neat stack of white linen scarves upon it. Sijjer removed his sodden shoes and laid one of the scarves over his head. He opened the inner doors to a high-ceilinged chamber. Sweet incense burned. The floor was covered with layers of carpets of gold and red. A skylight illuminated a central podium which rose to knee-height, and upon the podium sat a thickly bearded *granthi.* He was an old man clothed and turbanned entirely in white except for delicate wire-rimmed spectacles that rode the bridge of his large nose. He pored over the scriptures and hummed a monotonous tune.

Sijjer was absorbed by this scene for minutes or perhaps hours, his sense of time suspended. Rain drummed on the skylights. A candle flickered. Filaments of smoke dissolved. He retreated to the darkest corner of the room and sat cross-legged on the warm carpet.

Later the *granthi* folded his glasses and, chanting, covered the pages of the scripture with muslin and silk. He stood on legs bowed under the weight of an immense belly, came and sat next to Sijjer.

"*Sat-sri-akal,*" said the old man. He rocked back and forth on his haunches. "Oh, oh, it is terrible cold," he muttered.

"The rain makes it seem cold."

"Ah, the rain." He pulled at his beard thoughtfully. "You have not been drinking the rain, I think. And you speak like the Angrezi . . . looks like Punjabi, but speaks like Angrezi. That is a puzzle," the old man giggled.

"Has not drunken rain,
but looks like . . . pain.
Has drunken the *schrahb*,
and not quite Punjab" he intoned.

Then the *granthi* fairly shook with mirth. His face became a mass of wrinkles.

"I love poems," he said. "Don't you love poems? But I should have known you were a new man. You walk like Western Boot, Modern Shoe . . . you know, we walk like Old Shoe. Old Shoe and sometimes, No Shoe." He laughed heartily and pulled at long strands of beard.

Sijjer looked at his feet.

"Well, Mister Not-Rain Drinker, you like this place?"

"It's got a certain squat wartime charm . . . "

"Squot? Great Squot?"

"Squat. I was just joking. It's fine."

"Acha. Fine. But no priests. We have no priest here. Some *lok* come here looking for priests. *Sants*. I have to say, 'No *Sants* here, my darlings.' You looking for a *Sant* to help you? No, you know already. No *sants*. Just a place. Some people come here on Sunday. That's all. Once an *Angrezi* man come and I said, 'No God in here, my darling. Nothing big.' He was surprised. We say, 'God is everywhere,' not just at *Gurdwara*."

"That makes sense."

"They wrote sense, those gurus, nothing but sense, because they didn't know anything else, that's why."

The *granthi* rocked back and forth on his haunches and hummed a tune and a few words. "Has drunken *shrahb*, but not quite Punjab . . . " he sang. "I get hungry when it rains, don't you? Even old fat man get hungry when the rain comes. It would be better if the rain were food! You know *shrahb*?"

"Booze."

"*Shrahb* is fun. Makes a man forget. He sits in his field and the crops dry up and perish. He sits and forgets about his wife and hungry children."

"I don't have children . . . "

"And there are no fields here! Ha,ha. This place is not Punjab, is it?"

"I wouldn't know. I've never been there. I want to go . . . "

"Oh, you must go. It is one place which you should see."

"You must miss it sometimes," said Sijjer.

"Punjab? Aho. It is not a TV place. No Dallas. No Bugs Bunny . . . " The *granthi* was giggling once more, shaking with it. " . . . no Tchevrolet."

"I don't watch much television . . . "

"Then go to Punjab!," the *granthi* roared. "Why wait here? You're waiting and waiting and nothing happens!"

He stood with much oohing and aahing and reasserted that he was hungry indeed.

"The more it rains, the more hungry I am.
The rain should be food!
Rain come down from sky
Come in old man's eye.
It is not so rude
To wish rain could be food!

Like that one?"

The *granthi* beckoned to him and Sijjer could not help but smile as he reeled to his feet and followed the old man through a door and downstairs into a spacious kitchen. Immense, gleaming aluminum pots hung on racks. An old woman tended an oven. When the two men were seated, she brought a stack of hot potato-filled *prantai* and bowls of yoghurt and *dal*.

Sijjer dove into this offering. Strangely, when he was finished, he found that he was alone. The *granthi* and his plates had vanished. There was no sign of the old woman. From above came the *granthi*'s voice echoing through the temple, "Hoo, hoo, it is such rain!"

Sijjer cleaned his plates in the kitchen sink and listened to the rain drumming on the roof. His feet were dry and he was sleepy. He no longer reeled.

Punjab. Prito was there, old and alone. It became clear suddenly that it was time for him to go to her. If there was a place of spiritual rebirth for Jaswant Singh Sijjer, then perhaps it was the Land of Five Rivers, Punjab.

Sitting beneath the roof of the Gurdwara, Sijjer imagined the lush delta of the rivers, a battle ground, a garden of lovers, murderers, prophets. It was beautiful and romantic, and it touched him like a warm ray of sun.

Then that moment passed and it was tranquil in the kitchen of the temple. Without the voice of the *granthi* to be heard, an air of solitude descended. He passed through the main, skylit chamber, found his shoes and dashed through the rain to the VW bus.

III

Sijjer arranged vaccinations for himself, packed a flight bag and booked flights for Toronto with connections to London and

Bombay. Karla was gone once more. He waited for her, unwilling to ask Grey the whereabouts of his wife or tell him of his travel plans. He was sick with suspicion and fear. Finally he wrote her a note, packed up and left.

It was hot and sticky in Toronto. Car exhaust and smog-filtered sunlight gave the place a tomb-like appearence. The people on the streets were entrapped in concrete and smoke. They moved at a forced, nerve-wracked pace. Sijjer watched a car grind inexorably into the back of another car. The drivers struggled out of their seats and went forth to do battle. A child howled by its mother's side as she watched the men fight.

These were the facts. We are trapped into waiting. We wait and wait.

He tried unsuccessfully to phone Gurjit. One of the vaccines had made him woozy and hot. India would be just this, he decided. Hot, delirious and chaos. He ducked into a bar. Inside it was cool, perpetual evening. Mirrors and chrome gleamed smartly and a poster on the wall displayed the glowing body of a dancer. The pervading mood was one of recklessness. Business people wound their drunken lunches down and the bartenders and waitresses were gay.

Sijjer found a corner in which to slide back vodka and watch the afternoon progress. In time the place filled, a dancer appeared and danced the blues. People began to dance. A buxom woman fixed Sijjer with a look. In the next moment she had taken him by the arm and he drifted along onto the floor, moving to the voices and lights, not hearing the strains of music. The woman steered him to a table and bought him a drink. She said something about her place and a late night snack. Her voice was as soft as a kitten's purr. He wondered what had become of Mohan's bride. He thought of telling the woman beside him that she would fit into Mohan's bride's palm.

She kissed his mouth and they drank. He tried to call Gurjit again.

By the time Gurjit appeared, the bar was closed. Sijjer weaved as he followed his brother to the car. The buxom woman had disappeared.

Gurjit's car was a late model Porsche. "It's not mine," he said.

They piled in Sijjer's two suitcases and pulled away into a city night full of the minute activities of a sleepless, sweating downtown. Fire escapes groaned under the weight of tenement dwellers. On a corner two men engaged in a lethargic fistfight. Sijjer stared, certain that these were the two motorists he had seen eight hours before.

Down a street a man chased a woman dressed in a bathrobe. Her face, white with terror, turned back towards the pursuer and picked up the gleam of street lamps. Onlookers stepped aside to let the couple pass.

"What will he do to her?" Sijjer asked

"What?" said Gurjit. "Listen, Jassy, you picked a hell of a time to drop in unannounced."

"I tried to. You weren't home."

"After all that happened, I'm still here, Jassy. After I came out to see you and you took off and hid somewhere, after you came here and behaved so damn strange. After you skipped out of the funeral. After all that shit, I'm still here for you. But this is not a good time for me and I want you to know it."

The car slid slowly onwards. A cat glared at Sijjer from atop a postbox. They came abreast of the man chasing the woman. He was gaunt and looked as though he carried a knife. He was psychopathic, Sijjer thought. He wore a sweatshirt with a hood and his hands were tucked inside. The womans' robe had flapped open to reveal a torn slip. Her face was a mask.

"It's this woman I'm with," Gurjit was saying. "The owner of this fucking eighty grand toy. Going through hell with each other, I don't know why. She drives me nuts, the bitch."

Gurjit had changed. His resonant voice cracked with strain. His wore wrap-around, reflective sunglasses and his beard was unruly.

The liquor poured off Sijjer in a tide of sweat.

"She's got my number, man." Gurjit went on, "she's got my number. When you meet her, don't be surprised by anything."

Gurjit and his lover shared a townhouse in Yorkville. It consisted of four spacious floors, a Jacuzzi, tropical plants thoughout and an electric-doored garage for the Porsche.

Gurjit propelled Sijjer into a chair in a room, then vanished. A moment later Sijjer heard the sounds of a quarrel being conducted in loud, hissing whispers. Then a woman's voice: "I don't care!".

Gurjit returned, his face suffused with blood. He still wore his sunglasses, so Sijjer was spared the fury of his brother's scowl.

"Let's get out of this fucking place," Gurjit muttered. Then they were out again and Gurjit drove, seething. He took his hatred out on the Porsche, it seemed, locking up the brakes on corners and jamming the gearshift.

"I can stay somewhere else."

"Bullshit. Don't give me that bullshit now. You show up completely out of the blue. You show up pissed-drunk and looking as though you might croak any moment. Look at you! You been drinking continuously since we last met? You were pretty well gone then too. Fucking car! I hate this fat bitch of a car!"

The car pulled over suddenly, the brakes locked for the last time. Sijjer climbed out and listened from a distance to Gurjit's raging. Gurjit finished off his tirade by slamming the car door not once but twice before stalking away down the sidewalk. Lights flashed meanly on the reflective surface of his sunglasses.

"Everything fucking happens at once," he was fuming, "... pissed to the gills ... goddamn bitch and her fat bitch of a car ... "

Sijjer concentrated on walking soberly, conscious now of the state of drunkeness which welled up around him like a haze. It seemed that T-shirted, sweaty people floated at him out of doors and windows. He was sweaty and cold.

"What did you come to Toronto for anyway? You never told me what you're doing here."

"Transit. I'm in transit. I thought I'd ... I don't know what I was thinking ... I thought I'd better drop off here to see you ... "

"See me?" Gurjits' voice softened a bit at this. "You like Italian food?"

"Yeah, you know."

"Yeah, yeah. Why didn't you come and help me when I needed you? You too proud to cremate your own father? Trying to make some kind of point? To whom? Me?"

"You're too mad to talk. Let's talk it over later."

"Of course, I'm mad. What the hell do you think I should be. I needed you. Maybe the one time in my life when I needed you and what happens? You let me down. You never even explained or excused yourself. You never called. Didn't you know that it was important? Didn't you know that?"

"I couldn't do it. I hated him . . . "

Gurjit wheeled around and batted Sijjer across the side of the head with enough force to dissolve the haze with shocking suddenness.

"You goddamn dupe! You've always been such a dupe! You can't hate a sick, piteous old man. You can't hate your father. What are you? Are you so poisoned with self-pity that you can't forgive an old person their flaws? What the hell are you anyway?"

"Lay off, Gurjit."

Gurjit wheeled around again which made Sijjer duck. His head rang. He was only now registering shock and humiliation. . . .

Gurjit sat on the curb. With his sunglasses reflecting the lights of passing cars, and with his long beard, he looked calloused. "You're my only brother, I keep telling myself that. My only brother. Why don't you buy some new clothes for God's sake? How can you wear that trench coat in this heat? You look like some kook working on the Manhattan Project."

"I lost my job." He sat beside Gurjit.

"Incredible. Brilliant career move. What next?"

"I'm on my way to Punjab."

"Punjab?"

Gurjit removed his sunglasses for the first time that evening. He wore two black circles of fatigue around his eyes, like double zeros.

"Punjab? Did you pay for your ticket yet?

"Why?"

"I think you can get your money back still. Was it charter?"

"What are you talking about, Gurjit?"

"What do you want to go to Punjab for?"

"Our mother's there. Remember? Remember her?"

"Jassy . . . "

"I haven't forgotten her. Maybe everyone else has, but I haven't. I just realized the time had come for me to go to her.

After all this time, the time finally came. Isn't that strange? I've been writing letters to her. Got a stack of them. But I never sent them because I never got her address. I'm going to take them over there and sit down with her and read each one to her in order. I'll take her presents, some books maybe and all the money I have. She doesn't have anyone but us. We're going to sit and talk over all those stories she used to tell, and I'm going to ask to her to explain them the way I used to when I was a kid. We'll just talk things over, about Mohan and Bear and Karla . . . "

Sijjer did not go on. He was crying. Sitting on a curb in downtown Toronto, aware that passers-by stared and saw two grown, dark men sitting on the curb, one crying. Gurjit put one arm around his shoulders and held him the way he had done when they were kids.

"You know she's gone, Jassy. You know it. She's dead and long gone. You never wanted to talk about it, so I said to myself: that's okay, he'll handle it quietly and in his own way. Then time went on. I thought you'd accepted it all this time. Poor old Mohan never could talk about it either. It broke his ratty little heart. She just got sick and didn't say much, just went off back to her home to die. Mohan never could tell us.

"When I went to Punjab and found out she'd died years before, I couldn't come back. Couldn't function at all in fact. I just wandered around for awhile. Then I woke up one day and found that I'd wandered all over India still looking for something that would replace her. I'd be in a vast crowd in a marketplace and I'd see a face like hers. I wandered around for five years searching. It was bad at times. I got sick in one place and thought I would die. Typhoid, I think. The fever got so bad I lost my sense for a while and in the middle of this delirium Mother came to me. She told me a million stories, ones she'd never told us before, told them just the way she always did, and she told me to go home. She said I was looking for my home but my home was back here all the time. When I recovered, I wrote all the things she told me in two of those black books. You must have read it. I showed it to you, I remember."

"I couldn't read it."

"But you knew just the same, didn't you. It's too late to go back, Jassy. It's too late for you, and it was too late for me back then. Anyway, it's always too late. Everything we have, we hold in our hands right now. There's nothing in India that we can lay claim to. The people there don't care about you. No one there knows you or cares. You'll find some distant relatives somewhere, maybe even someone who bears a resemblence to you or me, and you'll wonder if there's something of you in them. You may want to see it. You'll strain to see it. But really there's nothing."

PART THREE

NINETEEN

The Lions

I

In Gurjit's study the indestructible black tomes of his journey occupied a separate bookshelf placed at the centre of the room. In the night Sijjer opened his eyes to see them hanging illuminated, their bindings worn to dull glossiness. Sijjer did not open the books, even after Gurjit told him that Prito was dead. And he had no recollection of having read them before. So there was this question: had he known, deep down, all these years of Prito's death? It seemed absurd that he had not. Yet nothing of the content of the books remained with him; nothing but the dreadful iron heft of them.

He swung his suitcase wearily into his house and paused, hearing voices. Karla came in, stopped when she saw him and said,

"You're back. What happened?"

"I want to know what's going on." He took up his suitcase as he spoke, as if that offered the choice of flight.

"Nothing is going on."

"I want the truth."

"There's no truth. Nothing's going on. I am in love with him. That's what you want to know, so I'm saying it. Nothing is going on."

She went into the kitchen. He followed, suitcase in hand.

"Where is he?"

She nodded in the direction of the deck, and Sijjer saw Grey through the window.

"I guess you want me out of your way. I bet you want me to just pick up and . . . How can you tell me that? How can you just do that to me?"

"I don't expect you to leave. In fact I'm moving back to my apartment. I kept my apartment this time."

Karla went to her room and shut the door. She emerged minutes later and went straight off without a word. Sijjer stood watching her go, his own bag still in hand. He set it down slowly and looked out the sundeck window. Grey was shirtless, asleep in the sun.

He took off his trenchcoat and poured himself a large drink. Then he moved to the other side of the house, thinking that Karla would come back. But the street remained empty through that drink and through another until he realized that she would not return.

After a long time he noticed the Lions profiled against the distant horizon. And he noticed something new. Upon the mountains were granulous black objects which slid from the crests to form a stream which emptied into the green forest at their base.

"You're looking kind of spooked," Grey said behind him.

"There's some stuff on the mountains. Rockslide, I guess," said Sijjer without turning.

"That's happens when you drink too much. Spooked. Ghosts in the head. I've seen it. Something out there keeps your head snapping around and your head is like it's on an elastic band and someone is yanking on it all the time."

"It's just the meltwater reflecting in the sun."

"Or sometimes it's something real about a place, not in the head at all. You get sensitive around it, then you want to pray to it without even understanding it. Praying to the land. But it's mostly native people do that. Nobody else feels the spirits that way. And you know why that is? That's because you have to have a spirit yourself so you can be in touch with the spirits out there. It doesn't happen in the head, so the white man can't understand it. It goes on in the belly, in the soles of the feet, in the hands. The spirit talks and listens and sees. I felt it when I was in the earth. It was a power down in the mine. You were right in the centre of it."

"You told me about it."

"So I did. So I did," Grey chuckled and turned to go.

"Listen," said Sijjer suddenly. "What do you say we go on a hike? You and me. You could probably use the exercise after all these weeks in the house." He looked at Grey.

Grey stopped smiling, "Hike?"

"Up in the mountains. See what that is up there. Rocks or water? Or think of it as a sort of prayer if you like. Climb up the peaks. It's not supposed to take more than an afternoon."

"What do you need me to go for?" said Grey.

"Thought you could show me how to climb. It doesn't matter. Forget it."

Sijjer's returned his gaze to the Lions. He saw the black things sliding down the face of the peaks. The Lions were disintegrating before his eyes.

II

A few days later Grey awoke early. For the first time in a month he felt whole. His muscles were warm and strength flowed through them.

He watched the rays of the rising sun touch the western face of the Lions, then went to Sijjer's room and shook him awake.

"Okay," he said. "I'll hike with you. We'll climb, just the two of us. But we go right now." He chuckled briefly. "It's your chance to make your claim, isn't it?"

Sijjer sat up and stared at Grey but found inscrutibility. He saw the face beneath the mask of humanity; the bottom half was crossed with shiny red scar tissue, one eye perfused with blood.

"What are you talking about?"

"You know what I'm talking about. Maybe you don't even know you know."

An hour later they were on the switchbacked road leading to the base of the Lions. Sijjer drove the VW bus up on the grass and set the brake. Grey shouldered a small pack he had filled with food and Cokes and set out at a slow jog.

Sijjer followed at a distance. He was in no condition for climbing. His thighs burned before he reached the trail into the woods. He watched the broad back disappear through the trees and then he was alone with the unfamiliar odours and sounds of the forest.

He had opened his letters to Prito during the last few days and had read through parts in which he had described Karla and little Bear. It brought memories and sensations and pain. There were some bad moments remembering little Bear as an infant, of the way he smelled and sounded. Then he had drunk to relieve the pain, but a terrible, resistant dagger had lodged in his chest. In his drunkeness he speculated that he had cancer.

So there was nothing to lose. He plodded through a wet bog and up over the huge root of a tree.

He must resist. He must fight. He had decided this the day that he had seen the disintegration of the Lions. Karla would not come back unless he fought. Just as Grey had resisted Radki, he must resist Grey. This much he had gleaned from the story of the mines. This was the way of things. Grey had learned from his enemies. From Dupray and Radki he had learned meaningless aggression. So now he had crossed Sijjer's line, and would take (had taken?) his wife. So it was clear. The rules were understood.

But the rules were not understood. Sijjer had only a vague idea of what course of action to take. Through the trees he saw the faded patch of blue that was Grey's jean jacket. And what did this stranger, this murderer, have in mind? He shivered.

Dead, dead, dead. He dropped one foot after the other and clumped down a slope into a dark ravine. His mind wandered.

How long had Prito suffered? What was he doing when she

died? He recalled the short time when Mohan had taken up drinking. It must have been then. Alone with two young sons . . .

Sijjer stopped to rest. Ahead of him the trail was silent.

Grey sat on a rock. He had taken a Coke and bread and cheese out of his pack and was eating. As Sijjer approached, he polished off the Coke and shouldered the pack.

They were above the forest now and the Lions towered overhead. The peaks no longer resembled lions, but were two colossal blocks balanced on the ends of two sloping ridges. There was no sign of the black particles crumbling away from the rock. There was no meltwater.

Grey spoke without looking at him. "You ever climb before? Me neither. I figure the trick is to make sure you don't look down. Talk to the rock as you climb. I'll lead off."

The east-most peak was shaded from the morning sun. From the corner of his eye Sijjer saw motion, a rapid descent into shadow. He looked at the place and saw nothing.

Grey was already on the first face. He stretched and searched for a route, then scrambled up the first twenty feet and waited on a ledge.

Sijjer moved up to the rock face. It was black this close. Basaltic rock, black and unforgiving. He noticed a wisp of cloud drifting by near the peak. Grey, grinning from his perch, beckoned him to climb.

He found a fingerhold and pulled himself up. Then, without looking back, he followed Grey's route. When he reached the ledge, Grey had already gone on.

This next climb was a high, almost vertical rise, more than twice the height of the first. Grey climbed ten feet, then moved transversely until he found a long groove which he followed as it angled upward. In the middle of it he stopped and his body went flat and rigid against the rock. He remained for a long time motionless, his head down, clinging flat to the groove. Then he climbed again, slowly. He made the ledge and pulled himself out of view.

Sijjer worked his way across to the groove, then rested. He looked up and felt suddenly drained of power. The air was thin.

He remembered Grey's remark about looking down and when he thought of this he could not help but look down.

The drop loomed beneath. He saw the canyon between the heads of the two Lions and below this the woods. He saw over the tree tops and down into the great channel of the sea, and beyond the shining city. To the west was the polished Pacific, broken by the motionless ripples from a passing ship.

He brought his focus back to the immediate height once more and experienced vertigo. He closed his eyes. When he did so, he hallucinated falling away from the rock and hurtling down the precipice. His eyes opened. The sun had swung past its zenith and now warmed the rock face. He began crawling up the jagged groove once more and did not look down until he gained the ledge.

This ledge was broad and smooth. Grey lay comfortably in the sun, lost in contemplation of the view.

"You decided yet?" Grey grinned confidently at him.

"Decided what?"

The other man shrugged.

Sijjer knew and did not know of what the other man spoke. He knew some of the rules of this game, but not all. Grey had challenged him. He had stepped over his line. It required a belief in the rules, a moral belief. It took, more than anything, strength.

"You go on ahead. My leg needs a bit of a rest. It's not much more to the top."

"I'm not in a hurry."

"It's a funny thing, how much difference open space makes. If you climb the same distance in a tunnel underground, you have a whole different feeling of the height. It's the space and light," said Grey. He looked over at Sijjer. "You ought to go on ahead, make the top."

"No, I'll rest here a while."

Grey swore. He looked at Sijjer, then looked away, the steam rising off of him. "Don't piss around. You don't know what you're doing, do you? You're gutless, you're spirit is shot. That's why you got no one. No one can stand a man with no spirit."

"You understand me no better than you know Karla."

"You wouldn't know how well I know her."

Sijjer stood up. A muscle in his eyelid began to twitch and flutter. He cleared his throat.

"Don't you know when enough is enough. You keep pushing and pushing. What makes you so sure I'll lay back and take it."

"You think I'm screwing your wife. You want to kill me, but you don't even know it. You don't know it, and even if you did, you wouldn't know how. And if you knew how, you couldn't do it anyway because I'm honest, but you're not honest. You just fool yourself and fool yourself your whole life through and it makes me sick." Grey turned his back and looked out over the sea.

It was Sijjer's chance. The other man stood less than a foot from the edge of the cliff. It required no more than a shove. The drop was a hundred feet. No one would know. If he did not do it, he might as well give up everything. That much was suddenly clear. He was playing for all he had.

Yet he still hesitated. Grey was right, he was sapped and drunken and weary into his soul. He did not desire life enough to seize it. Grey had known him, after all.

Without a word Grey went to the face and scanned it for the climb to the summit. He stretched for his first handhold, hauled himself up with one hand, found a foot and scrambled up the wall.

Sijjer turned and looked out over the panorama, his eyelid batting up and down like the lid of a pot on the boil. The sun on his skin no longer warmed him. His teeth chattered. Shivering, he reached for the first handhold, but it was too high for him.

A fluffy cloud swirled slowly around the peak opposite. The sun tracked above him in its arc as he watched it.

Sijjer sat down. Grey had known it was impossible for him to continue. Damn him. He looked up at the wall, considered his chances. He looked away again and rubbed his spastic eyelid. He would die. Grey had beaten him. Grey had known the game so much better than he — he had known exactly what he was incapable of. It had gotten away from him. Grey had tricked him.

His chest seared with pain and there was not a drink to be had.

Then he saw the flitting motion again, the plummeting shadow of disintegration. It was at a point on which his eyes had been focused, yet it eluded definition. Another plummet. It was a black bird, diving for prey. But no. What kind of bird was that big? The hair on his skin stood. It was odd. Did only he see it? Or had Grey seen it too.

"Hey," he called up the cliff, but he caught himself, sickened by a plaintive note he detected in his voice. Fear.

Another flitting shadow. He saw it this time. It was a large animal, a mountain lion. It sprang from the western peak into the gap, silently diving hundreds of feet.

Sweat bathed him. His mouth was dry, his legs rubber. He was freezing. To see and not be sure was terrifying. What was real? Was Grey real? Was the mountain real? A mountain lion appeared on ledge above, stretched in the sun. He had known they were here, had seen them from the city, which was absurd in itself.

Grey waited above somewhere, perhaps watching him, waiting to see what he would do.

He saw another silent cougar and decided to ignore it. He looked out over the panorama.

One could see the whole picture from here: the sun tracking across the sky towards the horizon, nightfall closing in from above, and the Lower Mainland spread out as flat as a map. The immensity of the view gave the illusion of great mental clarity.

In the corner of his vision another lion leapt. He saw the amber of its eyes, the gleam of saliva on its tooth.

He closed his eyes and imagined time marching forward. He imagined the past, the land before the city was built and the oceans before man had set eyes on them. He saw the dark anonymity of the land mass covered in forests, free of the imprint of man's endeavor. It scared him to think of the land, huge and lonely.

He opened his eyes to see a massive cat, sleek muscles flickering in the light, pacing on the ledge across from him. It bounded into space.

He clenched his eyes shut and attempted to place the moment in the great perspective of eternity. He concentrated on his small progression through time. But instead a single absurd image filled his mind: the image of himself with a shovel and heavy rubber boots, scratching the mud from a rainy ditch.

He shuddered and once more turned to search the rock-face for a way out. He spotted one place he could reach, but it led to a treacherous vertical section. The other option was to climb down. That meant conceding . . .

There were two cougars now, contemplating his plight from the opposite face. One paced, the other lay, licking its paws. They were mates; the female was pregant and rolled over to warm her belly in the sun. She would birth a litter on the ledge, the family would thrive. But no. Now she stood, crouched, leapt into the chasm. The male yawned and scratched himself, then followed.

Sijjer tried jumping for Grey's handhold. He touched it but could not get a good grip. He found another place and climbed for a while to find himself blocked by the smooth vertical face. He backed down. The sun was sinking; time was running out.

A mountain lion opposite bared its teeth.

Sijjer let himself over the lip and climbed down. At the bottom he waited for an hour for Grey. The appearance of this enemy, this thief, this friend, would present a last chance for redemption. But he finally drove home alone.

He never saw the man again.

TWENTY

I

When he felt sufficiently healed Grey ventured back to the Lower Eastside. In the taverns, he saw shock register in the faces of his drinking companions. The men had seen scars and mutilations enough; many were the victims of mining and logging accidents. But they forgot their usual self-deprecating levity when Grey appeared. Instead their bleary eyes widened and their expressions went soft.

The only one who failed to respond in horror to his disfigurement was the old medicine woman. She had moved her operations permanently, it seemed, and occupied a nook in the sidewalk on Water Street. The little terrier stood guard and when Grey passed, it yapped in recognition. The old woman murmered a few words in her tongue, bestowing blessings. He saluted in return.

He acted as though nothing were amiss, avoided his reflection in mirrors and ignored the reactions of old friends.

on a chair and pulled off his boots. He switched on the television and lay down and thought about money. In a sense he was rich, having the house to himself, but in fact he was broke. He remembered paydays at the mine, the way his wallet was stuffed with twenty dollar bills which he would not bother to count. Good, plentiful times. Now he could not scrape together enough for a meal. It was a crime for a man to be destitute in the city. Panhandling, which he had never liked, had not been helped by his scars. Grey had made the surprising discovery that strangers are less sympathetic to an ugly face than they are to a handsome one.

But he felt he had won the house and there was bounty in that. Bounty, though, tainted with bad conscience. Ultimately he realized he had brutalized Sijjer, if not physically, then in other ways, and he did not understand why he had done it. It had been done to him and he had passed the bad card on to Sijjer. He knew this. But he did not understand why it had to be so. It was beyond his control, which was a mystery. He wondered what Bernard would say about it. . . .

He was not surprised when he came back to the house to find Sijjer gone. He had given him three days to leave. During that time Grey had stayed on the mountain. At the outset he wished for Karla to return, but after a while he was glad she stayed away. The prairie fire, fleet and hot, that Karla had lit, had cooled when Sijjer had climbed down the mountain. Now Grey thought of leaving Vancouver. He overheard someone talking about Mexico one day and this caught his fancy. Then in a magazine he saw a photo of a Mexican volcano spewing smoke over a dense jungle, and beautiful women carrying water from a river. He thought of how he would travel and came up hard against his absolute lack of cash.

There was a television and stereo and other things in Sijjer's house to pawn. But the spoils were tainted by bad conscience. He had borrowed what he could for beer and food. He had resorted to plucking cigarette butts from the sidewalk.

There was a tap on the glass door of the sundeck and Grey sat up. He switched off the lights and peered into the dark. At the window was the distinct shaggy head of Dupray.

"I know you're in there," Dupray called out. Grey looked around for a weapon and and grabbed a meat cleaver which he placed on the table behind him.

He had wondered about Dupray these past weeks, not knowing what he would do when he found him. Now that Dupray had come to him, he was off guard. Instead of the expected surge of rage, Grey found his feelings were neutral.

"What do you want?"

"Come on, man. Open up. I ain't going to do nothing. Hey look, I'm even sorry for what I did."

Grey switched on the outer light and saw Dupray's toothy grin. Behind him Willy lurked on the stairs. Grey opened the door.

"Now that's better, ain't it," said Dupray.

"What do you want?"

"Oh, hey." Dupray saw Grey's face now and his grin became strained. "Hey, you got it pretty fine here. You're set up real good. Willy and me here are doing pretty well ourselves, ain't we, Will?" Willy crowded in behind Dupray, his nose twitching like a dog's.

"Glad to hear it. You still haven't said what it is you want."

"Social call. We were in the neighbourhood, as they say. Thought we'd see how you was. Um, fact is we thought you might be able to spot me a little loan."

"You just said . . . "

"Yeah, well. I ran a bit short of bread. Lost a lot in the fire. Everything, you might say."

"Yeah, you should have thought of that."

"Me? Hey, I might have beat on you, but you were the one who lit up the place. I call that even. Anyway, I'm ready to let it all go, if you are."

"It's not even at all, asshole. I didn't light your fire for you."

Dupray looked desperate. He had an urge to stare at the damage to Grey's face but made an effort to fix his eyes on his feet instead.

Grey remained calm. He felt vaguely disappointed that he had no urge to violence. He relaxed enough to sit down, the cleaver within reach.

"I don't have a cent," Grey said.

Dupray looked around at the television, the stereo, the pile of bottles by the door. A hard glint passed over his face.

"Hey. Who helped you back when you first landed here with no money, no job? Who gave you a place to stay and all?"

"I sure paid for it, didn't I?"

"All I need is twenty bucks."

"I'm broke."

"Ten."

"Search the place. I'm broke."

The glint went into Dupray's eyes and stayed there. "I don't see your girlfriend around anywhere."

He meant Francie. Grey had not seen her since before the fire.

"That's because she's not here," said Grey.

"Ohhh . . . " Dupray pulled up a chair and straddled it. He lit the butt of a cigarette. "Yeah. I got all over that business. I ain't mad with you no more. Heh. That one's not for me anyhow . . . She and you still getting it on?"

Grey shrugged.

"Yeah, I figured so. You're more her type. I figured maybe you two might be making plans or something . . . "

Grey shrugged again.

" . . . maybe to get married or settled down or something serious. Maybe planning to have kids . . . "

Grey watched the cigarette butt going down.

" . . . and a real job. Nice little place like this to live in. 'Course the big problem with all that is that you're such a sucker."

Grey stood up. "This time I won't turn my back for you, you bastard."

"Relax, relax. What's the big hurry? Whose place is this anyhow? Nice place. Nice furniture. Little sundeck. I like this. Didn't she tell you she's a two bit who'. Nothing personal, but didn't you know that?"

Grey had the cleaver in his hand before he felt the blood rushing to his head. Willy dove for the door and was gone, but Dupray sat still.

"You going to mess me up with that?" Dupray challenged him. "Hey, I come to give you a piece of advice, tell you the facts of life, like, and look what you do. You're all ready to mess me up."

Grey stepped towards Dupray. His flash of rage was shallow. It passed off quickly. He held the cleaver in his hand, but it felt wrong. But he wanted Dupray out of his sight. Then he saw that Dupray held a small twenty-two pistol in his hand.

"Go ahead," said Dupray. "Give me a chance to try this thing out. They'd probably give me some kind of reward for bringing you down. You're a hothead worse than me, man. That's why you're in trouble. Running away. Always running. What'd you do? Chop someone up? You use a meat cleaver before once?"

"Get out of here. Get out and leave me alone."

"The bitch is a hustler. What do you think about that, man? She's a hooker. That makes you nothing but a dumb asshole if you didn't figure her out."

Then Dupray went. When he was in the street, Grey heard the bray of his laughter.

II

The pain in Grey's leg began with a little pinch like a fine needle being pushed in above the knee. Then tiny waves of pain shot through the leg as though the needle were probing the bone. It grew hot and expanded and his leg throbbed. Then it died suddenly. He had thought to see a doctor about his leg, but doctors meant hospitals and hospitals meant questions. He decided that the pain would go away on its own.

He lay in the dark unable to sleep, waiting for the pain to subside. From outside came the rasping cough of an old person. The sound reminded him of old William. The strange thing was that every old man reminded him of old William these days. The further mystery was why he felt uncomfortable when he thought about him. William had not been much of a father to him. William had not been family. But then who was family? The problem, really, was that he was rootless as ever, a man without kin. Grey reflected that everyone needs kin — the awareness of that was painful. The only option was to make your own people. Find a girl, have a family. That was the way.

For the first time in his life Grey found this thought oppressive. He had always taken it for granted that he would father children. He loved children. But this dream had been trod on by Dupray, for in his mind, he now put the girl Francie in the role of mother to his family. It seemed to Grey that all along it was exactly as Dupray had said: he had plans for he and Francie. He now fantasized about marrying her, not remembering that he had not, in fact, thought of her in weeks.

So he tried to convince himself that it did not matter. What if she was a hooker? It bothered him only that it had escaped his notice. But why would she go with him if she was a professional? Did hookers have boyfriends? Hookers have pimps, not boyfriends. It seemed to him he knew the street well enough to know, yet . . . Not once had she asked him for money. Of course not. Hookers were mixed up teenagers, junkies, retards . . . Dupray was jealous, that was all.

The pain stopped, leaving a floating sensation behind it. With this sensation an idea came to him. It was simple. He would forget about Francie's past, whatever it was. He would take her out of it. It was probably those friends of hers who got pushed her into it in the first place. The ones at that crazy party. He would take her with him to Mexico and they would start fresh . . .

Grey began to feel good. He let himself be taken up by optimism. The future now seemed to hang before him like an enticing fruit to be picked. . . .

The next afternoon he went downtown to the Lamplighter. It was Friday and the bar was full. The bartenders wore teeshirts and trackshoes and slung beer along the counter. Grey drank thirstily and waited. It became dark outside and he asked the bartender where Francie was. The bartender shrugged.

He left the Lamplighter without paying, walked around in Gastown looking for Francie in bars and restaurants. Then he walked uptown. A girl in tight shorts asked him for a date and he asked her if she knew Francie. She pointed towards one of the big hotels.

Francie was coming out of the hotel lounge as Grey came

up. His leg began hurting just then and he could feel the blood pumping through the veins in his head.

She saw him and froze in mid-stride. "What the hell happened to you?" she said. There was someone with her. He came up beside her and stood waiting. Grey recognized him as John Pound, the one with the photo gallery full of Indians. Now Grey saw that Pound was a pimp.

"I'll see you later," Pound said to Francie.

"Sure, you go on ahead."

Grey watched Pound drive off in a foregn car which glowed with a spectral white paint.

"He didn't recognize me," said Grey.

"Who would. Aw, that pretty face!"

"Hey," Grey said, "why don't you and me do something tonight. Go for a walk maybe. I wanted to talk."

"I don't know. I'm pretty busy tonight."

"It's important."

"I don't know. I don't think so."

"What are you busy with anyhow?"

"Business. Just busy."

"But what business?" he persisted.

"My business. Look, why don't you go home, okay? You'd better leave me be. It's best."

She tried to hail a cab and then began walking towards the West End, her hair waving on her back like a flag. He moved along beside her, not knowing what to say to stop her. A little bubble of anger grew in his head as he walked. His leg throbbed.

"I know what you're doing," he said finally. "You don't need to do it."

"Do what? Oh, so you figured that out, huh. Well, who says what I need or don't need? You know, I thought you were a nice guy but it turns out you've got a big mouth just like everybody else. Big talker. What do you think anyway, Big Mouth? You think you're going to save me from something? Keep me from destroying myself? Or maybe you want to keep me in style, is that it? Who the hell do you think you are anyway?"

She had stopped walking now and was talking not at Grey but off into the street somewhere, her arms crossed and her hands stroking her shoulders. When she stopped talking, she lit up a cigarette and smoked it in a succession of rapid, shallow puffs. She tapped her foot and switched her head so that her hair moved like a cat's tail.

"Didn't you hear what I said?" asked Grey simply. "I told you you don't need to go on doing . . . "

"Look, fuck off, okay. You have suddenly become a real pain in the ass. Just go away and fuck off."

They were in the West End now. Cars cruised by in a slow line, car windows reflecting lights and people as weird curvatures. Francie stood staring out at the traffic. A silver Camaro pulled up, the driver calling out at her, and she went to the car and got in.

Grey found himself alone. He simply stood for a long time staring at the tail lights of the Camaro as it moved slowly up Davie Street.

III

He found a quiet place to sit and have a few drinks. The bubble of rage that had been floating in his head shrank after a while, and he thought he might be okay. He tried to dream up his Mexico scheme to pluck up his spirits but it was no good. He panhandled a while, then bought a mickey of vodka and wandered back to the hotel district. When he spotted the silver Camaro, he did not even realize he had been looking for it.

It was parked in front of a small building near the hotels. It too was a hotel, Grey realized after a moment, but one which he had not noticed before. There were no signs except for the name on a small plaque by the door.

Grey went and stood across the street for a time and looked at the windows of the hotel and drank his vodka. When he was finished, he threw the bottle into the middle of the street. His leg hurt.

The front doors of the hotel were metal with glass porthole windows. Inside an old man sat at a desk watching a game show on a portable television. Grey slipped by him and took to the stairs.

His leg lost its flexibility when it hurt and so now lagged behind and caused Grey to lurch up the stairs unevenly. He came to a hall with four doors, listened for a moment then crashed heavily against one which sent it banging aside, pieces of lock metal sprinkled about like stars on the dark floor. Grey sat down in the empty room. He was breathing hard. Around him there was a stuffy quiet in which he sensed or imagined the scampering of rodents and muffled television voices. There was a momentary feeling of having been in the place before. He recalled lying on the floor of Bernard's house waiting for something to happen to him and it occurred to him that nothing had ever come of it. Nothing had ever happened to him, really.

There were voices from the next room. Grey went into the hall and lurched against the flimsy door, bursting through it. There were two men in this room, naked in a red-lit pose that looked almost modest. One man cupped his hand over his sex, the other hunched his shoulders and pitched his head forward like a bull about to charge. Grey pulled the door closed after him, then it opened and the man charged out. Grey punched him once, in the throat and with his full weight behind it. Then he turned away and had his shoulder against the third door before the naked man hit the floor, coughing and gasping. This third door broke into splinters that Grey kicked away. It was lit by a bare bulb. A man lay sleeping inside. The stench was rotten, as though someone had died.

Grey skipped the fourth door and jolted up the stairs. He hit the first door of the next floor at a trot and it buckled in like cardboard. Grey froze. Francie was on the bed, her dress around her ankles. Around her neck she wore a studded dog leash which strained tautly in the hands of the owner of the silver Camaro. They stared at him and he at them. Over the surging of his heart Grey heard a commotion from below. He noticed that the Camaro owner had pressed his jeans. He had buckteeth and a large gold ring. His blue eyes were vacant and benign and they appealed to Grey in fear. His hand in the loop of the leash slowly descended.

"You come away now," said Grey softly.

Francie did not move. "What the hell do you think you're doing?" she said coldly. She abruptly pulled on her dress. "If you don't leave, you're going to have more trouble than you would ever want."

He missed the coldness in her voice.

"You come with me now," he repeated.

With the leash trailing behind her she stood and ran by him out of the room and down the stairs. She stopped to see the naked man leaning, choking, against the wall, then went on down into street and across it to an apartment block. When she came out, she was followed by a massive old man with long white hair. A cowboy with sunglasses and a baseball bat overtook Francie and the old man on the stairs.

When the cowboy stormed into the room, he saw Grey's fists driving like two pistons into the face and torso of Francie's trick who had stopped raising his hands against the onslaught. His fists kept pumping even after the cowboy delivered a blow to his back. Grey broke his attacker's headlock by stomping on his foot. He turned quickly and knocked the bat away. He took one further kick at the Camaro owner and scrambled out of the room. He stopped when he saw the staircase was blocked by the old man and headed for the staircase at the other end of the hall. He dove up one flight, then up another half-flight and cranked open the firedoor to the roof.

When the air on the roof hit Grey, his leg coursed again with pain and he sucked in his breath. He shut the door and hobbled on the gravel roof. The surface of the roof was black, the only light coming up around the edges from the streets. The pain sobered him. He swung over the metal edge onto an adjoining roof, dropping a few feet and pitching onto his hands. He found the door to the roof. It was locked. Behind him he heard the firedoor of the hotel cranking open. He went to the corner of the roof and peered over the edge into the street. On the street side there was a small balcony near the corner. Past that, four floors down, was the alley. Grey considered this for a moment until he heard someone jumping down from the hotel roof. He edged himself over carefully, his good leg first and let himself hang. He looked down on one side and saw the wet reflection from the alley floor, looked on the other side at the little balcony a few feet down. He let go. His bad leg hit on the parapet and sent a shock up his spine. Then he fell. He saw a flicker of a window go by as he rolled over in space and he had a moment to see the alley rush up to meet him. Then he hit, landing in the soft stinking mash of wet cardboard, paper and trash of a garbage bin.

IV

Grey had one dollar. He kept playing with it in his pocket as he drank beer after beer. Finally he pulled it out and unravelled it on the bar so that the bartender could see it when he came near. Grey stank of trash.

Each time he thought of himself climbing out of the garbage bin he wanted to laugh. He thought of the way his mother had shed death. He was oilskin! He had waited for something to happen but again there had been no reply. He had stood in the alley listening to the voices on the roof, then walked boldly out to the street, saw the ambulance come and then stood watching them load a man into it. It was the owner of the Camaro, Francie's trick, an oxygen mask over his face and blood spattered on his creased jeans.

Grey pressed the green bill flat on the bar and thought, "Tomorrow I'll be in Mexico." He pictured himself in white pajamas astride a mule.

"What's that?" said the bartender looking at the bill.

"That's for you. For the drinks."

"The hell it is," laughed the bartender. "You owe me twelve bucks."

"I thought I had more . . . " Grey began but the bartender was already on the phone calling the police. Grey looked down the bar and saw only the moon faces of strangers staring at him. He hopped off the bar stool and made for the door with his dollar crumpled in his fist.

The streets were quiet. The cars that moved up and past him did so with a cushioned grace and precision. In this stage of his drunkeness the elements of the universe fit perfectly together, were comprehensible and harmless. The treachery of friends, poverty, uncertainty and homelessness were part of an unrelated, distant world. In this mood Grey would drive a car at a hundred miles an hour and feel invulnerable. He would repel the bartender and a squadron of policemen if they came for him. He was prepared to leave for Mexico that moment, even if Francie spurned him. He had the urge to go to the hospital, find the man he had beaten and apologize to him, feeling the other man would understand.

Instead he headed back to the hotel.

It was late. As he walked, the last bars closed down and stragglers spilled onto the street. At a familiar corner he recognized a sleeping lump in a nook by the sidewalk. It was the old woman asleep under her rug, the terrier watching over her. A light rain fell making the scene cold and forlorn. Grey imagined the medicine woman in her youth. He imagined her taking instruction from her mother: how to cook and care for a child. He grew morose. He brought forth the crumpled dollar bill and tucked it under the rug. When he looked up, the old woman was awake and eyeing him. She sat upright and took out the bill and, laying it flat on the wet sidewalk, smoothed it carefully with a flat palm. She beckoned him to sit. He squatted and the old woman began to chant as she dug out her shiny bones and tossed them onto the bill. She examined the bones, then gathered them and placed them firmly in his hand. The bones were oddly heavy, as though they were made of ivory or pearl. When they touched together they made a loud clicking.

"Keep," she said to Grey. She smiled and her old eyes closed down to slits. "For you," she said thickly, then she lay down under her rug once more.

The bones clicked in Grey's pocket. As he walked through the rain, he put his hand on them to feel their smooth heaviness. They buoyed his confidence; he knew they were magical.

He found himself once more in front of the hotel. The place was quiet now but he scouted for signs of policemen or the huge old man he had seen on the stairs. He was about to slip into the hotel when a car came around the corner behind him and slowed down. Grey passed the metal doors and kept walking, clicking the bones in his pocket. The car pulled along beside him.

"Look who's here," said the driver. It was John Pound.

Grey stopped walking and faced Pound. His hair was slowly soaking up rain and cooling his skull. He was aware of blood flowing hot through his brain, then cooling as it ran under the wet hair.

The car was a two-seater Mercedes Benz. Inside and out it was white so that Pound looked as though he were sitting in snow. He smoked a cigarette and smiled with the corners of his mouth.

Grey began to walk again and the car rolled quietly along beside him with Pound talking from the window.

"You look like a wet rat, you know. Ratty clothes, ratty face. I can smell you from here. Ratty smell.

"Hey, what do you think of the wheels? I just took delivery. Mercedes 450 SL, in case you don't know. A perfectly made little machine. You know how I got it? Connections. And I'm good at business. I make some money and I use it to make more. You know what the secret to making money is? Don't take bad risks. Just good risks. Make good connections. Let people know you're dependable. That's all. It doesn't take much. You listening?"

Grey kept walking, the rain cooling him.

"You could learn something from this, my friend. Police were looking for you. Still are, I guess. Turns out you are one very unpleasant person. Very unpleasant. You beat up a friend of mine. Nice friends. Connections. You break in on parties uninvited. All of it very bad for business."

"Couldn't give a fuck."

"What did you want with Francie anyway?"

"Where is she?" Grey stopped walking.

"You know something about her? She's smarter than she looks, that Francie. She knows who to go to in a pinch. That takes intelligence. She doesn't hang around losers. She can pick them out. She's been hustling since she was thirteen and she'd be dead now if she wasn't damn smart. Yes, my friend, she is smart and she's also the best damn little whore a man could care to own."

Grey heaved a sigh. He felt the aura of peace and freedom, of anticipation and invulnerability dissipate all at once. He clicked the bones in his pocket and felt tiny quiverings in his leg as if it were talking to him.

"Shut up," he warned.

"You don't like my story?" Pound laughed smoothly. "I've got loads of stories. See, this guy came to my place a while back. Handsome stranger. I asked him for permission to take his picture, asked him just that simple favour, and he turned me down. But I took the photo anyway when he wasn't looking. Came out really nice. Then this friend of mine, a cop actually, saw the picture and said he knew the guy. Imagine that."

Pound's face hung in the dark interior of the car like a mask. The mask buzzed and talked. It reminded Grey of those Hallowe'en masks that kids wear with the elastics that go around the head. He clicked the bones in his pocket and looked up the street, the mask talking and his leg talking.

"So the thing is," Pound was saying, "it turns out the guy I photographed is wanted by the police. My cop friend recognized him from one of those police drawings. Wanted for something pretty serious, I guess. Deaths of two miners somewhere. And the real funny part is when my cop friend asked me where I saw the guy I told a lie. Imagine that! I said I bought the picture in L.A. Told him I never met the guy."

Grey watched the twinkle of Pound's cigarette and clicked the bones loudly in his pocket.

"But it's funny how a few scars can change a man," said Pound. "You know, if I saw you like you are now, I'd never even think of hanging you in my gallery. That's just the way people are. If you're nice looking, nice smile, nice teeth, nice skin, you get everyone's attention. Everyone likes you. People want to know you. They love beauty. Women fall head over heels. But when you're face is a scarred mess, those people don't have the time of day. It's just the way they are. I guess you noticed that, huh?

"I think the best thing for you is to go off somewhere, my friend, and die peacefully. And in the meantime, if you see Francie sometime, you know, hanging around somewhere, you'd be better just to pretend she don't know you. In fact, she doesn't really know you anyway, so what's the difference. She doesn't know you, and she sure as hell doesn't care. Best thing is for you to just pack it in, my friend. It's the best for everyone."

Pound's mask had become mournful. He drew up the window of the Mercedes and made a slow U-turn. Grey seized a trash barrel from the end of an alley. He picked it up over his head and heaved it at the Mercedes as it pulled away. It crashed onto the street, strewing bottles and cans. The car glided off unscratched.

"Fuck you!" screamed Grey. "Fuck you to hell!"

V

A cold sea rain fell in the streets. Rain soaked Grey's jeans and ran down his face along the scar line. His head throbbed with fatigue and strain. He did not try to return to the hotel now but walked aimlessly downhill into the harbour area. As he walked, he tried to revive his sunny fantasy of Mexico once again but found the image cool and difficult to sustain. Mexico shrank out of reach. It was becoming like the other dreams that blossomed in his head. He would chase them, and as he chased them, they dried up and shrank like flowers past their season. One day he would stop chasing and see them for what they were. Now he knew that without Francie Mexico would not happen.

He came to the abandoned pier he had stood upon the first day in the city many months before. He climbed the fence, stepped across the rotted timbers to the water and sat on the edge of the pier, legs dangling. Below, the water hissed and slapped the pier.

The night was endless. He had no idea of how much time had passed since he had plunged from the hotel roof.

Grey closed his eyes. He felt his leg ticking in contemplation, then the peculiar searing deep inside as the pain began. It ran up and down the leg, worse than ever before. It made him shake so that he gripped the wooden plank on which he sat with both hands clenched. By the time the pain died away, he was cold and sober and his muscles trembled lightly. He opened his eyes. The darkness and the rain were unchanged. The night was endless.

Grey thought of what Pound had said and realized he was in danger. If Pound knew who he was, then in time others would find out. The police would find out and then what? His mind was blank when it came to this. Never had he seriously considered what would happen to him were he caught. It had never seemed possible before this night.

He clicked the heavy bones together in his pocket and pulled them out. He felt each strangely shaped piece. Even in the darkness their whiteness shone.

He thought about Radki briefly, recalled him without pity or remorse. He felt again the anger that had blazed through him as he smote Radki with the scaling bar. Then the triumphant elation as he escaped. He went back over the sensations he had experienced coming to Vancouver, thinking of his disfigurement at the hands of Dupray. He thought about Sijjer, not dwelling on the climb or the way Sijjer had climbed humbly down the mountain, but feeling sorrow for his lust and compulsion.

Then a happy picture entered his thoughts. He saw himself and Karla hand in hand walking by a river through a lush valley. The sun shone, they stopped and drank cold beer. That was it. Karla could come to Mexico. Who needed Francie after all? The idea was perfect. He only had to convince her.

Grey rose and clacked the bones together in his cupped hands. He limped down the pier feeling his old optimism return. But when he climbed the fence at the end of the pier, his leg began to tick in warning and he sat suddenly on a curb. The bones were clenched in his fist.

That was how the policemen first saw Grey. They were in a van on a routine patrol. Near the harbour they usually found a number of rubbies, conscious and comatose, and these they deposited in the drunk tank or hospital. This late in the night the two officers sipped coffee and talked quietly as they pulled alongside Grey. The driver rolled down his window.

Grey was shocked to see the police van pull up. It was as though he had no sooner thought of the police than they appeared. He stood up quickly and made away as fast as his limp would carry him. The bones dropped from his hand.

"Hey," said the cop. "Hold on a minute." Grey stopped in

his tracks but dared not turn. He considered his options as the policeman opened his door and approached behind him. Grey counted off the footsteps. In one motion he turned and shot forth a low, concentrated punch with his left. Then his right came around in a short arc that snapped back the policeman's head and knocked him to the ground.

As he ran, Grey heard a clicking sound behind him. He moved in heavy, painful strides that seemed not to cover any ground. He headed towards the dark mouth of an alley.

"Halt!" yelled the other officer. "This is the police!" There was an explosion which raised the hackles on Grey's neck. But nothing happened. He ran on. He was close to the dark womb of the alley and his leg was wooden. Then for some reason he fell, pitching forward on his belly and face. He had heard no second gunshot, yet lay unable to move, hearing the clomp-clomping of police boots behind him.

His leg, for some reason, had stopped hurting. For the first time in days it felt normal. He focused one eye on a fat earthworm that inched its way along the gutter. How beautiful it was, pink-red and segmented with a slimy girdle. That would be the taster, Grey thought of the girdle. There were voices behind him but he did not move his head to face the men. The voices came from far off. From the hills across the water, or further.

"You hit him."

"Stupid son of a bitch. Christ."

"You better get on the blower."

"Christ. I was only trying to question him and give him these stones he dropped."

Grey heard the heavy clicking of bones in the hand of the cop. He was aware of someone kneeling over him. A hand tugged gently at his collar.

"Oh, man," said the officer. "Can you hear me, Mister?"

Grey was not listening anymore. He closed his eyes and heard a faint roaring. He knew the sound. It was the roaring of the stope as the blasting began. He had heard it a hundred times. It made a vibration like a small heat that came up through the rock, up through the steel soles of the boots.

But he was mistaken. The roar was something else. Before

his eyes there was the cone of a volcano sending a geyser of steam into the sky. Below was the thick, verdant canopy of a forest. The forest was alive with strange, beautiful birds. Women in brilliantly coloured dresses carried wash to the river. They carried it in baskets on their heads. Mexico! This was Mexico. This was where he was going.

Yet Grey knew he had missed it. He could not remember how he was supposed to get there. For a moment he had the compulsion to laugh at himself: he was getting stupid! . . .

Blood ran from him and seeped into the rain in the gutter.

TWENTY-ONE

I

Karla moved into the ancient, chaotic downtown flat in which her friend Sharon Sterns painted. To maintain herself she took a job as a waitress.

But there came a morning when she blinked open her eyes and perceived dissolution. She awoke on her pallet and foam and saw cracked plaster on the walls, smudges on the warped glass of windows and mirrors. She felt the hardness of the plank beneath her. Was this musty odour the perfume of her garden? Was the ache in her joints arthritis? She had become diverted from important goals, forgotten entirely her urge to write.

She went to the restaurant where she worked and quit her job. For the rest of the day she walked through the windy, towering downtown, through the tree-shaded West End, on through Stanley Park and along the sea wall. It was Saturday. The concrete wall and walkway which curved around Brockton Point were thronged with joggers, cyclists, clowns, lovers, children and dogs. Under the clear sky the sea was a deep blue laced with foam. Coloured sails flitted in the distance.

In this milieu Karla was miserable and lonesome. Her boots were cumbersome in the summer warmth and she worried that she was past her sexual prime. Men no longer looked at her the same way, glances summarizing her, dismissing her. And she hated herself for her vulnerability to that.

She ached when she saw couples with young children.

She stopped to rest at the marina. Sailing boats moved into the glossy swells. A man and a teenage girl maneuvered a ketch into the afternoon thermal, then rode it down the Narrows towards the sea. It could have been her father and her, a short time ago. Safe, glorious days! She had been under the impression that she would live forever! Sailing boats, sun-glossened waters and safe passages.

What had become of her goals, her ambitions? Shining Papa was old, his polished emanation dulled. He now sailed a rudderless, listing boat, becalmed. At the end the boat sinks. She was on that boat too, so was everyone.

An old man came and sat at the other end of Karla's bench. He wore an overcoat and a derby and looked crushed by anonymity. Karla had the feeling that no one had said a word of greeting to him in years.

"Hello there," she said with a kind smile.

The old man looked at her crossly, then marched away muttering.

Karla wept. She cried for the emptiness in her womb and for her Shining Papa on his listing boat, and she cried because her feet were damp and sore in her boots and her bladder was full and she knew there were no toilets.

She wiped her nose and said a brief prayer. She searched for a place beneath a boardwalk. Here she found a dead fish. It was the kind of place where she expected to find trash, feces, rats, or worse, and she was strangely buoyed up by the absence of these sordid sights.

She went home tired and at a loss. She looked over her makeshift desk at the disconnected pages of script noting that it was covered with dust. She picked up the first page of the introduction to an idea she had entitled Technology and Tomorrow: the Death of Culture. It was written a year before; it was the hundredth reading. With a disconsolate sigh she flipped through the other pages to discover a colony of fat silverfish devouring the paper.

II

She moved out of the studio apartment, rented a car and headed for the cabin in the Selkirks. As she drove, she tried to summon some optimism. Life, she told herself, was an adventure, the horizons of achievement distant. She had come of age, weathered the worst she could imagine. Were not the reins of her destiny in her hands? Of course. Yet the gnawing in her belly, of Bear, of Sijjer, persisted. Flaws in her crystal of hope.

She came to the pocket desert near Osoyoos. It was scorching in the late morning sun. It seemed as though the parched hills were devoid of life. Animal and plant had ceased moving. On the roadside a figure loomed up. A hitchhiker as motionless as the sunbaked rocks. Squinting, she almost passed him.

Perhaps because of the isolated place she slowed down. He was an old man, bent and wrinkled. He wore a broken cowboy hat pulled low, boots and hunting shirt. His hands were empty. The empty-handedness struck Karla as odd, reminding her of the drunks in the alley near Sterns' old studio. The empty hands were the first thing she noticed of the drunks. Empty hands hanging like discarded tools or hidden away in pockets. Or holding a thing awkwardly: their own peckers, or punctured cans of disinfectant. One of the old man's hands was out, a hammer of a tobacco-stained thumb pointed down the road.

But something else distracted her from suspicion. An intense midnight-blue aura leapt and contracted around him like a solar wind. She unlocked the door and let him in. He climbed in beside her, pulled out a well-chewed cigar, lit it and blew out swirling clouds.

The sagebrush and cactus turned to scrub and pine woods. Heat waves shimmered over the road.

"You sure are a pretty gal," said the old-timer.

"Nice of you to say so."

A moment later she felt a hand on her knee.

She was driving at that moment through waves of moving air and above them there appeared the figures of two boys tussling. They were brothers, these two; both had a thick, dark forelock and lanky movements. It was a mirage.

Karla looked at the hand on her leg and sighed. How strange were living things! This gnarled tree of a hand posed a threat! Yet it came from an innocuous-looking grandfather who shone with a radiance that put the sun to shame. She turned and was shocked to see that she had misjudged him. Suddenly he appeared tense with vigour and strength. The sinew in his neck stood out. His face glowed, his eyes flat and brown like two pennies. A magnificent light, peacock and twilight blue, fell away from him in streaks.

The car dropped onto the shoulder of the highway and skidded to a stop sending gravel and and dust flying.

"Don't do that," she said and removed his hand.

The smell of hot blood rose from him.

Above the road the brothers disengaged and engaged, grappling for holds.

"Willya lookit that, hey? Just like a pitcher show of somepin', said the hitchhiker. "In all my time I never . . . "

"Get out," said Karla.

"Yer gonna leave me here in the middle o' the moon?"

"I'm sure you'll be fine."

"Aw, I'll be nice. You'll see." He smiled and Karla saw rows of yellow horse's teeth. "I'll be real good." His hand scampered up her thigh and pressed firmly against her crotch.

The figures over the road enlarged. The smaller brother had gotten hurt; the elder chucked him on the shoulder and mussed his hair. They turned towards Karla and froze. Could a mirage see? Could they see how the gnarled hand zipped her down and slipped inside her pants like a thief? How her shirt was unbuttoned and her breasts exposed? How the whiskery-rough face rubbed her nipples?

She opened her door and tumbled out.

"Hey, we just got goin'!"

She had recognized the hands in the beginning. She had known. She now watched the hands pursue her out of the car, saw how they hung uselessly. Big, clawy things. They came at her, rough and sweating.

Karla ran, buttoning and zipping herself as she went, into the scrub by the road. She heard him coming behind her, labouring up the hill. She turned and saw the ominous contour in his pants. He threw off his hat, whooped for joy, and emanated a blue as radiant as Venus.

She ran steadily, climbed over dead logs and through gigantic spider webs that hung from the dying pines. The webs were thick and dusty and loaded with insects and one small bird that fluttered in spasms. She tore the web loose from the bird as she passed. Fatigue caught up with her as she ploughed through the silk. It stuck to her clothes. She slowed. Another bird hung dead and dessicated in the sunlight.

The place, she realized, was as deathful and profane as hell. She stopped amid the webs. Who was responsible for her destiny? Was it not she? She wanted to sit, sort through her thoughts and call a stop to the action. But there was a crash behind her and she bolted forward. Instinct turned her in a large circle, back to the car.

The old satyr was gone, lost in the dead pines and webs. Over the road the brothers looked on as Karla pulled back onto the highway.

When she had driven several miles she came to a gas station with a green patch of lawn on which two teenage boys practised judo. They waved and screamed as she passed.

III

The morning after Karla arrived at the cabin the air had a magnifying quality. She could see beyond the eastern range into the icy crests of the Rockies. The sky was limpid blue.

As darkness drained from the forests and sun touched the lake, she dragged the canoe down to the water's edge. She slid between the gunwales and paddled into the morning shadows. She paddled down a mile then came in close to shore and explored the nooks and bubbling streams. The canoe moved so easily that she had only to touch the paddle to water; it made no more noise than the sleek otter she followed for a way.

What more could anyone want but a perfect canoe and a flat lake? Life is an adventure. The horizons are distant! Yet the flaws scratched at her belly, droned in her ears like mosquitos. She was confined, trapped in the pine-wood webs by her sorrows. Bear, Bear, Bear . . .

She let the canoe float in the cove. The fish beneath her moved in a drugged, aimless pattern. She watched them, hypnotized. Life is an adventure! The horizons are far, far . . . She should have no regrets, no sorrows. The reins of her destiny were in the hands of whom?

The air changed, began to move, and the water became choppy. Grey clouds scudded in, bringing behind them darker cumulo-nimbus. She dug in her paddle and headed for home.

What further sorrows faced her? Maybe it was only the beginning. Yet she was a woman of mind, a woman of soul. She was strong, was she not? Did she not hold the reins of destiny?

Distant are the horizons!

She sighed and picked her way up the steep path to the cabin as the first drops fell. They pattered like rocks on her head. Water ran into her mouth. The season was late. Rain-rocks crashed into the foliage and splashed in the lake.

Were not all things in balance? Did the rain not balance the sun? Did not the blood pulsing through her veins balance the death of the pine-wood webs? Life was an adventure! Of course.

The light was blotted from the sky as she reached the cabin.

As she towelled herself off, she recalled how she had despaired once as a child. Her mother advised her to pray to God. She had tried prayer. But the prayers fell short. She knew God did not hear. Determined that her prayers work, she shut herself in a closet, wooden crucifix in hand. She pinched herself until she cried. She felt cleansed then: the prayers had worked. She repeated this tactic a number of times until Shining Papa found out, one day cutting herself with a paring knife and one time pricking herself on the feet and hands the way Christ was nailed.

As a child, pain brought relief. But it made no sense.

Life is an adventure, the horizons distant.

Karla took two Valiums from her handbag. She swallowed them dry and went to bed.

IV

When she awoke, the air was summery and a faint ray of filtered sun fell across her eyes. The forest resounded with the shrill of jays, the thumping of rabbits and the swish of upper boughs in the wind.

She rose and opened the cabin door. The light and warm air remained apart from her as though there were yet other doors to open. She looked at her hand and saw that it was translucent as morning mist. Her hair was unruffled by the breeze. In the fragment of mirror on the shelf she was wispy, her flesh sere. Her eyes were an indistinct wash of watercolours.

It occurred to Karla that she had died. She heard whispers in the trees, the forest creatures became silent, as if forewarned. Around her the lights and sound faltered and she was transported.

A wind touched her skin.

At the mouth of the tumbling water is the cove and the clustering of the village. They wear cloaks of fur of sea otter and seal and deer. Hair long and oiled. At the shore the men sing. Ocean canoes lie beached like foundered whales. They climb into the boats and paddle out, bows plunging through waves. Far out on the sea the harpoon throwers stand, then they throw.

If you close your eyes, you can hear the hit. You can hear the scream under the water.

She guts salmon. She slices the white bellies with a copper knife. Children come near, shouting strange words. Women watch from a distance and laugh. She carries the fish in a basket to the smoke shed and hangs it.

The sun is sinking, the village a darkening pit. Smoke from the fires rises straight up. Set back from the river is the longhouse. Over the entrance a wooden man supports a wooden wolf. Totem poles before the house are of eagle and bear and beaver. Dark circles around beaver's eyes, thatched tail held in front as a shield.

Back from the house are the redwoods supporting the clouds. She wants to run to them, knows she can escape. But they call her by name to the wooden house. Qwimii, they call. Seagull.

"Qwimii," says Grey and she stares at the surging blue penumbra.

"Qwimii," says the chief's son. He stands by his father. Old man nods. Nods slowly. Slow and evil. Snake motion. She knows the evil in the white cataract of his eye. Old one speaks to Grey, then to his son. The son looks at her and smiles. Cold smile. Fish smile. Grey is gone.

She returns to the hovel to sleep with the other slaves. Silent and wet. The cold and rain leak through the roof and she curls up with another girl. But sleep is interrupted by the scream of a mountain lion, a sudden silver moon thrown into the sky by Ququsin, the raven, and magic light which stirs the spirit of the bear totem so that he turns towards her and offers his side as a mother offers her bosom.

Slave. She wakes in the morning to climb the paths, her basket under her arm. From high over the inlet she sees the plume of a killer whale as it glides seaward. Above are the dark spaces between the mountain peaks. She drops her basket, berries red-spilling, and she runs, her name called behind her. Qwimii. Qwimii. She runs higher until the voices cannot be heard, then the path disappears. She is in the cloud atop the redwoods. . . .

Chief's son comes from nowhere, fish-smile, panting, hands empty and hard. The hands pull her shirt apart, knock her to the ground, separate her legs. He knocks her down and hits her when she fights to stand. He is on her, hands clutching and cold. She goes calm and grasps for a stone.

His body is eventually still, eyes rolled up. Fish eyes. Limbs shudder. Fish. Hands empty and clutching. Fish.

She flees up the mountain, straight up until the rain ceases. Icefields. Crevasses.

Then she sees, silhouetted against the sky on a crest of snow, the shaggy fur and razor claws. Around him the electric blue light spurts and surges. It is the bear. It is Grey, waiting for her, welcoming her home.

She moves towards him, climbing the jagged rock and snow. But when she gets to the top, she finds that she has pursued an illusion. There is no bear, no Grey, only the blue glow which scatters like smoke and is gone.

She finds herself free but alone amid a vast snow-field.

V

Karla awoke. It was early morning and only a trace of light entered the cabin. The rain had stopped. She looked at her watch and saw that she had slept for twenty hours through storm and night. A pristine morning unfolded once more. She felt the warmth of her wool blankets, smelled the must of the cabin. Her body was limp and sleepy. . . .

Outside a sleek doe grazed in the grass. She opened the window and called out to it softly. It responded by taking tentative steps toward her, then stared with huge, sympathetic eyes.

In her dreams she had dreamt other dreams. Was it possible to dream of dreaming?

She had lost Grey. He was gone. Inside her she detected the spot where Bear had come to life and gone forth. There was no emptiness now. Strangely. It was the place where Grey had dwelled.

Twice emptied, yet full.

The meadow and the doe were tinged with a vibrant yellow light. From the meadow came a rustling, ringing music, as though the living forces within the plants and creatures sang together. Adventure, they sang. Distant, they cried.

The air filled Karla's lungs and she drank of the oxygen. Outside her window was a doe in a meadow. Outside there was magic in the world.

TWENTY-TWO

I

The evening is thick with the threat of rain. Heavy presences hang in the air. A familiar eeriness advances through the walls, over the sills, slips along the floor. An essence, a whisper, a shadow. A flash of gold in the weeds.

He stands beneath a sky low and heavy. A breath tickles his neck. In the semi-dark something touches his hand and he jumps, then retreats inside, retreats to the bottle. Yet he cannot drink. The golden fluid swirls into the sink and he shakes watching it.

In the north, in the dying summer sun, the Lions look askance. What does one want? What does one wait for? One awaits death and then . . .

He studies his palm, tracing intricate lines. Lines millions of years old, passed on from the genes of non-men, passed on from the rocks. Blood of rocks. Blood of mountains. The lines transform as water touches them. . . .

The clouds breath in, the clouds breath out and it rains.

II

The war with the bottle had commenced gradually, beneath awareness. He drank wildly the days after the climb. Alone, he hated drinking, but drank anyway. Then he felt like a slave to his drinking. He hated that and still drank, fighting. He bought bottles and poured them into the sink, threw them whole into the trash, only to retrieve them and drink, hating that he drank. His body revolted. He was alone in the war, fighting himself.

Sijjer packed up the VW van and drove away from the house for the last time. He thought he had no choice but to leave. Grey had challenged him and won. Now there was nothing left to do but withdraw. He had no destination, no plan. He was resigned to everything except his drunkeness which he fought.

He followed the freeway south across the border, then cut off onto the old highway that hugged the American coast. With the war on, with a physical sobriety setting in, his reflexes were bad. There was little traffic on this road and he let the bus weave and roam the humped road. Washington slid by, then the air took on a bronzed quality and became warm. The Pacific stretched out like a great pool of quicksilver.

He fell asleep at the wheel during a rightward drift on the bent spine of the old road. The bus ran off the road and ploughed gently into brambles and a swath of thick grass. He awoke and reversed the van onto the road to find that the engine dropped its oil in a steady stream. It was late in the evening as he searched for the nearest town.

The road ran towards the sea, climbing a long hill. The VW bus faded halfway up and Sijjer let it roll onto the shoulder of the road. He stuffed some things into a canvas bag and hiked the rest of the way in.

The surrounding hills were sepia under a rising half-moon. Around him were neither lights nor movement. He detected the ocean shore in the air as a tangible denseness and he could hear the rumbling of surf. From the crest of the hill he saw a clustering of a buildings in the valley below and he trotted down the hill.

The town of Athlone was a single road with three streetlamps, a restaurant, filling station, store and motel. An office stood behind a bare flagpole implanted in a mowed lawn. By the light of the moon the outlines of houses were visible but no lights or sounds betrayed the presence of inhabitants. No dogs barked in alarm, no blue glow of televisions lit windows. Athlone was what Sijjer imagined a movie set to be. He half expected that, if he looked behind one of the buildings, he would discover that it was supported by scaffolding.

Then a dry cough of dusty wind blew up. It cut through the oceanic air like a knife, carrying a faint burning odour that caused the hair on Sijjer's neck to rise. A eucalyptus tree croaked out a warning: *Jiv-jis, jiv-jis*. From the corner of his eye he saw a shadow and a flicker of movement. He turned and saw a gaunt figure suspended in space. He knew the figure well. White-tinged hair, winged brows and jutting, bird-like features. The figure was surrounded entirely by blackness, and its attitude was of craning, peering as though trying to penetrate the light that separates life from death. The figure was gnawed and lonely.

It was Mohan. What was he saying? There was no sound, no signal. Mohan simply stared at his son, the image of an unfulfilled seeker.

Sijjer stared back seeing Mohan as he had never seen him. He felt pity instead of hate. Through the eyes of pity he saw a man locked up in pride and pain, a man who for most of his adult life lived in one house, but was homeless.

The image was a reflection in a store window. But it was Mohan nonetheless. Had he become Mohan? Was this the fate of adversaries? It seemed that all his life he had feared this. Then he stepped back, the hair on his back twitching. Mohan moved too, his face becoming indistinct.

The tree creaked, *Jiv-jis, jiv-jis*.

The reflection changed. The lines of the face transformed, the outline became a *chuni*. Suddenly the face of Prito emerged through Mohan's. She too stared. But her mouth opened and she spoke. It came out as a queer parched sound, a croak.

Jiv-jis, jiv-jis, she croaked. "Persist, persist." The cry echoed off the house fronts and went unanswered. Prito smiled, her eyes sad.

The dry wind became was overcome once again by a cool ocean breeze.

Sijjer turned away from the glass and moved down the street towards the sound of surf. A cloud moved in front of the moon, but in the dark he followed the sound and the steady slope off the road. His feet touched sand after a time, and the sand was vaguely white, then there were ghosts again, these ones rolling in from the sea.

He was suddenly exhausted. He was in the dark, in a place he had never been, yet he felt as though he were home. He stretched out on a bed of sand with his sack as a pillow and a tuft of grass as a windbreak, and rested.

III

He awoke from a sleep tinged in the early hours by the colour of steel and gold of dawn light. He put his head up and saw teenagers carrying surfboards down the dunes to the water. No one paid him any mind.

He picked up his sack, shook the sand from his clothes and stood, unable to think of a direction in which to turn. Only the sea ahead of him. It was the end of the road. He had no desire to journey further.

The beach was a five-hundred-metre stretch of sand between two massive, rocky points. A teenage lifeguard sat perched atop a high metal chair, the sand around him dotted with sunbathers. Among the field of waves that crashed towards shore, surfers crawled on their bellies up the steep waves to stand, crouch and tumble in the water. . . .

Sijjer took off his shoes and climbed one of the rocks that divided the beach. From here he could see a stretch of the coast to the north. It appeared as a long dusky, blue line of ridges and mountains that curved away into haze.

He sat on the high rocks and gazed out to sea at the

dazzling water. In his sack he found a bottle, wine he had saved in one last lost battle, one last capitulation. He took an unenthusiastic swig from it. It was sour and made his throat contract.

There was no such thing as a new start. There was no such a thing as escape. There was only oneself to face. And grief over shirked responsibilities, perhaps. Piara had said loved ones need caring for, chasing after, worrying after without a moment of negligence. But families cease to be. And what was a man without a family? A cold stone?

But whom had he betrayed? Karla? Bear? Had it been he who had let Prito, Gurjit, Karla and Bear drift out of sight?

He let the bottle slide down the rocky slope to the sand. It made him sick. He was poisoning himself. Where did this weakness come from? Spiritlessness? How was he to answer Prito's ghostly salute?

He stood up. Light struck his eyes and broke apart. In one of these beams lay a mystery. He brushed crumbs of lichen from his pants, wiped his glasses, and stared out at the ocean. There, far out to sea, were two heads rising on a swell. Papery, fluttering things drifted over the end of the point. They were butterflies of the plain white kind, meandering in a cloud between Sijjer and the water. Thousands of butterflies followed a child-like course, furiously fighting the sea breeze. When they passed the point, there were jewels of light in the water and the two shadowy heads appeared again. It was Bear, little lost Bear, clinging to Zeph. The two floated calmly up and down , moving out to sea on the current.

Sijjer clambered down to the end of the point, where his glasses slipped off and were lost between the rocks. He looked out to sea once more, imagined the sprint down the last tongue of rock and the dive into the waves after his lost Bear. He saw himself swim away never to return. The water would close over his head.

But then he saw something else. He saw that there was no panic in Bear's motions. In fact Bear was laughing, hugging his dog, his eyes bright with play.

Sijjer felt a tremor. It was an unaccustomed sensation, brilliant and warm. It was joy. Pure, irrational joy. Bear was laughing. Somehow this made sense. There was order to things that he had not sensed until now. And for the first time in a long time he was aware of the preciousness of vitality.

He turned away and walked back up the tongue of rock and up the hill to the town.

TWENTY-THREE

I

The truck driver dropped Sijjer in Surrey. From there he caught a bus into Vancouver and checked into an eastside hotel.

Coming back that way, he found a certain anonymity. He could have been coming to any city. He knew no one, had no roots. He stayed in his room and watched television and fought his war.

Afterward it was like a tranquil sleep. He stopped shaking. The pains in his chest vanished. Thirst faded to a background annoyance which he assuaged by drinking cases of ginger ale.

Weeks flew by, then the warm season ended. A mass of cloud moved in and the North Pacific rains of winter commenced. . . .

On this first day of rain Sijjer returned to his house. He found Grey's few clothes folded on the sofa beside a dirty dish and glass. A meat cleaver lay on the countertop. The lights were on, although it was midday. There was no sign of Karla.

Five days later the house remained undisturbed.

He returned to the old hotel. At first he kept a lookout for

Grey in the streets. After a week, he searched actively. He scoured the lower east side taverns and bars in turns each night: the Lamplighter, Leo's, the Balmoral, the Olympia, Star and all the rest. No one had seen Grey. One day he followed his own drunken trail to the burned shell of the house where Grey had lived with Dupray. He found the lot empty but for the blackened remnant of the foundation.

He walked along Water Street late one night and came upon a curious sight. An old woman sat upright on a blanket before a tiny flame. Beside her a small dog stood guard. There was no one else in the street at that moment and, when Sijjer came near, she summoned him. He hesitated, unsure. Her hair was matted and a single tooth protruded from her mouth. Her eyes reflected the flicker of the flame. She withdrew three stones from the folds of her blanket: one white, one blood red and one cupric blue.

Sijjer stared. He kneeled on the sidewalk.

She tossed the stones against the wall and scrutinized their positions. Then she beckoned him to come close.

Sijjer crept forward, his eyes on the stones. They could not be, but somehow were, his own.

"You," she whispered, "you."

The dog growled and the flame fluttered out, then sprang into existence again like a wellspring.

"Who are you?" she said. "You friend and enemy are one man fly. I know. Stone talks. One man kill, one man fly."

She took up the blanket, wrapped it around her shoulders, and closed her eyes. The stones she left on the step, their colours curiously vivid in the dark.

In the morning Sijjer went to the police station and discovered that Conrad Grey was dead.

II

From the hotel the Lions were obscured by the smog and the blanket of rain clouds.

Sijjer got Karla's address from her father. He waited outside her place one morning in the rain. When she came out an hour later, he fell in step with her. She stopped and faced him.

"Hi," he said.

"Hi," she said. "You're soaked."

"I don't mind. I'm warm, even in the rain. Anyway I lost that old trenchcoat."

Karla began to walk.

"It looked terrible anyway. I wore it so much I never saw what a rag it had become."

They walked along in silence for a few blocks. Water dripped from Sijjer's hair. His glasses were fogged.

"It's funny how a thing like that creeps up on you. Tiny little events like the fraying of a thread, spread out over time. We can't see small things over long periods. We're blind to it."

Karla looked at him, frowning.

"You can't take time for granted," he went on. "Time is event. Without event there is no time. Just a sea of non-event, all of it the same. All the faces the same . . . I found out Connie Grey died. The whole time I knew him seems to me like a long dream. "

"It was real to me . . . " said Karla. They were in front of a cafe.

"I'm meeting someone here, Jassy."

"Anyone I know."

"No."

"A man?"

"Good-bye." She turned, looked back from the door once, then went inside.

Sijjer walked up the street, around the block, then peered into the restaurant window. Karla remained alone drinking tea. She looked up once and seemed to see him. But she dropped her gaze and he went away.

He left her alone for two days, then waited in front of her place again.

"You don't believe in phoning?" she said when she saw him.

"You might not answer."

"That's right. I might not."

"Where are we going today?"

Karla stopped walking. "Jassy, you don't know what's going on. Do you know what you're doing?"

"No," he admitted. . . .

"The two of us have too many sorrows, Jassy. What's left besides that?"

"There isn't anything if you want it that way. Or there could be everything. It's up to us."

III

Dear Mother,

It's spring once again here; the flowers are so bright in the sun that they assault the eyes. . . .

Karla has moved away to her cabin for now, but she'll be back to stay. She is not the elf she was, for she will never forget our lost Bear. But in her eyes I see a spark of hope. She is pregnant, it turns out, by Conrad Grey. She is about to publish her first book and is at work on another. When we see each other, there are many things of which we cannot speak. It seems that, along with the sorrow and loss, Karla got some of the things she wanted.

What about me, you ask? I feel there are many pressing questions. About birth and death. About lost traditions. About finding a way without the love of one's mother. I have always feared that I am really not alive at all. I have feared that I am a stone. Without loved ones, without friends or community or tradition I fear to be alone. But I discovered that there is a vital core in me. Spirit, Grey called it. The spirit that Grey and even I thought had died in me. It is there. It's not the fierce flame of Conrad Grey, but it is there, flickering like the old magic woman's fire. Grey's flame burned so brightly it burned people. And in the end it was extinguished in violence. So it is, I think, as Grey might claim. There is no place in the city for a real untamed spirit. There is no place in the city for the old world spirits of forest and mountain. Maybe this is why I have moved to the country. I have lost faith in the city. There may be some corner for a man like me, a man without roots, rent from the old traditions of our people, but I could not find it. So I have started a life in this small town near the coast. Digging ditches is not as bad as I always thought it would be. It gives one time to think and appreciate.

I have begun to appreciate that we are ultimately alone. You would know about that. We enter the world alone and we leave it alone. There are periods in between when we find this painful. So alone, lonely and afraid, we find the confusion and mystery, the pain of love and family so valuable that we sacrifice anything to have it. It's strange that we cherish the pain so much that we burn up after it, like flying insects that venture close to the fire. So Karla will come back to me to live. Perhaps we will live as friends. Perhaps as a family. It will be another beginning.

Now it's time for me to go. I will take a walk down the street and down the hill to the beach and from there watch the sun go down. The sea will turn to black and the mountains will gleam in the last light of this day.

your son, Jaswant